RITE OF DEATH
The Damien Palmer Investigations
Book 2

I0689990

Stuart Holland

RITE OF DEATH
The Damien Palmer Investigations
Book 2

Chapter One

Damien Palmer looked out of the window of his study and observed it really looked like the cold, frosty mornings of winter had finally passed. The road was typical for the area. Along one side of the cracked and pot-holed surface was a line of terraced housing, a throwback to the thirties. Some of the properties revealed the care their owners lavished upon them, with replacement guttering and double-glazing. Even Palmer's own home, the sixth in the line, sported double glazing and a new-looking set of roof tiles, though the care had not been lavished by Palmer, but the previous occupant. Across the road a small grassy area enclosed by wrought iron railings brought a touch of fervent green to an otherwise very urban area. Beyond the grassy area, which was just large enough to walk across, was a row of terraced homes that matched the row in which Palmer lived. It seemed to Palmer, as he looked out of the window, the grassy area was a ray of hope in an otherwise forlorn part of the world.

Palmer surveyed the grassy area from his study window. He dwelled on the beauty and soothing qualities of the dew that had not yet risen from the luscious green covering. It made him feel good about the day.

The study was aptly named for along its sides were shelves of pristine, leather-bound tomes, a collection that Palmer had started as a child of no more than eight years old. The first volume of his collection, a well-thumbed version of Treasure Island, was possibly his most prized possession. For Palmer, it held sad memories of a loving father who had died tragically. He had died a few weeks before the book, a beloved family possession, had been handed down to the young Damien as a keepsake, much to the annoyance of his two elder sisters, Roxanne and Ophelia. His jealous sisters were, unlike the young Damien, not avid readers. They were more interested in outdoor pursuits.

And so, throughout the years, Palmer had kept the book as a memory of the father who for some reason had died of a brain haemorrhage. The memories of that fateful day came flooding back to Palmer as he looked through the window at the grassy area. There had been the breakfast where his father had quite suddenly collapsed, and then there had been the doctor. At that point the children had been ushered into the playroom. The events of the bygone years had never left Palmer's memory, though the details had on occasion become confused. Now, as he looked out of his window, he could almost picture the horse-drawn funeral carriage as it had come up the road bearing his father's coffin. Even now it seemed as though Palmer was waiting for the return of that same carriage, as if it would somehow set the clock back to the happier part of his childhood.

Then, as if resigned to the fact that the carriage would not return, Palmer turned away from the window. A large oak desk grandly occupied the centre of the room and between the desk and the window was Palmer's leather upholstered chair. The appearance of opulence was deliberate, and made possible by the extraordinary deductive talents of the man who had been looking out at the spring morning, reflecting on his own past.

Palmer sipped the cup of freshly made coffee as he once again turned to look out of the window. As he did so, his memory brought him back to the present and he reflected on the fact that it had been a quiet few weeks. This time of year always was. After the New Year rush of enquiries from people believing their partner might have been unfaithful at a Christmas or New Year party, the remainder of the winter period was nearly always quiet. Palmer had long since discovered that most such enquiries were unfounded, probably triggered by the insecurity and paranoia that generally sweeps through people's lives as the New Year starts. He had often mused on the possibility that such a condition was also responsible for the strange situation where people found it necessary to spend vast sums of money on items in the sales, when they had lived perfectly happily without the same items for the past year or more. It had been a source of some amusement and interest to him for many years.

Now, as he looked out of the window, he began to keep one eye on his watch as if waiting for someone. He had been watching this way for maybe five minutes when a man dressed in the uniform of the postman walked down the short path that led to his front door. He heard the letters fall on the doormat outside his office, but his attention remained focused on the path that led away from his house. He sipped some more coffee.

On his desk lay a copy of a tabloid newspaper that was some weeks old. It was a local paper, the kind that is distributed free every week, but it was not from Palmer's own area. The paper lay on the pristine blotter that covered much of the surface of the desk. Beside the paper sat a black box. Palmer had not yet turned on his laptop computer and in fact he had not yet started work for the day. The grandfather clock that stood in the hallway sounded the hour. It was eight o'clock.

The morning post lay untouched on the doormat as Palmer continued to look out of the window. Having heard the eight chimes from the clock his patience began to wane. He did not usually accept clients so early in the morning, but then his expected guest warranted his urgent attention. It was always an annoyance to Palmer when people turned up late for meetings, and it was particularly annoying when the meeting was so early in the day.

Finally, after a further five minutes, he saw the man walking down the road. He was a short man, wearing a long dark coat to keep out the cold air of the morning, and he wore a flat cap on his head. To Palmer his appearance was incongruous with his professional status. As the man walked, Palmer noticed he had a slight limp in his left leg. He recognised the man immediately, but waited behind the net curtains until the man had actually stepped onto the little path that led to the front door. Only then did Palmer retreat into the hall and collect up the small pile of mail, which had arrived several minutes earlier. As he left his office, he carefully placed the empty coffee cup on the edge of the blotter.

He waited until the doorbell sounded before he turned the handle and faced his guest.

'Good morning, John, how are you today? Not too cold I hope.' Palmer sounded friendly as the two men shook hands. 'Do come in.'

'Morning, Mr. Palmer.' The voice was deep, unusually so for a man of such short stature.

'Damien, please, I insist. These are not your offices and we're not with a client. Here, let me take your coat.'

The short man took off his long coat, placing leather gloves in the pockets as he did so.

'Thank you, and in answer to your question, I am actually feeling very well, if not a little confused. Also, for your information, it is still damn cold out there.' Palmer shut the door.

'My office, please do go in. Would you like coffee, tea perhaps?' Palmer was almost effusive as he showed the shorter man into his opulent study.

'Coffee would be very nice.'

'One minute and I'll be right back.' Palmer left the shorter man rummaging in the rigid attaché case that he had brought with him and walked down the short hallway into the kitchen. The percolator was already full of fresh coffee and it took Palmer only a few minutes to prepare the drinks. It was a common ploy of his to allow his clients to gather their thoughts in his office while he went off to the kitchen to make coffee. When new clients visited him it gave him time to form an initial opinion of them. In the case of John Manning there was no such need. Palmer had spent many hours conversing with the man over the past few years, had dined with him on occasion, and regarded him as almost being a friend. In Palmer's particular line of business caution was always exercised over the term friend, and if pushed he would have said that Manning was still an acquaintance.

'Coffee,' Palmer enthused as he pushed the door to his study open. Manning was sitting in the 'interview' seat facing Palmer's desk. Palmer carefully placed the tray on the blotter between them and sat down in his leather swivel chair. He turned slightly to look at his client. Both men took a mug of the steaming coffee and sipped the contents before placing the mugs back on the tray.

'Now, John, what can I do for you?'

'I don't know really; inspiration, perhaps. Are you familiar with the John Burnston murder case?'

'Only what has been reported in the newspapers, I'm afraid. It's a case of battered wife inflicts revenge on bully of a husband, or something like that, isn't it? I got one of my contacts to do a bit of digging after you phoned me. He came up with this article.' Palmer reached out and picked up the old newspaper. He turned to page five and spun it round so his client could read it. Below the article he pointed to, Palmer noticed there was an appeal for a witness to come forward in connection with a death the previous October. The dead woman was only in her mid-twenties and she had blond hair. Her body had been found in the local park and to date the police had not tracked down her killer. Palmer knew little about the case though he did recall she had been stabbed repeatedly. It was a bizarre murder but it was not the focus of Palmer's attention. That, for the present moment, was directed to the much larger article at the top of the page.

'So, what has this got to do with me?' Palmer spoke evenly as he looked at his guest.

'Well, the wife has asked me to represent her. And that is where the problem starts. Seeing as the police actually caught her standing over her husband, who was lying in a pool of blood, holding the murder weapon, you'd think she'd plead guilty.'

'Yes, it would seem reasonable,' Palmer agreed with growing interest. Indeed, the short man now held Palmer's undivided attention.

'Well, she is absolutely adamant that she didn't do it and she wants to plead not guilty.' At this point Manning paused and took a sip of coffee. It was almost a dramatic pause, but the coffee made the pause too long, and for a moment it seemed as if the short man was going to struggle to make his request. 'Basically, Damien, I need some help, because if I am to proceed with this case on that basis I need something to work with, and quite frankly we've been working on this for a month now and we've got nowhere.'

'I see. And when you say we, who exactly do you mean?'

'Myself, of course, and a research assistant I have working for the practice. Also, I have to admit,' and again Manning paused, though this time he shuffled uneasily in his chair, as if embarrassed by the revelation still to come, 'I tried Expert Investigations a couple of weeks ago, but they drew a blank. So, all I have left is the best - you!'

'I see.' Palmer placed his hands together with the tips of his index fingers touching. Then he raised his hands until the index fingers touched his mouth. He looked hard at his client, weighed up the

11

situation, and considered the options open to him. Finally, after several seconds, Palmer smiled a slow, thin smile.

'Well John, as it's you, and as I like hopeless cases, you're on. But it won't be cheap. To do this properly will cost quite a lot.'

'That's not a problem. My client is paying me privately, and there are undoubtedly enough funds to cover your expenses too.' The short man looked evenly at the private investigator, though the solicitor was evidently still apprehensive about the whole meeting.

'In that case, I will require one thousand pounds up front and I will invoice you as necessary.' Palmer sounded decisive, like the businessman who now held his quarry in a position whereby it would be difficult to back away from the deal.

'A thousand, that's a bit steep, isn't it?' Manning questioned the investigator, though his question sounded more out of habit than any surprise.

'Possibly, but from what I have read there is going to have to be some considerable efforts on this case if we are to get anywhere, and time is money, so they say. I'll be blunt. This case could cost your client over two thousand in investigation costs alone. And, I have to say it at this time, there can be no guarantee I'll succeed in proving your client was not the killer.'

'Very well, the funds will be transferred to your account this afternoon if that's okay. Now I have a dossier here that contains some stuff you will need to know. It's not much, I agree, but it might help.'

With the deal struck, Manning visibly relaxed, though his somewhat chubby face had turned a slightly darker shade of crimson. The study was a warm room, but not sufficiently so to account for his ruddy complexion.

'Excellent.' Palmer took the manila A4 sized envelope and opened the flap. The contents were indeed sparse. There were two pictures. The man, lying in a pool of blood, was evidently the deceased. The picture of the female was, Palmer presumed, his wife.

'That's the happy couple,' said Manning as he watched Palmer take the pictures out of the envelope and examine them.

In addition to the pictures there were a few pages of notes, a report, pathology report, and a few other notes that Palmer decided to ignore for the moment.

'So that's it. A copy of the police report, a couple of pictures, and the other report, all four pages of waffle, is presumably from Expert Investigations?' The question was meant to be rhetorical but Manning was pleased to confirm Palmer's findings. 'They were a lot of use, weren't they? Let's hope I have better fortune. Now, John, I need to talk to your client at some point. Could you arrange a meeting for sometime tomorrow afternoon?'

'Yes, that should be possible.'

'And when is the trial?'

'Well, we've already had the committal. The trial itself is set for 13th April, so that gives you just under two weeks.'

'Christ, they've moved quickly on this one.'

'Yeah, but to the authorities it's an open and shut case. To be frank, Damien, I'm inclined to agree with them, and unless you come up with something quickly, that is exactly what it will be.'

'So you think your client is guilty?' Palmer looked sternly at the shorter man, scrutinising his reaction.

'Well, on the balance of the evidence we have so far, yes. At least that is what any reasonable jury would conclude.' His voice sounded unconvincing and Palmer detected a degree of apprehension in his tone.

'But,' Palmer tried to lead the solicitor.

'But, there is something about the woman. I don't know what it is, but there is something. When you meet her you'll understand what I mean.'

'Fair enough, now I take it the scene of the crime is no longer cordoned off?'

'No. Actually our client, Heather Burnston, has a sister, Rachel, who is looking after the house while she's awaiting trial. I can arrange for you to meet her there so you can have a look round. Not that there'll be much chance of you finding anything after the police investigation.'

'You never know. How about two this afternoon? I have some other things to sort out first.'

'I'll do my best. How can I contact you today?'

'My card,' said Palmer as he handed his business card over the top of the desk. 'It has my mobile number, home number, and e-mail address on it. You should be able to get hold of me. If my mobile is off then you can always leave a message on my answer-phone.'

'Good. In which case I had better let you get started. And thanks, Damien.'

'Don't thank me yet, that can wait until we get a result.'

'Fair enough. I'd better get to the office. Anything else you need, just ring me.'

'I will.'

The two men stood up and Palmer showed the shorter man to the hallway. Standing in the hall, Manning donned his long coat and fished the leather gloves from the pockets.

'One more thing before I go. Although the press are obviously interested in this case, there has been no indication given out as to which way she is going to plead and reporting restrictions are not in force. I'd like to keep it quiet if possible.'

'That's not a problem. Now, with luck, I'll hear from you later.'

Palmer opened the door and ushered his guest back out into the cold. As soon as the man had turned back onto the pavement, Palmer closed the door and returned to his office.

Chapter Two

Coffee was something Palmer relied on heavily. He claimed it helped him to think. As soon as Manning had left, Palmer recharged his cup in the kitchen before returning to his study. He sat in his leather chair and picked up the few pages of documents he had been left with. He scanned the report from Expert Investigations. It was, as he had surmised a few minutes earlier, a large volume of waffle with little of substance. Palmer knew of the firm and knew also that they were considered to be good. This lack of success, and their feeble attempt to dress up the fact they had discovered nothing of any use, only added to the foreboding that Palmer began to feel over accepting the case. He looked with more interest at the other reports.

At 12:32 pm on January 26th the police had received an anonymous telephone call alerting them to the victim's house. The house was located in Wimbledon Village, not a particularly up-market part of the village but not the sort of property to which such attentions were usually directed. The panda car had pulled up outside the house, which was semi-detached. The house was in good condition. A new roof, double-glazing, and recently painted rendering indicated the owners had ensured their dwelling was as comfortable and smart as possible.

In front of the house was a short garden with a path leading to the door. The house was the left of the pair, and to the side of the house was a garage. It was a typical, 1930's style, semi-detached dwelling.

Sergeant Cranshaw pressed the doorbell and then, receiving no response, knocked on the door. Still there was no reply so he bent down and peered through the letterbox. At the far end of the hall was a door that was closed and so, at the time of looking through the letterbox, Cranshaw could only guess at the room beyond the hall. The hall carpet was a light beige colour, except that the carpet near the door was stained very heavily with a much darker colour.

Cranshaw realised what the colour was and stood up grim-faced.

'Better get some assistance,' he looked at his colleague, a fresh-faced WPC by the name of Juliet Trensham. She was a new recruit and Cranshaw knew already that this would be her worst experience to date. We will need medical assistance and some backup.'

'Serge.' The woman turned and spoke urgently into her radio. As she did so, Cranshaw felt round the door. He surmised that it was not particularly strong.

'Right, you'd better stand back,' he called out to his colleague. As she stepped back, Cranshaw put his considerable weight to bear on the door. With the third attempt the door gave way. The interior of the house was surprisingly quiet.

Cranshaw, followed closely by the WPC, walked quickly up the short length of the hallway. He stopped short of the stain on the carpet, and bent down. He touched the stain and sniffed it.

'Blood,' he said gently. He turned to look at the WPC, not sure what to expect.

'Blood,' she repeated in a matter-of-fact, professional voice. 'I think we should try to see where it's coming from, don't you, Serge? Oh I get it. I'm new and you're worried about me. Don't be, I've seen loads of this stuff before. My dad works on a farm. I've seen more than you have I should think.'

'Sorry, Trensham, I didn't know that. Now, don't step in it.' Cranshaw gently turned the handle on the door and as gently pushed the door open. It gave way easily. The kitchen floor was tiled, with the tiles coming up to meet the hall carpet. As Cranshaw opened the door it was immediately evident that there was a lot of blood. It covered the tiles near the door. More blood was splattered up the sides of the floor cupboards and some even reached the ceiling. The door was pushed further open and Cranshaw stepped back in horror. As he did so he nearly knocked the WPC off balance.

'Christ.' It was all he could manage as he turned green and ran back down the hallway.

In the middle of the kitchen floor was a man. He was face down in what was a very considerable pool of blood. The blood had soaked through his boxer shorts and his white shirt. There was, quite literally, blood everywhere and in the midst of this gruesome discovery stood a woman. She, barely five feet tall, stood over the body, a serrated, long bladed, kitchen knife held in her right hand. The knife, like much of the kitchen, was covered in the man's blood. The woman held the knife with a firm grip, seemingly oblivious to the arrival of the police.

Even as Cranshaw stepped backwards, the WPC pushed past him. Careful to avoid the blood she stood at the kitchen door appraising the situation.

'Mrs Burnston?' She called out gently. 'I'm WPC Trensham. My colleague and I have come to help you, but first we need you to help us. Can you hear me, Mrs Burnston?'

The woman standing over the body nodded slightly.

'That's very good. Now what we need you to do is to put the knife down. Will you do that?'

Again the woman nodded.

'Okay then. Just reach out to your right and put the knife on the work surface.'

Suddenly, and just as the woman reached out her hand there was a commotion in the hallway. With the element of surprise on his side, the photographer had gained access to the scene through the unguarded doorway. Now, with Cranshaw still gagging behind the front door, from the horror of the scene, the photographer reached up and pointed his camera in the direction of the kitchen. Then, just as the woman reached out her hand, the flashlight of the camera disturbed her.

The WPC reacted first. She turned round to face the intruder.

'Christ, have you people no sensitivity. What are you doing here?'

'We got a tip off.' The photographer was already backing away from the scene.

'Get out of here and wait outside. Now,' her voice was still calm, and authoritative, 'or you will be arrested,' she had continued. The photographer knew better than to argue, and still unable to comprehend either the horror or his good fortune he turned and ran.

Just as quickly as she had turned to face the photographer, so she turned back to face the woman. The woman, still standing over the body, was now visibly shaking with the knife still held in her hand. Trensham observed that tears now stained the woman's cheeks.

'Mrs Burnston, can you hear me? Mrs Burnston?' The WPC's voice remained even, and calm. By way of response, the woman nodded slightly. 'Sorry about that, but he's gone now. Now, you were about to put the knife down, weren't you?'

Heather Burnston nodded. Slowly she reached out her hand until it hung over the kitchen work surface. Then, and very slowly, she loosened her grasp on the handle. Slowly, painfully slowly, she opened her fingers until the blood stained knife fell onto the work surface.

'That's very good. Now, come towards me. Try not to step in anything, just come towards me.'

Heather Burnston looked up with a dazed expression on her face. Slowly, and almost mechanically, her feet started to move. She paid no regard to what lay on the floor. It took her five blood-soaked steps to reach the door to the kitchen.

'Okay Mrs Burnston, I need you to take off your shoes and to step onto the hall carpet, beyond the stained carpet. Can you do that?'

Again Heather Burnston nodded her head. Her shoes were of a type that can be slipped off very easily and it took her only a few seconds to step onto the hall carpet.

'Serge, where's the backup?' Trensham turned to look quickly at her superior. It was probably inexperience on her part but it gave Burnston a moment of inattention. With a desperate lunge, she pushed the WPC forward, knocking her off balance. With the open door, Heather Burnston suddenly realised it was a chance for escape. As she ran to cover the five or six steps needed to reach the door, Cranshaw looked up at his WPC and understood what was happening. Even as he turned he yelled,

'Look out.' As he called out, he pushed the broken door back into position. In less than two seconds Heather Burnston was sprawled on the floor, her escape route closed. In a few seconds her wrists were handcuffed behind her.

The sound of sirens filled the air shortly after her escape bid, and eventually she was led from the building to a waiting police car, to the interest of the small group of onlookers that had gathered by this time.

Palmer paused at the end of this part of the report. He re-read it twice, soaking in the full horror of what had happened. It was only when he was sure he had understood the scene that he rose from his chair and made himself some more coffee.

When he returned to his office he continued to read the document. It went on to describe the scene of the crime in greater detail, but Palmer was already aware of the horrific nature of the attack on John Burnston. Then he picked up the pathology report. It was short and concise and indicated that death was a result of the multiple stab wounds. It described in detail each wound and pointed out that whilst a few wounds would have required considerable force, a number of the wounds were little more than mere scratches. The report also mentioned that one of the deeper wounds had severed the aorta, and doubtless accounted for the large volume of blood that had poured out of the body. After he had scanned the report, Palmer picked up the telephone as he once again read the newspaper article.

Eddie Marston was someone Palmer truly counted as a friend, and moreover he was a colleague of some years standing. Palmer had first met Marston several years earlier when he had been working for another investigator and Marston had been looking for work. Marston had just recovered from being stabbed eight times in a bizarre attack related to an ex-girlfriend when Palmer first met him, and there had been something about the rather short, not quite cockney, man that had endeared him to Palmer. And so, over the years, their friendship had grown. Palmer had come to learn much of the man, his past, his weaknesses, and his strengths. Yet, for all this, Palmer had managed to keep much of his own sad, abused, childhood to himself.

It was this rather short, bespectacled man with the somewhat chubby face, who heard the phone ring in the sitting room of his rather drab and dreary single-bedroom flat early that morning. He managed to answer the phone after the third ring.

'Eddie, sorry to trouble you, it's Damien. How are you?'

'Not so bad considering it's still not ten o'clock. You know I'm really a night owl.'

'Yes, I'm sorry. Look, something's come up. Are you available to do a bit of wandering round and asking questions some time later today?'

'Sure. Where do you want me to go, and what's it all about?'

'Well, it's a bit complicated and I haven't worked it out yet. How about you come round here at twelve and we go and have a pint up the road?'

'That sounds good to me. Twelve it is then.'

'Good, I'll see you then.'

The telephone went dead as Marston replaced his receiver. It was true, the morning had barely begun, Palmer's clock showed the time to be approaching half past nine.

Palmer turned his attentions to the computer and in a moment it had sprung to life. It took a couple of minutes before Palmer was able to select the program he wanted to run. He inserted the precious CD in the drive on the front of the laptop and waited for it to start. When it did so, he used the keyboard to enter his query. In a moment the computer screen showed the only two occupants at the address he had typed in to be John Burnston and Heather Burnston. He pressed some more keys and the display changed. The screen indicated that the information related to business listings, but under the heading the screen simply stated that nothing had been found. Palmer scrawled a few notes on a pad of paper that he had taken out of the desk drawer while the computer had been starting up. When he had finished writing he drummed out a further command on the keyboard, located the information he wanted, and requested the information was printed. Finally, having made these enquiries, he turned the computer off.

He turned his attentions back to the dossier he had been given by Manning and carefully replaced the pages in the manila envelope. As he did so, he observed the smiling, happy, picture of his client. Her red-brown hair was shoulder length and she had an attractive face. Palmer noticed that she appeared quite slender and that her arms seemed somewhat thin. Perhaps, he thought, it was a trick of the camera, but it looked as if she had suffered some bruising around the left eye some time before the picture had been taken.

The pile of letters that had been delivered that morning remained unopened on one side of his desk. Now, with some time to spare, Palmer turned his attentions to the mail. Carefully he slit open each letter with his gold-plated letter opener. Deftly he withdrew the contents of each envelope and scrutinised it. There were, inevitably, a few bills that would need his attention in due course. There were also a couple of payments from clients.

The seventh envelope was opened and Palmer was extracting its contents. He noticed that the name and address on the envelope had been hastily written. Palmer withdrew the letter, a single page, and unfolded it. The words on the paper had been cut from some book or newspaper and the message was crude.

'THE BURNSTON WOMAN IS GUILTY – LEAVE IT AT THAT'

Palmer let out a low whistle as he carefully reread the simple message. He held the paper in his hand as he began to pace up and down the room. It was typical of his nature that he'd pace up and down his office searching for a reason. The carpet was well-worn but not thread-bare, evidence of his trait.

'How the hell,' he muttered to himself, 'could anyone know I'm involved in this? I only took on the case an hour ago, and yet this was sent yesterday! Must be someone connected with Manning, or Burnston herself, but how?' Palmer paced the room again, back and forth, searching for the answer that simply wouldn't come.

'It can't be Burnston. She's in jail and with very limited access to the outside world. Okay, Manning said he'd discussed this with her, a couple of days ago, but that doesn't give her time to get the word out, and why would she want to anyway?'

As he spoke to himself he stopped pacing and turned on the spot to face the window. It still looked cold outside as Palmer looked at the grassy patch across the road. After a moment, he turned from the window and smiled thinly.

'Manning,' he hissed, 'it has to come from someone in Manning's his office. He phoned yesterday morning to arrange this, so someone on the ball in his office could have sent this. That doesn't leave much choice. It must have been his assistant or the secretary, but why? And why do it this quickly? Why blow their cover in such an obvious way? Why make it so obvious and put me on my guard? It doesn't make sense.'

Palmer paced some more, his thoughts now clearly focused on the solicitor who had visited him earlier. He looked again at the envelope. The postmark was local, but then so were the solicitor's offices.

Palmer decided to take a walk. The sun was out and the morning was beginning to warm up a little but it still demanded that he wore his long winter coat and a grey scarf as he set off up the street following the same direction that Manning had taken a few hours earlier. It was now just after ten o'clock and the strength of the sun's rays had begun to warm the cold spring air. Palmer walked with the stride of a man of purpose. It took him only a few moments to walk past the other five houses in the terrace and leave the patch of grass on the other side of the road behind him. The next few roads he turned into were similar to his own, streets lined with small, functional, dwellings.

In his hand he held a white A4 sized envelope. It was part of a plan he had conjured up a few minutes earlier and he hoped that his familiar presence at his destination would be less suspicious on account of the envelope.

The walk lasted barely ten minutes before Palmer stood outside the door to the offices of Clarke and Manning, solicitors. It was a dingy door for such an organisation. The dark wood panelling needed a coat of varnish, and the brass plate identifying the firm had long since needed to be polished. Palmer pushed the door open to be greeted by the familiar set of stairs. The actual offices were on the first floor and Palmer had long since got used to the flight of stairs that led him to the reception and waiting room.

'Good morning, Mr Palmer, have you come to do a swear?' The ritual was familiar to Palmer. It was not uncommon for him to visit these offices a few times a week for the purpose of swearing an affidavit, usually relating to some kind of document, called Process, which he'd had to serve on some poor individual.

'Good morning, Carol, yes I have.' Palmer was used to the firm of solicitors and the receptionist was a familiar face to him. They had, in fact, had the beginnings of a relationship a few years back. The relationship had failed because she was too passive for him, but they had stayed friends. Then, about six months later, the cool woman now seated opposite him had chosen to inform the sleuth that she had just become engaged to another man. Now, as Palmer looked at her, he began to wonder whether she had changed from the passive, almost frigid, person he had known. She certainly looked radiant and it appeared her marriage was working well. He was pleased for her.

Palmer was almost sure she was not the originator of the letter he had received in the post that morning, but his experience in this business had taught him caution and he could not afford to give her the benefit of the doubt.

'Mr Manning has a client with him, but Mr Clarke is free. One minute and I'll check if he's available.'

'Actually, if it's all the same to you, I'd prefer to wait for Mr Manning. There is something else I need to talk to him about – something that happened several years ago that he handled. So I guess it's a sort of professional courtesy to broach the subject with him again.'

'Oh yes, of course. His client shouldn't be much longer.'

'Excellent. At least I can kill two birds with one stone, and hopefully I'll only get charged for the swearing. Anyway, how's life?' The question simply showed their continued friendship.

'Oh, not so bad I suppose. Clive's had a promotion, so he's being kept really busy.'

'Is he still in computers?'

'Yes. Design analyst now. Sounds awfully complicated to me, but he seems to cope quite well. Don't know how well he'll cope with the baby though.'

'You're pregnant?' Palmer could not help but sound surprised.

'Yes, it's just over two months. Don't tell anyone though, please, not even Mr Manning. We haven't told the family yet. We want to get the first scan done and make sure everything is okay, so please don't say anything.'

'I won't, I promise. That's great news, isn't it?'

'I suppose so, but I'll have to leave here I guess.'

'I don't see why. You'll get your maternity leave and then it's up to you.'

'Yeah, but between you and me I can't see myself as a working mother. I know some women manage it, but I don't think I could. I'd just want to stay at home and look after the baby.'

At that moment there were footsteps outside the office and a client, unseen to Palmer, descended the stairs to the street.

'That's Mr Manning's client. I'll ring through for you.'

The receptionist pressed a button on the switchboard console and spoke into her headset.

'Go on through, Mr Palmer,' she said in a voice that was not quite as friendly as it had been a few moments earlier.

Palmer did as requested and knocked politely on the door of John Manning. He was still holding the A4 sized envelope in his hand.

'Come in,' the voice behind the door beckoned, and to the trained ear it would have sounded confused.

Palmer entered the office and carefully shut the door behind him before speaking.

'Are you sure that thing is off?' He pointed at the intercom on Manning's desk, and spoke with a deliberately soft voice.

'I'm absolutely sure. Why? My secretary said you'd come to do a swear.'

'I know. Forget that and look at this.' Palmer opened the A4 sized white envelope and deposited the contents on Manning's desk. Manning picked up the envelope that had already been slit open and emptied the contents. Just as Palmer had done earlier, he unfolded the single sheet of paper. The message was still the same:

'THE BURNSTON WOMAN IS GUILTY – LEAVE IT AT THAT.'

'John,' Palmer continued after a short pause, 'I hate to say this but you have someone in this office who wants to ruin this case.'

'You're not wrong. This is awful. When did it arrive?'

'It came in the morning post. It was actually lying on my desk while we were discussing this case. It's a shame I hadn't opened the post before you arrived.'

'You mean someone knew I was asking you to get involved. That's impossible. Apart from myself, and Mrs Burnston, only my secretary would have had a chance of knowing, and that would have needed a good guess. When she phoned you on my behalf, I swear she had no idea what it was about. In fact, she still doesn't.'

'Well, someone does, and I've wracked my brains but I can't see how it can be anyone other than someone connected with this office.'

'I know, I know. Could it have been Burnston?'

'I did consider it. But you only talked to her the day before yesterday and she couldn't have got a message out that quickly. Not only that, but why would she? After all, she's banking on me proving her innocence.'

'True. Well, there are only two people in this firm that could be the person. There's my secretary, Carol, but I doubt it's her.'

'I doubt it,' said Palmer, evenly.

'And then there's the research assistant, but she didn't know I was getting you involved, or at least I hadn't told her.'

'I'll bet it's your research assistant. In fact I'll lay odds on it.' Palmer sounded surer of the matter than he felt at that precise moment. With Manning's next question he wished he'd kept quiet.

'And why do you say that?'

'Not sure really,' Palmer tried feebly to think up an excuse. 'Perhaps your secretary knew you were coming to see me and told your research assistant quite innocently or something like that.'

'I suppose that could be the answer. Anyway, it will take time to find out. For now we'd better be careful.' Manning sounded worried.

'I agree. We need to find out if this is an empty threat or something with substance.'

'And how do we do that?'

'Simple. We carry on as if it didn't arrive and see what happens next. By the way, did you have any luck fixing up the meeting for this afternoon?'

'Yes. Actually I've just left a message on your answer-phone. Two o'clock is fine with Rachel Connors, that's Mrs Burnston's sister. You have the address?'

'Yes, the address is in just about all the reports, including the one from Expert Investigations.'

'Well, in that case we had better get on.' As Manning spoke, Palmer replaced the letter and its envelope in the larger envelope and turned to the door.

'One thing, John, where is your research assistant today?'

'It's her day off.'

'And her name and address, just out of curiosity?'

Manning wrote the details down on a square of paper and handed them to the sleuth.

'Thanks, John, I might just have a look around and see if anything comes up.'

'If it does, let me know, won't you?'

'You'll be the first to hear, I promise.'

For the second time that day the sleuth and the solicitor parted company and Palmer made his way back towards the reception room. The door was open and the secretary sat at her desk. Palmer smiled perfunctorily at her and waved his farewells. She carried on typing, the headset making conversation difficult.

In a moment, Palmer descended the staircase that led to the street and began his walk home.

Chapter Three

The mid-morning shoppers were out in force when Palmer left the offices of Clarke and Manning. Palmer had developed a habit of always looking around him as he left the premises. In the past his caution had served him well and now the habit was almost second nature to him. He glanced first in the direction he intended to walk. There were people busying themselves around the local shops but nothing that would arouse suspicion. Then Palmer looked in the opposite direction.

At first Palmer saw nothing that raised his interest. Someone was crossing the road. There were a couple of window shoppers were all female, nothing of interest. He was just averting his gaze and turning to walk down in the intended direction when he spotted something. It made his stop momentarily. Across the road, standing in the doorway of the antique dealers was a woman. Instantly Palmer sensed danger. She was pretending to look in the side window but Palmer was sure she was watching the doorway he had just stepped out of. It was like a sixth sense and for some unfathomable reason he was sure she was watching out for him. Perhaps, he considered, she'd even followed him from his home to the solicitors.

He made up his mind and turned towards the woman, though he did not cross the road. He walked slowly, keeping one eye on the antique shop, the other straight ahead of him. He passed the antiques shop and continued walking for another twenty paces. Only then did he stop to ostensibly look in a shop window. After several seconds he turned away from the window and as he turned his line of sight fell once again on the antiques shop.

The woman, who Palmer considered was in her early twenties, had vanished. He walked back down the street and gazed inside the window of the antique shop. She was in there now, talking to the shop owner. As Palmer continued walking he wondered if he was experiencing the onset of paranoia. Was she really watching him after all? Perhaps not, but Palmer still felt uneasy about the situation.

He walked even more briskly now, with the stride of a man in a hurry. He crossed three roads and turned two corners before he stopped and waited. He was nearly home now and he still felt uneasy. He waited two minutes before she walked past the end of the road. As she did so she glanced down the road, evidently spotted Palmer and decided to continue walking.

Palmer knew it was the same woman. She had the same hair and the same coat and even at the distance from which he spotted her, there was no doubting she was the same woman. Palmer redoubled his stride, walking with the pace of a determined man. He crossed the final roads and finally entered his own. He doubted he was being followed now. After all, the woman must know where he lived so she would have been able to guess that was where he was heading.

He arrived home nearly twenty minutes after leaving the solicitor's office. With haste he removed his coat and scarf and entered his study. The empty coffee mug was still perched on the end of the blotter and the red light on his answerphone was flashing, indicating a message was waiting for him. Palmer ignored it as he turned the computer on. Only when he had entered his user identity and password did his attentions turn back to the mug. The computer completed its start-up procedures while Palmer went to the kitchen and recharged the mug with coffee. He returned to the study to find the computer ready and waiting for him. As he had done earlier that morning he selected a program and pressed the relevant keys.

While he waited for the computer to start the program he pressed the 'play' button on the answerphone.

'You have one new message,' the disembodied voice dispassionately advised him. There was the electronic sound of a 'BEEP' before the message began.

'Mr Palmer, good morning. It seems you do not understand simple messages.' The voice was male, evidently disguised and with no discernible accent. The person spoke evenly, almost in monotone. 'We know you received the letter this morning. Please can I tell you again that the Burnston woman is guilty as charged? If you persist in following this case then I am afraid that I cannot remain responsible for your safety. Good day.' The message ended and Palmer was given the option to listen to it again, which he did. The second time he listened he made some notes on his pad of paper. The notes were almost illegible but they contained the gist of the message and a few observations about its delivery. After he'd listened to the message a third time, Palmer deleted it. He turned his attention back to the computer.

This time he entered the name of the research assistant he'd been given by Manning. He waited for the program to search its database.

After maybe thirty seconds, and with a low whistle, Palmer noted the results of the search. He compared the address on the screen with the one he'd been given by Manning and observed their difference. As was his custom, he began to pace the length of his study, holding the two pieces of paper in his hand.

'Why,' he asked himself, 'would a research assistant give her employer a false address? Or is it simply a question of the database being out of date?'

There was only one sure way to find out, and Palmer made a mental note to find out as soon as possible. He looked at the two addresses and wondered which, if either was correct. If the Wimbledon address was true then it opened up all sorts of possibilities. If the Putney address was correct then that surely meant his earlier assertions were misguided. Palmer paced the length of the study a few more times and then placed the two addresses on his desk. He looked at his watch and decided there was no time now to discover the truth about them.

Palmer sat down in his leather swivel chair and once again picked up the documents he had been given earlier that morning. He read them again, with the trained eye of one experienced in detective work, with the mind of a person trying to find the slightest clue, and with the instinct of a gambler determined not to be beaten by the odds. He read the pages slowly, one at a time. He read the pathology report, and it was not pleasant reading. He read the police report. He scanned the report from Expert Investigations and he looked at the photographs. As he did so he became more and more convinced that the clue he was looking for lay within what he was reading. It was something that had been overlooked. It was as if the clue that was present in the documents was there only because something that should have been there was not.

After he had read the documents he sat back in the leather chair and closed his eyes in concentration. He sat this way, in total silence, for several minutes, his brain reaching out into the contents of the documents trying to find the vital missing clue. After maybe half an hour his eyes opened, and for nearly the first time in his life, Palmer was close to admitting defeat.

With this feeling came frustration. Instinctively he knew the clue was there and it frustrated him that after his period of deep thought he was no closer to unveiling it. He stood up and walked round the office before turning to gaze out of the window. The clouds had begun to close in and it seemed that the forecast of rain from the weatherman the previous evening would be proved correct. In the hall, the grandfather clock chimed eleven times.

Out on the grassy area two children were playing. No more than toddlers, they ran happily as their mother walked behind them. Their presence was a welcome break for the sleuth and he watched for some minutes as the children played around their mother.

After a while, Palmer looked away from the window. There was work to be done. Palmer looked back at the papers on his desk. He looked at the note warning him to stay away from the case, and he looked at the notes he'd made from the message on his answerphone. He searched for the reason for their existence – it was a reason that continued to elude him.

***

The grandfather clock in the hall chimed noon and as the last of the echoes faded into oblivion the sound of the doorbell reverberated through Palmer's office. He was still frustrated but had spent the last hour checking through another case that he was involved in. It was much less complicated than the one that had occupied his thoughts for much of the morning and he hoped to have it resolved in a few days.

Preoccupied as he was, it took him several seconds to react to the sound. As he stood up from his leather chair the sound penetrated his office for the second time. Before the caller had time to press the bell for the third time, Palmer reached the front door and opened it.

'Eddie, is that the time already? Come in, I won't be a minute.'

'Hey, you look hassled, and that's saying something.' Eddie Marston had never been one to hide his feelings and his expression fully justified what he sensed. Palmer looked perplexed, if only because he was.

'Well, I've got a lot on at the moment, which is why I gave you a call. Essentially I need some help making some enquiries, and they're the sort of enquiries that are right up your street.' Marston and Palmer had been friends and colleagues for several years, years that had taught them mutual respect for each other's capabilities and limitations, years that had taught them to trust each other, and years that had made their friendship genuine.

'So, do we talk here or down the pub?'

'Down the pub I think. I've spent enough time in here this morning. Then, when we come back, I'll give you any documents you need.'

'Fair enough.'

'Give me two minutes and we'll be off. Go in and take a seat, I just need to tidy some things up first.'

'Okay.' Marston entered the study and sat down on the interview chair. He looked around him, more out of habit than anything, for he had long ago memorised the major aspects of the room, and it was one of his gifts in life that his memory very rarely failed him. However, he took a certain degree of satisfaction and pride in congratulating himself that he had remembered everything correctly, so he took a few seconds to look around.

After a couple of minutes he heard Palmer descend the stairs in the hallway. A moment later he entered the study. As he did so he spoke.

'Is everything where you remembered it?'

'How did you know I was doing that? Yes they are.'

'You do it every time you come here. Still it's nice to know your memory is as good as ever. It

39

may pay dividends in this case I'm going to tell you about. Shall we go?'

As if by way of reply, Marston stood up and made his way towards the door. The walk to the pub was a short one and in less than five minutes the two men were sat round a small table in one corner. Their appearance seemed somewhat strange, for the rest of the pub was empty and they could easily have sat more in the open, but Palmer had decided seclusion was appropriate. On entering the pub they ordered lunch. Then they sat at the table and tasted the bitter for the first time.

'Not bad,' said Marston, appreciatively, after the first mouthful had been swallowed. 'Actually, it's pretty good.'

'Yes, they do a good pint here. The food's not bad either. Now, and I hope this doesn't put you off lunch, I have to tell you about this case.' Palmer went on to describe the early morning meeting with Manning. When he mentioned the Burnston murder, Marston nodded his head.

'You've heard about it before? Palmer was intrigued.

'Yeah, some local news reports a couple of months back. So how come you've got involved with it now?'

'Well, as I said, Manning came to see me. Basically, Heather Burnston has asked him to defend her and he needs my help.'

'Defend her?' Marston almost spat out the words. 'From what I remember she was caught at the scene holding the murder weapon!'

'Quite so, and if you speak any louder we might as well broadcast our involvement to the nation as well. Now, Manning says she is denying being the murderer. For what it's worth I've read the report and seen her picture and well, for the moment let's just say that something doesn't feel quite right. I don't know what yet, but there's something about it all that makes me half believe her.'

'Oh, come on, Damien, the cops have her banged to rights. Not even the greatest detective in the land could deny that.'

'Not on the face of it, but I say again that something doesn't feel quite right. So, here's what I want us to do. We ask around and build up a picture, that sort of thing. And we are very careful and very thorough. Manning's already involved Expert Investigations and they failed to get anywhere, so people may be a bit on the suspicious side. Hence the reason we need to be careful. Then, in a couple of days, we see how far we've got and take it from there. I'm going to the scene this afternoon.'

'What do you want me to do?'

'Go to Wimbledon and make some discreet enquiries. Pretend you're a long lost relative or something, and find out whatever you can. Concentrate on the neighbours, both sides of the house and across the road, and also see if there's a corner shop. If there is, then talk to whoever is behind the counter. You know the routine. Also, get me any car index numbers, makes, and so forth that you see parked round there. And then it's down to anything else you can think of. Remember, and this is in the reports I'll let you have a copy of, this crime probably happened sometime just before twelve on January 26th this year. It was a cold day, I checked with the Met office. Also, it was an unusual event for people round that way, so someone must remember something. If they do, no matter how insignificant it might seem, we need to know about it.'

'Fair enough. Is there anything else, before the food arrives?'

'Well, if you can get some pictures, then great. Oh, and don't forget, I'll be visiting the house at two o'clock. Just ignore me, and I'll ignore you too.'

'Right, here it comes.' Marston was sitting facing the kitchen area and he observed the young waitress walking towards them. As she walked, her hips wiggled, Marston presumed as a result of her high-heeled shoes.

'Lasagne?' She queried as she approached the table. Palmer nodded and moved his half full pint glass away from where the plate needed to rest. As the waitress leaned over to place the food in front of Palmer, he noticed she was quite a pretty young girl in her late teens. She had long, mousy-coloured hair that had been tied up at the back for her work, and although she was slim, and her arms thin, she was curvaceous enough to attract his attention for longer than was polite. The focus of his attention went unobserved by the teenager.

'And lemon chicken?' she said, needlessly, as she placed the second plate of food in front of Marston. 'Enjoy your meals.'

Palmer smiled sweetly at the waitress. 'Thank you and we will.' The waitress turned and wandered back in the direction of the kitchen.

'Eddie?'

'Yes?'

'Are we getting old, or are the waitresses these days getting younger?'

'We're getting old mate.'

'Yes, I thought so.' Palmer piled a portion of the lasagne on his fork and began his meal.

'Anyway,' said Marston after a couple of mouthfuls, 'if the cops have a picture of her standing over the body holding the murder weapon, how do you propose to prove she didn't do it?'

'Don't know, yet. It's just something Manning said this morning. It was something about her being adamant that she's not guilty, and that was after she'd been briefed thoroughly on the situation. Either she isn't guilty, or she's deluded, or she's having us all on.'

'She's probably having us all on. I really don't think I'm going to find out much that isn't known already.'

'Probably not, but it's worth a shot. Who knows what your enquiries might give rise to. There might even be a pretty waitress involved.' Palmer targeted the next piece of Lasagne and paused as he chewed on it. As he did so, he smiled at the observation he had made concerning his friend. 'This is good, how's your chicken?'

'Fine.' Marston pretended he had missed Palmer's quip about the waitress.

'Anyway, have you got anything lined up for this evening?'

'Nothing planned. I'll probably have a quiet night in with the telly or something. What about you?'

'Supposed to be seeing Karen at eight, but I tried phoning her first thing this morning and I couldn't get through, not even to the answer phone. Still, she'll be at work now and I don't really like using that number. I'll catch her later.'

'You two have been together now for some time, haven't you? Is it getting serious?'

'Yeah, time is marching on. We're still pretty casual about things but I suppose it is getting heavier as time passes.'

'She'll have a ring on her finger next.' Marston grinned, for he knew Palmer well.

'She might do, but it won't be mine. We've got a long way to go yet, and a few skeletons to let out of the cupboards.'

'Like your flings?'

'Yeah, and her flings too. I told you ages ago that we were pretty casual about that sort of thing. It happens to suit us both so we don't pry too much, and nothing's changed on that front so far as I'm concerned.'

'Well, don't go ruining a good relationship by being careless.'

'Thanks Eddie, I won't, believe me. Now, I have to get on with things. I have an appointment at two and I'm not particularly looking forward to it. Going to murder scenes doesn't do much for me I'm afraid.'

'Yeah, well, rather you than me mate. Who are you meeting?'

'The client's sister, apparently she's been looking after the house while her sister's remanded in custody.'

'That might be a bit longer than she thinks if you don't come up with something.' Marston's voice was sober and thoughtful. 'There is one thing, though. Something I heard about years ago. If you hit a main artery the blood spurts out, doesn't it? It's a bit like squeezing ketchup out of the tiny hole at the top of a plastic bottle, isn't it?'

'Yes, I believe so. So what's your point?'

'Well, if she had stood over him and stabbed him, and if she'd pierced an artery so the blood spurted up to the ceiling, she'd have probably got some of it on her own clothing, wouldn't she?'

'Yes, she probably did.'

'And that's my point.'

'What is?'

'Well, I saw the same picture that everyone saw from that local photographer. Okay, it was black and white and it was several weeks ago, but I don't recall seeing any blood on her.'

'Christ, are you sure?'

'Not totally, but my memory's pretty good on that sort of thing. Do you want me to check it out?'

'No. You stick to Wimbledon. If I get time I'll try to chase that one up. If not, it's something for another day.'

'Fair enough, I guess you'll have to go back to the paper to locate the photographer?'

'No need to. I should be able to order a colour version from the paper. We'd have it in a couple of days.'

'That might help prove things one way or the other.' Marston sounded pleased his train of thought had included the observation he'd locked away in his memory.

'Well, if she's covered in blood it would help the case for the police. If, on the other hand she is clean, then it doesn't help them. But it doesn't prove she didn't do it. Remember, she might have just been standing to one side at the time.'

'True, I suppose. Anyway, it might help.'

'It certainly might, and Eddie, it's a good idea. I hope you're right. Look, I'd better get moving if I'm going to get to Wimbledon for two. Are you ready?'

'Yeah, now I need that paperwork you were going to give me.'

Palmer and Marston drained their glasses and walked the short distance back to Palmer's house. It took a few minutes for Palmer to select the relevant pages of the reports. He handed them to his colleague and waited patiently as he read them. It may not be entirely accurate to say that Marston had a photographic memory, but he was extraordinarily good at remembering things he'd seen. It took him less than five minutes to read the half dozen pages before he handed them back to Palmer.

'That was pretty much like I remembered the press reports at the time. There's a bit more detail, but nothing of use to me. Interesting that Manning didn't have any pictures though.' Marston looked evenly at Palmer as he spoke.

'Yeah, I'll have to talk to him about that. I might actually go into Wimbledon Library and look on the fiches while I'm there. It'd be quicker than waiting for a picture order.'

'Okay. I could do it, if you wanted?'

'There's no need to. You'll be busy snooping around. I don't expect to be at the house for more than about twenty minutes. The police will have taken away anything that might have been of use to us. It's more of a formality really.'

'Fine. Well, I'd best be off.' Marston stood up and walked back into the hall. In a moment the two men had bid each other farewell and Palmer turned back to his study. When they'd returned from lunch he'd noticed that the answer phone was flashing but, as he always did when he had company, he chose to ignore it. Now, with Marston on his way to Wimbledon, Palmer turned his attention to the message that was waiting for him.

'Hi, darling, it's Karen. Hope you haven't been trying to contact me at home but the stupid machine ate the tape yesterday. If you're still coming over to me tonight then there's no need to call me, but if there's a problem could you ring me at home after six thirty. See you later.' The message ended with a sound that was only vaguely similar to the kiss that had blown down the mouthpiece. Palmer looked at his clock and realised he was going to be late for his two o'clock appointment if he did not hurry.

Chapter Four

Palmer had never been known for driving slowly, and at times his friends had cause to be concerned for their own safety. Palmer, though, was a skilled driver and he had even been accredited with an advanced motorist certificate. This particular afternoon the traffic was light and it took him only a few minutes to reach the Tibbet's Corner roundabout where the A3 artery into London crosses the main road that connects Putney to Wimbledon Village.

As Palmer joined the roundabout, the first drops of rain landed on his windscreen. As they did so, he realised that the lighting conditions had deteriorated quite suddenly, to the extent that some of the other vehicles using the road had elected to turn on side lights. He joined their number as he steered the car onto the road that skirted the side of Wimbledon Common. He passed the familiar turning that would have taken him to the windmill. Then, after slowing for a driver that was displaying 'L' plates, he finally reached the village. He turned right and headed towards Raynes Park.

The road was narrow and twisty and Palmer had to drive considerably more slowly. It was just two o'clock when he found the turning he was looking for. The houses were lined up in pairs of semis. The neat front gardens were small and the planners back in the 1930's had built off road parking or garages for all the homes. Palmer now selected a low gear as he searched for the house he wanted. He passed number 19 and the road began to slope steeply downwards towards the main town of Wimbledon. Suddenly there was a space in the parking bays that had been marked out along much of the road and Palmer took the opportunity to stop.

He turned to look in the back of the car and picked up the top-opening brown case that he habitually took with him on such visits. He pulled the bag over to the passenger seat and rummaged inside it for a few seconds. Satisfied, he opened the car door and in a moment began the short walk back up the road. He found the house he was seeking and walked up the drive to the front door. He pressed the doorbell and waited, looking exactly like an insurance salesman on a call. As he waited, he looked at the neat, bronze, number 19 that had been screwed to the central panel of the door.

The door opened slightly and Palmer stepped forward.

'Mrs Connors?' He enquired. 'I'm Damien Palmer.' He reached out a hand in greeting. The woman opened the door to allow him to enter. As she opened it, Palmer could not but help admire her. Whilst his client, Heather Burnston, was short and almost painfully thin, the woman standing before him was genuinely stunning and Palmer estimated that she was at least five feet eight inches tall. She had flowing, naturally blond hair that reached down to the small of her back and, without being as thin as her sister, Palmer considered that she would have had a better than even chance as a model. Her beauty took him aback slightly, though he recovered quickly.

'You'd better come in, Mr Palmer.' Her voice was silken, and there was a depth to it that was almost seductive.

Palmer did as she requested and the door closed behind him. She showed him into the lounge and they sat down.

'Now, Mrs Connors,' Palmer began though he was immediately interrupted.

'Please, do call me Rachel.' Palmer was sitting in the armchair and the woman on the large sofa. She began by sitting back in a relaxed manner, but as she spoke she sat up and leaned forward. As she did so it became obvious that her designer clothes, which were of a loose fitting, were also provocative under certain conditions.

'Now, Rachel,' Palmer continued, 'I understand from your sister's solicitor that you and your husband contacted him as soon as Heather was arrested back in January?'

'That's right.'

'Forgive me for asking, but how did you choose him when his offices are about ten miles away?'

'Oh, there's no secret. My husband, Warren, has a business out that way and the firm uses the solicitors. So when this came up it was a natural choice.'

'I see, obvious really. And what does your husband do, exactly?'

'Well, if I say he's a photographer but not the run of the mill kind, does that tell you what you need to know?'

'For now, that's fine. Just curiosity really, but why does he need a solicitor for that?'

'Well, there are a couple of reasons really. Firstly, it's a partnership. James, that's his partner, and he, were at school together. Now, Warren's the photographer, but James is good at computers and things that are technical. So they set up this business and it works well for them. I actually met Warren when I went to have some pictures done. That was ten years ago, and I was nineteen at the time.' She smiled seductively as she remembered her first encounter with her husband-to-be. 'We started dating and after a couple of years we teamed up. Their premises include a studio and all the usual things.'

Palmer smiled back.

'Now, Rachel,' he began as she leaned slightly closer to him, 'what do you think happened here?'

'I'm sorry, and it's most rude of me. Can I get you a drink first?'

'Tea would be nice, if you have any.'

'I can make it in a minute. We've kept most things here and I just bring milk and whatever when I come up. I won't be a minute.'

'Actually, do you mind if I come and have a look at the kitchen while you're making it?'

'No, be my guest. We've had all the mess cleaned up. We even had the hall carpet replaced. Luckily we managed to find the same carpet, so you'd never know.'

'I read the reports. Did you clean it up yourself?'

'Well, Warren did the worst of it. He's more used to blood and things. Once the worst had been done I came over and gave it the woman's touch.'

She stood up and Palmer followed her curvaceous body into the kitchen.

'It's all cleaned up now and you'd never know anything happened here.' She was still talking with her deep, seductive tones. It was beginning to have an effect on Palmer. He was a man who went much on first impressions and his views on meeting the woman he was now following had been very favourable indeed. In fact he found her deep, silky voice, very hard to ignore.

Palmer took a quick look around the kitchen as she filled the kettle. It was a medium-sized room with a square floor space of about ten feet. The floor was tiled and the kitchen units and work surfaces surrounded three of the walls, except for the gap on the outside wall where the door to the garden was situated.

'I gather the garden door was locked and that the key was on the inside,' Palmer continued the conversation.

'I believe so. It's certainly the way I'd seen things when I'd been round before. Heather was always worried about getting out if there was a fire, so they always either left the keys in the door or near to it.'

Palmer had been examining the back door in detail. It was a modern door, double-glazed and metal framed. The door was split horizontally into two sections, with glass panels top and bottom. He leaned over and examined the bottom of the doorframe. As he did so, he didn't hear the woman walking up behind him. He straightened and instantly felt her body behind him as his back touched her.

'I'm sorry,' he said immediately, 'I didn't know you were behind me.'

'That's all right. I shouldn't have been peering over you quite so closely. I just have this fascination about what you people do.'

'Well, in this case, not a lot. Just checking the door is as secure as it looks.'

'And is it?'

'Oh yes. It's top quality and is very secure. Not only that but it has multipoint locking so it would be very difficult to force an entry.'

'So, if I keep it locked, we're quite safe?' Palmer missed the change in the sense of what she was saying. He turned round to find her standing only a very short distance from him. Her lips were open, seductively, invitingly. As he turned to face her she reached a hand up and gently touched his face.

'You detectives are supposed to be such tough men. But actually you come across as being really kind and gentle and you have soft skin.' Her words were spoken slowly and, if it were possible, she reached a new, higher, level of seduction in the tone of her voice. Palmer was not used to this kind of approach from his clients and he stood there stunned for a fraction of a second too long. He stood there, amazed that this siren had managed to uncover his weakness in just the few minutes he had known her. She was rapidly uncovering the hard mask he wore each day of his life. It was this that made him stand stunned for the fraction of a second.

The woman, who was not much shorter than him, reached forward to kiss him. As she did so, he looked towards the floor and met the view offered by her loose fitting jumper. The contact was not particularly passionate but it did convey the woman's intentions. Palmer recovered now and stood back.

'I'm sorry, Rachel, but there's work to be done. And anyway, it wouldn't be right, you being a client.'

'But I'm not your client, my sister is, and we do have the house to ourselves.'

'But, but, you're a married woman!' Palmer was struggling to protest at her advances. Somewhere, something was urging him not to protest too strongly.

'So what, he hasn't wanted me in ages. He's preoccupied with his precious business and he doesn't have any time to treat me right. Anyway, I reckon he's at it, so why shouldn't I be, and you're the most gorgeous looking guy I've seen in ages.'

'If you're suspicious you could always hire someone to check him out.'

'What, someone like you?' She was still standing only a few feet from the investigator. She laughed slightly.

'Yes, someone like me.'

'Would you do it for me? I'd pay you, of course. Money is no object.' She took half a step towards Palmer who instinctively stepped backwards. His shoulders touched the back door and he realised he could retreat no further.

'I could do, if you are sure.'

'Well, it would be rather fun to know what the old man does when he's not with me.'

'We can discuss that in a few minutes. Do you mind if I just finish off what I came here for?'

'Sorry?' Her voice was surprised.

'Yes, remember? I came here to see if I could help your sister.'

'I hadn't forgotten. What else do you want to see?'

'Well, I presume that Mr. Burnston's own things, like his clothes, are still here.'

'Oh yes. Warren and I have done some sorting out, but we don't know what Heather's intentions are, so we've put all his clothes and things in the spare room.'

'Care to show me? It could be helpful.'

'Follow me.' The woman led the detective out of the kitchen and up the stairs. She was some feet ahead of him and as she climbed the staircase Palmer realised that the skirt she was wearing was not only very short but it was slit down the middle of the back to the extent that it was almost indecent. Trying hard to ignore this, he looked around as he climbed the remaining half dozen steps. He spotted the loft access in the ceiling at the top of the stairs. It was typical of such houses and was not of consequence.

'The master room is here,' she said, pointing at one door that was closed, 'and the spare room where we put all John's stuff is in there. I'll leave you to it if you don't mind.'

'Thanks,' Palmer responded as he opened the door. He was greeted by a single bed, upon which had been piled high a mountain of clothes. On the floor beside the bed was an attaché case, a modern one with combination lock.

Palmer closed the door carefully and began his examination. He located two suits and found they were empty. The rest of the clothing was more casual and it was evident the woman and her husband had very carefully checked each item some time ago, so Palmer turned his attention to the attaché case. Not surprisingly, it was locked. Undaunted, Palmer spent a few moments turning the dials of the combination lock. Suddenly he felt the lock yield under the light pressure that he was exerting on the tumbler as he turned the dials. In a moment the lid sprang open.

It seemed that his efforts were in vain. The case contained only a few papers upon which had been scribbled some indecipherable notes. Palmer held the papers up to examine them and after a moment carefully folded them and placed them in his own pocket. As he did so, he carefully closed the case and relocked it. He looked once more around the room and decided that there was little point in conducting a more detailed examination. If there had ever been anything worth finding it had long since been removed from the room, though he doubted there had ever been anything that would help him.

In less than five minutes, Palmer stood once again on the landing. Rachel Connors was nowhere to be seen, so Palmer tried the door of the master bedroom. As the door opened he realised that it was a mistake. The room itself was immaculate. The large Emperor sized bed occupied the central part of the bedroom. A couple of oak coloured wardrobes filled the back wall and the neat bedside tables with reading lamps completed the furniture, with the exception of the oak coloured dressing table that filled the area of the bay window. As the door opened Palmer noted the furniture and then his attention was distracted by one further observation.

Palmer had already realised that Rachel Connors was an attractive woman, and that she had seductive charms. Now, as she reposed on the bed, his observations were confirmed. The short skirt had been seductively made to ride a little higher than was decent, and the woman had chosen to remove the loose fitting jumper she had been wearing a few minutes earlier. She was lying on her left side watching the door, her head propped up on the arm that was supporting her. Palmer could not help but notice once again her womanly charms. She had full, yet firm breasts, and she was clearly aroused.

'Don't be shocked, Mr. Palmer, I'm not. I'm used to doing this sort of thing. Remember, it's how I met my husband?'

'Oh, it was that kind of photo shoot. I did wonder.' Palmer sat on the edge of the bed as she beckoned towards him. As he sat down, she sat up and draped her hands over his shoulders. As she did so, she sat up until her breasts filled his line of vision.

'Do you like them?' Her voice was soft and deep.

'They are attractive, as you are. Now what are you expecting to happen?'

'I'm hoping we can discuss terms for having my husband followed.'

'I don't do that kind of negotiation,' Palmer offered lamely, though his brain was now totally confused concerning this woman. By some miracle of professional aplomb he stood up and backed away from the woman's advances.

'Well, in that case I'll just have to pay you,' she said with a hint of regret and rejection in her voice.

Palmer was not unused to these kinds of experiences. He had, over the years, gained a reputation amongst his lady friends for being a good lover. However, what was happening to him this particular afternoon was seriously out of line with the professional approach he had decided was appropriate in such circumstances. Even with that approach he still found it hard to resist the lure of the semi-naked woman sprawled out for his pleasure on the bed. Finally his sensibility won the day.

'I'm sorry,' Palmer sounded disappointed as he faced up to the reality of the situation, 'but I don't do this kind of thing with my clients. It's nothing personal, but it would be totally wrong.'

'It's me that should apologise. I guess it's a case of abstinence makes the heart grow fonder and well, when I saw you, I just wanted to see if I could attract a man like I used to in the old days. I guess I haven't lost the knack, have I?'

'No, you certainly haven't. So, you're not upset or anything?' Palmer's voice was one of relief.

'Good Lord, no. Look on it as an experiment or something. Now, before you go I really do want to discuss having my husband followed.'

Palmer could hardly believe what he was hearing. This extraordinarily attractive woman had just attempted to seduce him, and now she wanted him to investigate her husband's own misdoings.

'Okay, but we'll talk about this downstairs,' he said after a moment. With that he left the bedroom and went down the stairs and waited in the lounge. He heard her go to the bathroom and it was perhaps five minutes before she followed him down the stairs. When she entered the room it was as if nothing had happened.

'Now, Mr Palmer, have you seen all you came to see.'

'I think so. As I expected, there's not much left after the police investigation. Now, are you sure about your husband?'

'I'm quite sure. If he's having it away with some young thing I don't see why I shouldn't have a bit of fun as well.'

'Like the way you tried with me this afternoon?'

'Yes, and no, now what do you need to know?' Her seductive voice had vanished and her tone was now more business-like.

'Your address, what he does, where he goes, car type and registration number, and a picture would be useful?'

Rachel Connors spent the next ten minutes discussing her husband with the detective. As she wrote down her address and telephone number, he noted she was left-handed. She described the car in detail and his place of work. She also casually mentioned that her husband had told her he would be going out the following evening at eight o'clock, though he had not told her where. Finally she pulled her bag up from the side of the settee and rummaged inside. Her hand came out holding a slightly worn picture.

'And this is him.'

'Excellent. Can I keep this for now?'

'Certainly, now the only thing we haven't mentioned is cost.'

'Well, I suppose you'd be looking at about two to three hundred if it's an easy job, and upwards from there. But,' Palmer rubbed his chin thoughtfully, 'if I were to do it as part of my investigations into your sister's case then we could cut it down a bit.'

'Why would you want to investigate my husband in connection with her case?' For a moment Palmer thought she sounded anxious. The moment passed.

'Oh, I wouldn't. It's just that I could do it to show I've been thorough. There would be one proviso?'

'And what's that?'

'I'd have to include something on you as well. Otherwise it would look odd. You know, make it look like a routine investigation of the sister and her husband, that sort of thing. Looks good for the report but it would just be dressing. The real work I do on your husband would be just for you. That way I can hide the costs.'

'Okay. When will you do it?'

'Well, from what you've said, I'll probably make a start tomorrow. I should be finished in a few days if all goes well. Now, unless there's anything else, I'd best get a move on. It's nearly four o'clock and I have some other things to attend to.'

'No. Nothing else and I ought to be getting home too. It's only a couple of minutes' walk, but the house has to look right for when Warren gets back or there's trouble, and I'm not into that sort of thing this evening, if you understand me.'

'I think so, and what time does he usually get home?'

'It could be any time after five o'clock. It depends on his work load, or at least so he tells me.'

Within a matter of a few minutes, Palmer was standing on the doorstep saying his farewells, careful that any observer would see precisely what he wanted them to see. The door closed respectfully behind him as he continued his journey down the path.

As Palmer walked the short distance to his car he felt in his trouser pocket to make sure the sheets of paper he had removed from the attaché case were still there. He smiled to himself when he found they were secure. Apart from Rachel's presence, it had been a disappointing visit, with little of interest to the sleuth. Doubtless the firm of Expert Investigations had also visited the house and they too, according to their report, had found very little, though it had taken the author some four pages to say it. Now, as he left the scene of the crime, Palmer began to understand their disillusionment. He surmised that this was going to be a particularly awkward case to crack, always assuming that John Manning's client wasn't the guilty party.

After his inspection of the kitchen it seemed unlikely that anyone could have gained access through the kitchen door. It was double glazed with a multi-point locking system that made the door one of the safest on the market. Not only that but the police report had been quite specific that there had been no signs of an attempted break-in, either through the kitchen door, or any other door or window. As he had looked at the kitchen door, Palmer had been forced to conclude that whoever had killed John Burnston must have had legitimate access to the house. It was not looking good for Manning's client.

Palmer regained the warmth of his car and in a few moments was joining the traffic into the heart of Wimbledon. It took just a few minutes to drive the short distance and Palmer was grateful to almost immediately locate an empty parking bay. He paid for an hour and made his way to the redbrick building that boasted the legend above its doorway of 'Library'. He pushed the door open and went inside. His visit was one of purpose and in less than ten minutes he had located the newspaper article that interested him. In a further ten minutes he was back in his car with a copy of the article neatly folded on the passenger seat.

It was probably the first time in the case that Palmer had been tempted to believe Manning's client. Despite all the evidence against her, when Palmer had taken his first look at the picture he had whistled softly to himself, much to the annoyance of the ever-attendant librarian who'd given him such a hostile look that Palmer had immediately apologised. The whistle had been an involuntary reaction, for the picture confirmed Marston's earlier recollection. The black and white picture clearly showed dark stains of blood on the kitchen work surfaces, and it showed the pool of blood surrounding the victim. What the picture also showed was Heather Burnston still holding the knife as she stood over her deceased husband. Yet, apart from one or two possible tiny stains, her clothing seemed to be almost completely untouched by the sanguine deluge. It was the first ray of hope for Palmer, but as he had said earlier to Marston, it didn't prove she hadn't committed the crime.

Chapter Five

It was nearly five o'clock when Palmer returned to his car. The traffic was building for the onslaught of the rush hour and Palmer joined the growing stream of traffic ascending Wimbledon hill. He had one final task to complete before preparing for the evening. He'd left it until now simply because he knew the person he'd be visiting would be out until after the children returned from school. Now, at five o'clock, he could be reasonably certain the person would be in.

Palmer drove for ten minutes in the traffic and pulled off into a side road at the top of the village. This would take him only a few minutes but it had been waiting for a couple of days and he knew the solicitor would soon be asking questions. He found the front door and pressed the doorbell.

After a minute a child opened the door.

"Yes, mister," he said, the evidence of his tea still round his mouth.

"Is your mother in?" Palmer asked the boy quite gently. There was no need for alarm, no need to create drama.

"Yeah, who is it?"

"Tell her I want to speak to her, please," Palmer smiled disarmingly. The boy slammed the door shut and ran off into the house. A few moments later a somewhat harassed looking adult opened the door.

"Sorry about that," she started. "It's just that he's not supposed to open the door to strangers."

"That's very wise." Palmer smiled again. "Now, are you by any chance Mrs Janice Reed?"

"Who wants to know?"

"I do. Sorry, I should have introduced myself. I'm Damien Palmer and I am what you could call a Private Investigator."

"So, why do you need to know?"

"I have some good news for the right person."

"Well, in that case, Mr Palmer, you'd better come in."

"You are Janice Reed?"

"Yes. Hang on while I get my driving licence to prove it." The woman shut the door behind Palmer and left him standing in the hallway looking at her grubby eight year old son. She returned in a moment and handed the licence to Palmer. "So what's this good news?"

"Just a minute, Mrs Reed, I need to make a few checks first. Do you know a certain Doris Engelbrook?"

"Yes, dear old thing, she lives out Sutton way. She used to live next door until they put her in one of those awful homes. Used to look after her here, visit her every day and so forth. That was until about four years ago when she got too frail and got put in this home. I haven't been to see her for six months now. I must try and go there soon."

"I'm afraid that's a bit late. Mrs Engelbrook died a month ago. I've been employed by the solicitor who's handling her affairs to locate you as one of her main beneficiaries. It seems that your dear old lady has left you a considerable sum of money. Now, before you get too excited there are some formalities to go through. They're all here in the envelope. You need to contact the solicitor as soon as possible and make an appointment to go and see him."

"Why didn't he write to me directly?" She asked, dazed by the news.

"Because Mrs Engelbrook did not have your address in her effects and her sole survivor, a grandson, was less than helpful, or so I understand. Now, I'm sorry if this is a bit of a shock for you. Are you going to be all right or is there somebody I can get to come and sit with you?"

"No, I'm fine. My boy will look after me." She sniffed as a tear trickled down her cheek. "Did she suffer?"

"No, I don't think so. She passed away during the night I believe."

"Oh, that's good. Poor old dear, nobody seemed to want to know her really."

"Yes, the home said she got very few visitors."

"Do you know what she has left me?"

"No, not exactly, all I've been told is it is a considerable sum of money, that's all. You can read into that what you will but as she was elderly I wouldn't get too excited if I were you. Now, I must be going. All the information you need is in the envelope and I've included my card in cases you need me for anything in the future. I will be calling the solicitor's in the morning to let them know I have contacted you."

"Well, thank you, Mr Palmer, wasn't it?"

"Damien Palmer. Sorry you didn't know about Mrs Engelbrook, I assumed you must have heard, seeing as it was a month ago."

"No. I don't get out much not with my kid to look after and a job to keep down. It's not been easy since his father left us."

"No, it can't have been. Anyway, I wish you well, Mrs Reed." Palmer was standing by the front door and opened it as he spoke.

"Thanks again, Mr Palmer."

"Good bye now." Palmer turned and walked down the path to his car.

***

Marston's afternoon passed swiftly. His journey to Wimbledon Village took place sometime before Palmer's and he followed much the same route to his destination. As with Palmer, he located the house that had been the scene of the crime but, unlike Palmer, he made no attempt to enter the building. Having located the road, he turned the car round and swiftly drove away. He headed back towards the village and parked in a side road. The rain began to fall and Marston formulated his own plan of action. The newsagents shop on the main road was his first target. It was a small shop and the only one selling papers in the area. Marston felt sure this would be a good point to start his investigations.

As he pushed open the door a bell sounded inside, attracting the shop assistant's attention. She was a short woman with jet-black hair. She looked as old as the shop yet her smile as Marston walked up to the counter made the investigator feel more comfortable.

'Hi,' he began, 'I don't know if you can help me, but I'm trying to locate an old friend of mine. I know she lives round here somewhere, but I don't know exactly where.'

'Well, there are nearly two thousand people around here. Why do you think I might know her?'

'I don't know really. I just remember the last time I was over, and that was about ten years ago, we went into a newspaper shop, and she paid her bill. And, unless I'm mistaken, you're the only one round here, so I thought it might be here.' Marston was speaking with a phoney southern accent, almost Australian, but not quite.

'Well, I'll try. An old friend you say? Why didn't you bring her address with you?'

'Actually, I do have it on me. Well some of it, only the bit that used to have the address and instructions isn't readable anymore. I dropped it in a pool of water a couple of days back and the ink ran quite badly. This is all I've got left I'm afraid.'

Marston handed the smudged paper over to the woman. 'Not much use really, is it?'

'Let's see. Name's Heather, number 19 Rid... something or other, and it's right off the village roundabout then left and something else.'

The woman scratched her head for a moment.

'You don't know her surname do you?'

'Well, her maiden name was Fox. I know that because we went out with each other for a few years. She got married some years back and wrote and told me and sent me these instructions. I came over a year or so after the wedding and found the place, no problem. This time though I can't seem to find it. I guess things have changed a bit over the years.'

'You don't know her married name, do you?'

'Something like Brenton, Bursham, something like that.' As Marston spoke the woman's eyes opened wider. Marston knew he was having the desired effect.

'Not Burnston, by any chance?' the woman's curiosity got the better of her.

'That's it! So you do know them!' Marston sounded relieved and if anything his southern accent was improving with practice.

'Know her, yes. Half of the country knows her name. Haven't you heard?'

'Heard what?' Marston judged the tone of apprehension to perfection, yet still maintained his phoney accent.

'Well, it's not really for me to say.' The woman was clearly having second thoughts about what she should say.

'Oh, go on, it can't be that bad, and Heather said she'd stay in touch.'

'She can't.'

'She is all right, isn't she?' Marston's voice was becoming more apprehensive by the word.

'Sort of, I suppose, but you really don't know, do you?'

'Know what?' Added to the apprehension was now a degree of impatience.

'Well, a few months ago now, January time, her husband was killed. It was in all the papers.'

'Good God, why didn't she write and tell me?' The feigned surprise was perfect.

'She couldn't, because she was arrested for killing him.' The woman sounded almost apologetic.

'She was what?'

'I said,' her sentence went unfinished.

'I know what you said, but that can't be right. Heather would never harm a fly.' Indignation now followed apprehension in his voice.

'That's as maybe, but they say the police found her at the scene holding the knife that killed him. Not only that, they've been in this shop several times together, and they were often rowing. She only had to say the slightest thing wrong and he'd fly at her.'

'Poor old Heather, I wonder where she is? I ought to go and visit her.'

'Papers said the trial starts in a couple of weeks. You might find a copy in the library if you're lucky, and it might tell you where she's being held.'

'I'll give it a try. So you reckon her husband was a bit of a thug then?'

'Oh yes. She's been in here a few times with a cut lip and bruising round one or other eye. From this side of the counter you don't like to ask what happened, but it was pretty obvious.'

'You mean she was being knocked around, poor kid?'

'Yes, I don't know why she stayed with him actually. She was always so nice and polite and friendly. Shame it had to end this way.'

'Did you ever get to know the husband that well?'

'Not really, though he was a bit of a loud mouth, or so the gossip was saying after his death. There was one ugly rumour that went round.' Even as she spoke the words the woman put her hand to her mouth as if she had said too much.

'Go on, I'm interested in anything that might help poor old Heather.'

'Well, and I don't know if it's true at all, but the rumour was he'd been having an affair and his wife found out about it, and it was the affair that made her lose control.'

'That doesn't sound like Heather to me, but I guess people can change over the years. Doesn't seem much point in finding out the address now seeing as no one will be at home. Anyway, thanks for telling me all about it. You've saved me some time. I'd best get off down to the library and see if I can find out where she is.' Marston turned and was walking back towards the door when the old woman called him back.

'There was one other thing that I heard,' she called out with a leering tone in her voice.

'And what was that?' Marston turned but did not approach the counter again.

'I did hear that he was involved in some kind of sect or something years back and that maybe he'd conjured up something then and it had come back to get him.' The woman laughed and waved Marston away. 'Some people will believe anything,' she chortled to herself as he left the shop.

It was true, and Marston knew it for sure, that desperate people will sometimes believe almost anything. But he was not desperate and her final divulgence seemed unnecessary. It was, thought

Marston, as if she was trying to lead him away from the truth, a truth that he and Palmer had only a few days to find.

Marston left the shop and made for the direction of the scene of the crime. His intentions were already formed in his mind and they did not include actually visiting the scene. After all, that was Palmer's job.

It took Marston a couple of minutes to reach the road he had turned round in sometime earlier. The rain had eased now and was little more than a fine drizzle. He walked down the road carefully and passed number nineteen. As he did so, he spotted Palmer's car and noted the bonnet was still hot. Marston made a mental note to include the fact in his report. It would show he was paying attention to detail, something Palmer had always stressed as being of vital importance in undertaking surveillance. Marston walked down the road, and then walked back up it, until he reached number 21. He walked up the short path to the front door. The house was typical of the road, a semi-detached 1930's style building. Unlike the house next door, its windows had not been replaced and it badly needed a coat of paint on the exterior woodwork. Marston mentally noted down all these details before the door was answered.

In response to the ring on the doorbell a short, plump, middle-aged woman with a ruddy complexion opened the door to inspect her visitor.

'Yes,' she beamed, glad that she had someone to talk to. Marston summed up the situation from the tone of her single word and the enthusiasm and warmth with which she spoke. She was a lonely woman who relished company, and she was the perfect person for Marston to talk to this particular afternoon.

'Oh hi, I'm David Fox.' Marston's phoney Australian accent was clearly intriguing the woman. Marston continued, 'I don't know if you can help me but I'm looking for my sister's house. I'm sure she lives round here somewhere.'

'Well, dear, that all depends. I've lived here for about thirty years now, so I know most of the people, unless she's only just moved in.'

'No. She's lived here at least five years. Got married about ten years ago, which was when I went to Australia. Been travelling round Europe for the past six months and thought I'd get in touch. I know she's round here somewhere, but for the life of me I can't find the bit of paper I wrote her address on.'

'Well, if you tell me her name, I might be able to help you.'

'Gee, thanks, well before she got married she was known as Heather Fox, but I guess you'd only know her by her married name. Truth is I haven't got much of a memory and we only ever wrote once or twice a year. If I remember right it was something like Brenton, Bursham, something like that.' As Marston spoke the woman's eyes opened wider. Marston knew that for the second time in less than an hour his tactics were paying off.

'It couldn't have been Burnston, by any chance?' The woman was still smiling though Marston detected something else in her voice.

'That's it, Burnston, so you do know her!'

'I should do, she's been my neighbour for over five years. You'd better come in.'

'So she lives next door. Well, thanks for your help, but I'd better go and see her. I haven't got long before I have to get on the move again. Once again thanks for your help.' Marston made as if to turn away from the woman but stopped in his tracks as she spoke.

'But she's not there.'

'Are you sure?'

'I'm one hundred percent sure. Now, do you want to come in, there's something you should know?'

Marston feigned surprise and made to enter the house. 'Everything is all right, isn't it?' His question was framed with just about enough degree of concern to pass any credibility check that the woman might have been making.

'Sort of, now would you like to come in, or do I have to tell you on the doorstep?'

'Thanks, I'll come in.' Marston deliberately looked grave about the situation.

'You say she's your sister, hey?' The woman continued once they were in the living room. 'Funny, but I don't remember Heather ever mentioning having a brother.'

'Probably because I sort of left under a cloud, which was why I went to Australia. But we did stay in touch, you know, birthdays, Christmas, that sort of thing. I guess she saw me as a bit of a black sheep, which is why she didn't mention me.'

'Well there's something you ought to know, and I'm afraid it will be a bit of a shock too you.

Heather is under arrest. She has been for a couple of months or so now.'

'Under arrest! What is she under arrest for?'

'Murder. You really have no idea, do you?' The woman continued, noticing that Marston had gone quite pale. Indeed Marston's act was almost worthy of an Oscar.

'None at all, what happened?' he stammered.

'Well, one day in January the police turned up at her front door. It seems like they'd been tipped off, or something. Anyway they found your sister in the kitchen holding a knife, and standing over her very dead husband.'

'That's not like Heather, well not the Heather I used to know. She was such a quiet little creature. There must be some mistake.'

'Well, the police are pretty sure it was her. Her trial starts in a couple of weeks now. I have to go to court as some sort of witness. Don't know what good I'll be, I'd gone to stay a few days with my brother when it all happened. Best I'll be able to say is that they were always rowing about things and there'd often be these banging noises late at night. Then, the next day, her face would often be all bruised. Poor thing, I can't say I blame her, he was such a brute.'

'Really, it's funny how she never mentioned it when she wrote. Oh well, that's brothers for you! The last people you confide in, I guess.'

'Anyway, there was something else about John. He was a bit strange. Like he'd often go out and get drunk and start shouting at her when he got home again. I remember one particular evening, sometime just before Christmas I think it was. He'd been out

75

and obviously came home the worse for drink. It didn't take long for the shouting and swearing to start I can tell you. Anyway, in amidst the tirade of abusive language he used, and if you don't mind me taking out all the swear words, he said something about how she should never have gone through, what was it, oh yes, the rite of the first hour, if she didn't want to be a member of the group. It didn't make any sense to me at the time but I can't get those words out of my mind.'

'Sorry, what was that rite?'

'I think he called it the rite of the first hour. Do you know what it means?'

'No.' Marston committed this piece of information to memory, a memory that had never yet failed him.

'Well, I'm sure Heather once told me he was involved in a group of some kind and they did weird things. It was a long time ago and I can't remember much.' Marston thought she was probably lying, but it had already been a useful meeting and he wasn't about to press her on the subject.

'I suppose these shouting matches, or whatever, didn't happen to occur at certain times of the month, or week, did they?'

'Not really, but I suppose they happened most on a Friday or Saturday night. I always thought it was after he'd been down the pub.'

'You're probably right. Anyway you've been very helpful. I don't suppose you know where my sister is being held, do you?'

'Sorry, but I do know that your other sister does.'

'Other sister, oh you mean Rachel.' As Marston said this the woman visibly relaxed.

'Yes. She lives round hereabouts somewhere. I could get her address for you next time I see her.'

'No need, Rachel never blamed me like Heather. We've stayed in touch, well up until I started touring Europe about six months ago. I've got her address written down in the little book. Shame I didn't put Heather's in there too. Anyway, Mrs,' the sentence went unfinished as Marston paused.

'Miss Simpson, as in Edward and, but absolutely no link I'm afraid.'

'Well, Miss Simpson, you've been a great help, and I couldn't think of a nicer person to have to tell me such awful news. But I mustn't keep you, and I ought to get round to Rachel's and see how she's coping.'

'Seems okay to me. She's been round here quite a lot with that husband of hers. They've been clearing up after it all, that sort of thing. Actually I rather thought she might have been there earlier, but I couldn't be sure. Sometimes I can hear her pottering about.'

'Oh, I see. It's been really kind of you, but I must get going. Time is marching on and I have to fly over to Germany in the morning. What with this news I just must get to see Rachel before I go.'

'Of course, and if I see her I'll tell her what a wonderful brother she's got.'

'Thanks.' Inwardly Marston cringed at the thought and muttered a silent 'shit'.

Having bidden his farewells with the required degree of profuseness, Marston walked back down the road. He noticed that Palmer's car was still there and decided it would be worth waiting to see what happened after Palmer left.

He walked the short distance back to his car and drove back round the corner. Parking was much easier at this time of day and Marston had no problem finding a parking bay that gave him a reasonable view of both number 19 and number 21. His wait was not long. After barely five minutes he saw Palmer leave number 19. Although not a religious person, Marston silently prayed that Rachel and Miss Simpson would not meet up in the next day or so as otherwise their cover would be blown. He watched as Palmer drove away from the scene, and Marston considered that Palmer might not even have known he was being observed.

After five minutes, Marston was about to drive off himself when a woman appeared from the driveway to number 19. She turned away from Marston and headed back up the hill. In a moment Marston decided that the easiest way to follow her, seeing as she was on foot, was to leave the car where it was and walk after her.

Cautious that she might suspect she was being followed, Marston walked on the opposite side of the road, careful not to get too close, and careful also to make sure he kept her in view. He need not have worried for her thoughts were clearly elsewhere.

At the top of the road she turned left and for a moment Marston was worried that she might turn round and spot him. She did not turn but carried on her walk oblivious to her pursuer. She walked for nearly five minutes before disappearing down a driveway. Marston was nearly one hundred metres behind her and by the time he had reached the entrance to the drive she had disappeared. Assuming it to be her own house he noted down the number and road name and walked back to his car.

Once in the car he pulled his mobile phone out of his pocket and dialled the Palmer's mobile. Palmer's mobile was obviously switched off at the time because Marston reached its answering service.

'Damien, this is Eddie. Thought you'd like to know I've completed the enquiries for today. Also I followed the woman after you'd left. Not much to report there. It looks like she went back home. I'll ring you in the morning and e-mail you a more detailed report later. Bye.'

It was Marston's night for the club, something he looked forward to. He'd meet up with some old acquaintances and make small talk. Almost certainly he'd play a few frames of snooker, perhaps throw some darts and definitely sink a few beers. With his work complete for the day, Marston began his journey back to his drab, grey, flat.

Chapter Six

Palmer arrived home a little after six o'clock that evening. It had been a worthwhile afternoon and he now had a little over an hour before he needed to leave for Karen's. She was his girlfriend of several months and they enjoyed each other's company several times a week. They were, as Eddie Marston would describe it, 'becoming an item'.

As was his custom, the first thing Palmer did on arriving back at his home was to turn on the coffee percolator. Even at this time of the afternoon Palmer felt the need for an infusion of caffeine. He claimed that it settled him despite the protestations of his doctor that he drank far too much of the stuff and far from settling him it did, if anything, make him more edgy than he would otherwise be. Palmer had on a number of occasions listened to the good gentleman's advice and upon leaving the surgery forgotten it. It was a habit he had grown accustomed to and switching on the percolator was an almost automatic action whenever he entered the abode.

Palmer was already feeling edgy. The mysterious watcher outside the solicitor's offices earlier in the day, the warning messages, his meeting with Rachel Connors and then the visit to the library had left him with a pain in his stomach, a gut feeling that something was wrong somewhere. He just couldn't work out what it was that was causing the cramps in his abdomen. As the percolator heated up the coffee he hoped the brown liquid would help him.

The second thing Palmer did was to go into his office and take out the sheets of paper he had removed from John Burnston's attaché case earlier that afternoon. He looked at them carefully but the handwriting was even worse than his own and there was little that he could make out. It seemed that the writing was deliberately bad, as if the writer was trying to retain some secrecy about the contents of the sheets of paper. Palmer examined each of the three sheets in turn. The scrawl was equally bad on each sheet.

After a few minutes, Palmer put the sheets on his desk and went to pour a mug of the freshly brewed coffee. It took him only a few minutes before he returned to his office. As he placed the mug on a coaster his vision focused once again on the top of the three sheets of paper. As he looked at the document he had an idea. He picked it up and turned it so that the room light, which was on, illuminated the document from behind. This only served to confirm the illegibility of the writing. Palmer let the paper slip from his fingers while he was holding it to the light. The document fluttered down onto his desk. Carelessly, he picked it up again and held it back in position. He started to curse himself softly for now holding the page back to front, and then stopped in his tracks for in amongst the scribble he could now just make out a few words.

The words, though significant in that they were words, made little sense to the investigator. Quickly Palmer inverted the other sheets of paper and held them up to the light. He whistled a low, soft whistle as he stared at the contents that were now revealed.

From the first sheet of paper, Palmer recognised three female names; Sonia, Michelle, and Daphne. Against each was a number, a single digit. In addition Palmer located what appeared to be the initials 'IR' against Sonia's name. It made little sense to him. On the second sheet of paper were the same three names, and these were each linked to an eight-digit number. Finally, on the third sheet of paper, were some more names. Palmer noted the details down and scanned the pages for more clues. Then, convinced that he had extracted the information available, he put the papers in a plastic wallet which he placed in his desk drawer.

Having completed this exercise, he sipped the coffee that had been waiting in the mug on the coaster. He seemed not to notice it had gone cold. His attention was still focused on the case.

His eyes were focused on the shelf of leather-bound and gilt-edged books when the telephone rang. His thoughts were focused far away and he seemed not to notice the attention-seeking tones coming from the device just behind him. The answering machine cut in and the caller left a brief message. All the time Palmer's gaze remained in the direction of the shelf of books.

In fact, Palmer had long since learned the techniques associated with deep, inner concentration and some minutes before the telephone had attempted to intrude on his thoughts he'd entered a state of mind which the uninitiated would have immediately called a trance. His own preference was to describe these instances as periods of focused concentration, for Palmer's mind was far from blank. A billion neurons in his brain flashed miniscule electrical signals through the pathways of his memories as if trying to rekindle something of huge significance from the dim and distant past. In reality Palmer was trying to focus his mind on the current case, a feat that eluded him.

Suddenly the electrical signals of the neurons touched an area of his memory and a case came to mind. For a brief moment, it was all that it took, the details of that case came flooding back to him. It was right at the beginning of his career as a sleuth and Palmer had been working under the auspices of a more experienced investigator when the case had come about.

The case concerned an eighteen year old girl who'd gone missing from some disco held in a hall local to where she'd lived. Palmer recalled the anguish of the case and the helplessness he'd felt. He also recalled the reaction of his mentor and the lack of interest he'd shown. Palmer, being a more passionate person in those days, had used the case as an excuse to ditch the mentor and set himself up in business.

It had been a strange case in many ways. The case involved a typical teenage girl. As Palmer had discovered, there was nothing unusual about her. She lived quite happily at home with her parents and was bright and well-liked at school with her sights set firmly on a University place after her gap year. Her A-Level studies were going well and she'd gone with a couple of friends to a disco one Friday night. Sometime during the evening the girl had been slipped some kind of drug, probably in a drink. No one was clear whether she had then wandered off on her own or whether she had been led out of the hall. In any event it seemed that she had been abducted. What was particularly strange about the case was the fact that a few days after her disappearance she had returned home apparently suffering from amnesia. In those few days, Palmer had spent time talking to the girl's parents, her friends at the Sixth Form College and others with whom she was acquainted.

Upon her return, the teenager had little recollection of where she'd been or what had happened to her. What did become clear was the fact that it had been a harrowing experience for her and Palmer recalled that her abductor had never been captured.

Then Palmer's memory recalled something about the case he had noticed at the time, something that had been of no significance all those years ago if only because it had nothing to do directly with the teenager who had been the subject of the case.

The girl had been mixing with a certain group of kids, some of them extremely attractive. Palmer recalled there had been one youngster who'd been less than concerned that her friend had been abducted. It had seemed to Palmer that it was quite likely she'd known more than she was prepared to divulge and there was something else, something Palmer's memory was trying to bring to his attention. The neurons were working hard, searching, trying to rekindle the memories concerning the case. Suddenly Palmer remembered the tattoo on the girl's shoulder. It had seemed insignificant because it was typical of the day. The dark ink was clearly visible on her shoulder and now, as Palmer recalled the meeting, the girl's presence seemed very real to him. He could almost read the lettering now as she turned towards him. As she did so the word became clear. There, on her shoulder was the word ' EROS '. It was an interesting word, referring to the euphemistic phrase 'sexual love', and it was part of the scene of the day to wear such a tattoo. Although the vision remained in Palmer's sight for several seconds it seemed illogical and even began to irritate him. This irritation interrupted his pattern of thoughts and as Palmer climbed back to a higher level of consciousness he wondered why that particular scene had come to mind when he had, after all, been trying to focus on the events surrounding the John Burnston murder.

As he came out of his reverie, Palmer turned and seemed almost surprised by the flashing red light on the top of the answer phone. Almost without interest he pressed the button and waited.

'You have one new message,' the disembodied voice electronically informed him.

'Hello, Mr. Palmer, my name is Andy Fielding. I have a problem I think you could help me with, in as much as it involves finding someone. I'd very much appreciate it if you could phone me back sometime in the next twenty-four hours. My phone number is,' and the message continued to reel off the number. As it did so, Palmer noted the details on his pad of paper and added the number at the end. To make sure he had noted the number correctly he listened to the message for a second time before wiping it from the machine's memory, a memory that could not be recovered in the future, unlike his own.

With the picture of the girl's bare shoulder still vying for his attention, Palmer looked at the clock and decided it was time to get ready for the evening. He pushed back the leather chair and took the half empty cup of cold coffee back to the kitchen. In a minute the shower was turned on and the water warming up while Palmer arranged his chosen attire for the evening. He undressed carefully and looked at himself in the mirror. For a man in his mid-forties he was quite good looking. Okay, the six-pack muscles had disappeared. Actually they had never really existed, but his body tone was good, and though, as he looked in the mirror, he considered he could afford to lose a few kilos in fat, he was quite fit for his age. He considered, with the evening ahead, he needed to be. It was partly his physical energy that kept his relationship with the woman he was going to visit very much alive, and he prided himself that he could still achieve the push-ups and sit-ups he had trained himself to do in his twenties.

As he looked in the mirror, Palmer saw the scar tissue on his right upper arm. It was an old wound that had resulted from a moment of carelessness and it had not healed well. The scar had faded with the passage of time but Palmer would never forget the memories of that fateful evening. On paper and even after the initial reconnaissance it had looked as if the job was going to be routine. Serving restraining orders had never been one of Palmer's preferred tasks, even before this incident. Since the event he had learned to be more cautious and it was one task that he carried out as part of his profession that he always felt nervous about.

This particular restraining order related to a somewhat overweight couch potato who went by the name of Ricky MacDonald. During the initial stages of locating this particular couch potato, Palmer had learned that the man was better known around the estate where he lived as "Rick the Brick". He had, it appeared, a reputation for violence and most people on the estate were happy to stay clear of him.

His nickname had arisen from his days as a youth. He and a select group of like-minded thugs had taken to hurling bricks through various house windows late at night, creating an air of fear and even terror amongst the more upstanding citizens who were unfortunate enough to coexist with the gang of youths.

Eventually the couch potato had grown up and settled down with a woman. During their brief partnership, Ricky managed to break both her arms and battered her senseless a couple of times. With due diligence, she had decided to leave him and now lived a few streets away. Her departure from Ricky's home had not deterred him from hounding her and even battering her one further time. The court order Palmer had to deliver was a legal attempt to stop him from injuring her again.

Palmer knocked on "The Brick's" door on the fateful evening. The door was opened by Ricky himself. He was holding a vegetable knife in his right hand and a partly-peeled potato in the other. He smiled at the unexpected visitor.

'Hi,' Palmer began, 'are you Ricky MacDonald?' He could have played it more cleverly, trying to trick the man into divulging his real name, but he decided Ricky MacDonald wasn't likely to cover up his identity. He was too well known around the estate to do that.

'Yeah, who wants to know?'

'Damien Palmer, Mr MacDonald, thanks for confirming your identity to me. I'm acting as a bailiff on behalf of Thordle and Harris. They are a firm of solicitors. I have been asked to personally hand you this document, which you can now consider duly served.' Palmer was breathing heavily by the time he'd finished speaking, the adrenaline pumping through his body.

Palmer knew as soon as he reached out his hand that "Rick the Brick" was not a happy man. Instead of taking the court order as he should have done, he reached out and used the vegetable knife to slash through Palmer's coat and down his upper arm.

Palmer had had no choice but to let the document drop. Feeling the nauseating pain in his arm he'd turned to leave.

'The courts still consider the document served. What's more I'll be going to the police over this.' Palmer grabbed his arm and watched fascinated as his blood seeped out onto the arm of the coat. He knew the injury was serious and that he had to get away from the house he'd been visiting. As he half-ran down the corridor away from MacDonald's house he heard the couch potato behind him shout,

'And you can tell the whore, if I get any more hassle I'll fix her good and proper.'

There'd been several expletives used in the phrase but Palmer decided to ignore them as he looked at the scar in the mirror.

From the house he'd made it back to his car and called for an ambulance. The ambulance had taken what seemed like ages to arrive, but in reality it had been only a few minutes. Palmer was weak from the loss of blood by the time it arrived and could only vaguely remember the trip to hospital and the operation to repair his arm. It was all a few years back and he at least had the grim satisfaction that the couch potato was now being entertained at her Majesty's pleasure, partly for slashing Palmer and partly for battering his ex-partner for a final time. Palmer turned from the mirror and instantly recalled the picture of the girl's shoulder and the single word etched across it. It was as if he was being prompted by some external force to understand the significance of what he had recalled whilst concentrating back down in his study a few minutes previously.

Palmer was not in a hurry and enjoyed the feel of the water as it jetted from the showerhead. He washed slowly and deliberately, a man with much on his mind. When he had finished he towelled himself dry and dressed. As he did so, the clock in the hall chimed seven times. As always, Palmer had found the water pressure from the shower therapeutic, and it helped relax the muscles that always seemed to get so tense when he was involved in a case.

Finally ready, he descended the stairs and partly closed his office door. The pad of paper remained on the desktop's blotter ready to remind him the following morning. Palmer left his house and, having carefully double locked the front door, began his journey to Sutton.

***

As Palmer began his journey, his hostess for the evening was making her own preparations. Karen Shaw's flat was comfortable but not overly spacious. The sitting room combined with a dining area off which the kitchenette was modern if functional. The flat boasted two bedrooms with the master bedroom having an en-suite shower room, and there was a separate bathroom. It was not that Karen needed two bedrooms but the pile of equipment, books, and other articles she had amassed over the years needed somewhere to live.

The oven gave off a warm sodium-light colour as the casserole bubbled steadily within and the woman turned her attentions to the bathroom. The water was hot and steam was rising onto the cold mirror, condensing as water droplets contacted cool glass. On the surface of the water lay a deep cushion of white foam. Into this foam the woman stepped carefully. She had an attractive body and was relatively tall for a woman, being just over five feet and nine inches. She had a slender figure and her 36C chest only added to her beauty. Her mid-back length sandy hair swirled seductively around her body as she twirled round in the bath.

She sat down, gently teased the white foam over her skin and smiled to herself as she contemplated the pleasures of the evening ahead. She had always liked to dress up for her lover. Perhaps it had something to do with the twelve years that separated them, and perhaps in that age gap was the secret of their passion. Although good at her job, Karen hated having to be the dominant force. Now, as the foam played around her naked body, she carefully washed herself and as the bubbles rose in the casserole that was cooking in the oven so, deep within her, bubbles of pleasure began to rise to the surface as she contemplated the evening ahead.

She bathed slowly. She had no idea how he would react to the request she would make, and this insecurity only added to her excitement. It was an excitement that continued to play through her body as she washed and then towelled herself dry. It continued as she delicately splashed on the sweet fragrance of the alluring perfume.

The excitement continued to ripple through her as she pulled on the figure-hugging black number that showed off all her finest attributes. On such an evening she was the kind of woman who wore no bra. Because she knew what effect they had on her lover, the suspender belt and black stockings had become desirable items for creating the mood. To complete the ensemble she had decided to wear the black G-string he had given her as a little present sometime in the past. When she had finished dressing she looked at herself in the bedroom mirror and smiled with contentment.

In the kitchen everything was under control so she sat down with a glass of white wine that she poured from an expensive looking bottle. She didn't need courage to ask her lover for the favour, but she figured it would be a whole lot easier if she had at least one glass of wine inside her when she did.

***

Palmer had barely closed his front door when his suspicions were aroused. He looked round quickly but could see nothing even though he was sure he was being watched. He walked down the short pathway leading to the pavement and looked up and down the street. It was dark and the street seemed to be deserted yet to Palmer it felt like a dozen eyes were watching him.

In the gloom of the streetlights he peered out onto the grassy area. He waited for some moments until his eyes had adjusted to the lighting conditions but still he could see nothing. He walked across the road for a closer inspection. Finally, convinced the grassy area was devoid of any humans, he crossed back over the road and walked the several yards to his car.

A car was parked on the far side of the green to Palmer's terraced house. The occupant was invisible to Palmer but she knew the moment he left his house. She watched as the hall light was extinguished and waited a few seconds before she opened the car door and stood up. Beneath the streetlight across the patch of grass she saw Palmer walk towards her. She froze and sank back into the vehicle, closing the door quietly.

She waited a further five minutes before leaving her car once again. By this time Palmer had walked to his car and started his journey. The woman walked nonchalantly across the grassy area and straight up to Palmer's front door. With a gloved hand she pressed the doorbell. Inside she heard it ring. She waited for half a minute and then rang the bell again. There was no answer.

Turning from the house she looked at the mobile phone in her left hand. She pressed the buttons and put it up to the side of her head. In a soft voice and with breath that was visible in the cold evening air, she spoke.

'He's gone out.' A pause then she spoke again. 'Yes, I'm sure he's out. The house is dark and I've rung the doorbell twice. He's taken his car. It's not where it was parked ten minutes ago.'

There was another pause as the person responded to her message.

'So, what do you want me to do? Sit here and wait, or go there?'

Another pause.

'Okay. I'll get back on the road. Talk to you later.'

She replaced the mobile phone in her pocket. Rubbing her hands together for warmth she crossed back over the grassy area and regained the relative warmth of her vehicle. She knew where she was heading, she had a map. What intrigued her was how the person she'd been talking to had known the address. Still, she surmised, it was not her job to go asking too many questions. She was on trial and had to show willingness and a degree of trust, after all she didn't want to fall foul of the man she'd communicated with – at this stage in their relationship that would be a disaster.

She started the car and pulled out onto the road. Following the same route Palmer had taken a few minutes previously she headed for Wimbledon. The traffic was light and she made good progress. Through Wimbledon, past the one-way system and down into Morden she journeyed. From Morden she swung left and continued towards Sutton. Twice she stopped to look at the map. This was unfamiliar territory to her. As she entered the outskirts of Sutton she made a wrong turning, had to pull in and cursed herself when she realised her mistake. She swung the vehicle round, mounting the pavement as she performed the reverse manoeuvre, and corrected her mistake.

She finally arrived at her destination at ten past eight. Parking her car in the road, she walked round the block of flats and smiled to herself when she spotted Palmer's vehicle in one of the parking bays. She returned to her car and took the mobile phone out of her pocket once again.

'It's me again,' she almost whispered. 'He's arrived at the place you said he'd probably be going to. His car's round the back and no sign of him. He must be indoors.' She paused to allow the man at the other end of the phone reply.

'So, what do you want me to do now?' Another pause while the man contemplated his response.

'What, all bloody evening?' She retorted. 'I mean, until what sort of time?'

She waited for his response.

'Eleven! That's nearly three hours. I'll freeze to death in that time.'

The man on the other end of the phone was unmoved by her claims of discomfiture. His voice remained impassive as he repeated the requirement.

'Very well, master,' she said, 'eleven it is.' She switched off the mobile and sat back to listen to the radio.

Chapter Seven

The buzzer on the intercom sounded at one minute to eight. Karen was almost walking to the internal phone before it sounded. It was as if she could predict the precise moment her lover would arrive, possibly because of his uncanny sense of punctuality, but possibly there was something else. Some months earlier she had ruled out the strange phenomenon that some folk called 'body chemistry', it was not that. Perhaps, she thought on occasion, it was some deep-seated psychic ability that she possessed.

'Hello,' she spoke into the phone.

'Karen, it's me, Damien.'

'I'll let you in.' She pressed the button on the side of the phone and somewhere on the ground floor a buzzer sounded as the outer door was released. She unlocked her own front door and went back to the lounge. After a minute she heard him at the door.

'I'm in the lounge, darling. Make sure the door's shut.'

Palmer entered the hallway of the flat and closed the door. He turned and pushed open the lounge door. She lay there on the settee, open, waiting for him. Stretched back on the seat with her chest pushed forward, stretching the tight material of the skimpy black number, she was propped up on one elbow, a glass of wine in one hand with a seductive grin on her face.

'Do you like it?' She asked more out of conversation than anything. The effect was exactly what she had planned and it was immediately obvious that Palmer was interested.

'You look wonderful.' He spoke softly as he walked into the room. He reached forward, careful not to disturb her glass of wine, and their lips met. They met for several seconds.

Finally he stood up and said, 'I brought you these. I hope you like them.' From behind his back he proffered the bunch of a dozen red roses. As he handed them to her he mused that the tint of the petals closely matched her lipstick.

'Oh, Damien, they're gorgeous.' She sat up now to receive the gift, and placed her glass on the low coffee table. 'They're so sweet and my favourites.' She kissed him again.

While she went to put the flowers in water, Palmer helped himself to a glass of wine and sat down. In a minute she returned with the vase of flowers. Placing the vase on the windowsill she went and sat next to the man. They looked at each other passionately and their lips met again in a longer, more passionate embrace than when Palmer had first arrived.

The embrace lasted for a full two minutes before Palmer pulled away.

'That smells good. What is it?'

'A surprise, but you'll like it. Anyway, how are you?'

'Oh, I'm not so bad, how about you?'

'Well, apart from the boss being a right sod and telling me I just don't have control of the department, I'm fine.'

'So it was one of those days, hey?' Palmer sounded genuinely interested in the beautiful woman who had edged closer to him while they had been speaking.

'Yeah, it was one of those days. Are you working on anything interesting at the moment?'

'Well, I suppose it is interesting. I've picked up the Burnston murder case. Have you heard about it?'

'No, but I'm intrigued. Is it a good one:'

'Not really, I'm afraid. Wife caught at murder scene with murder weapon still in her hand and now she's pleading not guilty. Solicitor has asked me to do some investigation. That's about the size of it really. I doubt whether I'll come up with much on this one.'

'Hmm, does sound a bit tricky, still you never know.'

With that, Karen Shaw gave the man an affectionate peck on the cheek as she stood to go into the kitchen. As she stood, Palmer admired her beauty for the umpteenth time since he had entered the door. She was wasted in computers – he was sure of that. She deserved so much more. Then it dawned on the investigator that he actually knew very little about the woman. For sure, he knew about her job. After all they'd met when he'd attended a seminar on the Internet that she was running. He also knew a little about her childhood and her wild teenage years. But in reality he knew precious little else. She was as much of an enigma to him as he knew he must be to her, after all he had told her very little about his miserable childhood.

'Dinner will be about ten minutes,' the siren in black stated as she returned to the living area. 'Hope you like casserole.'

'Love it, especially if you've cooked it.'

'You know, Damien, this is the umpteenth proper meal I've cooked here for us. When are you going to show me your culinary skills again?' She smiled sweetly but Palmer sensed there was more to the question than the blatantly obvious.

'Well, if you want to risk it why don't I do a meal next week sometime? By then this case will be wrapped up and I'll be able to spend some time thinking about it.'

'That sounds good to me. Now, I have a little favour to ask of you.' She hesitated as if not sure how to proceed. But then, her short visit to the kitchen had been more to do with plucking up the courage to face the situation than out of any need to check the food that was cooking. As she spoke she leaned into Palmer so that her chest was almost touching his arm and her face was a very short distance from his.

'Go on,' Palmer looked back at her with a measured degree of uncertainty.

'Well, I don't know quite how to put this, it's a bit delicate you see.' She paused more out of her own insecurity than anything else.

'Oh come on, Karen, we've known each other for a while now. You can trust me you know!'

'Okay. Well you know that when I went to school I went to a Convent?'

'Yes, you've told me that before.'

'Well, at this Convent the headmistress was a real disciplinarian.' And Karen continued for the next five minutes narrating her experiences at the hand of the dragon in a habit. It soon became evident the harridan of discipline stood for no nonsense and that the cane was frequently used for all kinds of misdemeanours. Indeed, the actions of Sister Clemence were as clearly imprinted in the woman's mind as they were when she had first experienced the length of wood for her own crimes.

As she spoke, Palmer nodded his head with the wisdom of one who had travelled the same journey. When she mentioned her personal experience of the cane, Palmer simply replied, 'Oh.' It was as if he was unsurprised by this revelation, as if such things were commonplace in those days. Karen continued to narrate her story. Finally Palmer interjected,

'So where is this leading us?' Palmer sounded interested as if he had gleaned the gist of what she was trying to tell him.

'It's simple really. After that caning I realised that something inside me makes me want to have to be submissive. So I was wondering if you wouldn't mind being a bit dominant somehow tonight. I just feel after the day I've had, I need someone who can take control of me. Does that sound odd?'

'Not really,' Palmer smiled gently.

'Not that I want you to cane me or anything,' she added quite quickly, 'but just to be in control and do what you want to do, and if necessary make me go along with you.'

'Hmm,' Palmer's voice had changed as if he had just been handed a very large gift and he didn't know why. 'Tell you what, I'll think about it over dinner, but no promises.'

'Okay, it's just that I've never trusted anyone with this before and I thought you might be the right person.'

'I might well be, but part of the game is that you won't know until it starts to happen. Now, I should think the food is cooked. Do you want a hand with it?'

'No, you just go and sit at the table. It will only take a moment to serve it.' Karen sounded slightly disappointed that her request had met with such an inconclusive response. It was a response that had been deliberately understated by Palmer, a response that was a part of the game he was even now starting to play with the woman.

The meal was good. Karen was more than adept in the kitchen, and almost as skilled as Palmer. A fine bottle of red wine accompanied the repast. Palmer had noticed it when he came into the flat and now it afforded him the chance he was looking for. The meal was virtually over when Karen reached over to top up his glass. As if unaware of what she was doing, Palmer lifted his glass to drink from it. The wine dribbled down the glass onto the clean, white, tablecloth.

Palmer put his glass down on the table and with a twinkle in his eye said,

'I think you've had enough to drink. Look at what you've done.' His voice was calm as he stood and walked round the table behind the woman. 'Now, before this soaks in, you'd better clean it up.'

Karen had caught the look in his eye and realised immediately that this was the point where Palmer was going to take control for the evening. The thought thrilled her as she went into the kitchenette to retrieve the damp cloth. She returned to find Palmer standing beside the table.

'Now, Miss Shaw,' he began, though the sentence went unfinished.

***

Eddie Marston was on his second pint of the evening and had already won his first frame of snooker. He was on a roll, having scored a fifty break. He personally didn't rate his game particularly highly but then he never rated anything he did with much credit.

The unofficial tournament was using all sixteen tables in the hall, though as each round progressed more and more tables would be freed up for occasional players. Marston sat on a stool at the side of the bar waiting for the second round draw to be made.

'Nice break,' Phil Marsh commented as he wandered over to where Marston was sitting.

'Thanks, Phil,' Marston replied. 'Fancy joining me?'

'Sure.'

'What's your poison?'

'Pint of bitter, mate.'

Marston ordered the drink and took a mouthful of his own. He was used to these evenings and knew just how to pace himself. Two pints, then something soft, and then alternate the beer with the soft drinks. He doubted he'd get past the next round, there were some good players in the tournament, but then again he might strike lucky.

'So, how's life treating you, Eddie?' Phil Marsh had known Marston for many years through their association with the snooker club.

'Not bad. Getting some work through from various sources that keeps me busy.'

'Yeah?' The question sounded genuine.

'Yeah, deliveries, that kind of thing.'

'Oh, right. And are you still with that blond I met in the High Street a couple of months back?'

'Oh, Wendy, no we split up. I've got another one on the boil now. Anyway, how are you doing?' Marston was never one who liked to divulge too much of his personal life.

'Fine, I've got a new job on security at this warehouse. This bloke I got introduced to a while back put me onto it. Which is just as well, really, seeing as the wife is expecting our first kid.'

'Congratulations. So, this warehouse security thing, what do you have to do?'

'Just keep an eye on the place, people coming, people going, deliveries, that sort of thing. Best of all it's only during office hours. They have a night guy that does all the out of hours stuff. It leaves me free for the evenings.'

'True,' Marston smiled as he took another mouthful of beer. 'It's been a few months since I last saw you here – thought you must have been working nights?' He continued after the beer had been swallowed.

'No, just been busy.'

'What, decorating and things?'

'No, it's nothing like that. Do you know Pete Adams?'

'No,' Marston replied after a moment of thought.

'Oh, well, really nice bloke. I met him down the market when I worked there. He's involved in this group that ferries the old and infirm around from place to place. I've helped him out a few times. Really rewarding stuff and you don't half hear some funny stories.'

'I'll bet, their often the worst, the blue rinse brigade.'

'They're not all like that, but tell you what, mentioning brigade has reminded me of something. One of the old guys, though I've never actually met him, is an ex Major or something. Utterly respectable on the face of it, walks with quite a limp and has a big old house in Wimbledon. Anyway, one of the old dears we ferry around quite a lot once told me he's a right letch, runs some kind of brothel she reckoned. Apparently he's always hosting orgies and the like. I mean, the guy must be about seventy!' Marsh almost laughed. 'Still, these old ones often have the best gossip to spread.'

'I'll bet you get a lot of that?'

'What?'

'Gossip. Look, I'd best get down to the bottom for the draw. Are you coming?'

'No, I'll sit here and wait to see what table you're on. Good luck.'

Marston took his half-empty glass and walked down the middle of the two rows of snooker tables to where the small group of people were gathering for the second round draw. The rumour he'd just heard stayed with him and he marvelled at the outrageous things some people would imagine so that they could tell a story, any story, just so long as it attracted attention. Doubtless, Marston thought, she must be a lonely old lady, one who had few friends. Still, there was often some truth in the stories that got told by such people and she must have some knowledge of the ex Major. By the time he'd walked the length of the hall, Marston was convinced there was something more than pure imagination in the woman's yarn.

It was Marston's lucky evening. Two frames later he was through to the last four – the semi-finals. The group of onlookers had grown as the tournament progressed, the unused tables remaining empty. The favourite, Bill Grantly, had been knocked out in the previous round and nobody rated his victor, Ian Hermann. Ian was about ten years younger than Marston, his next opponent. These single frame matches were always the same – unpredictable.

Marston lost the toss and was put into break. It wasn't a great break but the cue ball ended up back in the balk area. Hermann was getting nervous. He hadn't expected to get this far and he knew most of the onlookers would be rooting for Marston. He hit a clean ball, missed the target red going into the top left pocket by a couple of inches and the cue ball clattered back into the pack. Marston smiled as someone in the crowd shouted,

'Come on, Eddie.'

And that is precisely what Marston did to. It took him nearly ten minutes to build the seventy-four break and it was a frame winning score. Hermann never returned to the table and conceded while sitting on his stool.

The second semi took longer, a real needle match where both players were noted for the quality of their safety play. Marston watched, intrigued. There was no real money to be won in the tournament it was just one of the matches the club ran from time to time. Marston knew the fifty quid would be mostly spent on the winner's round of drinks – assuming he won it.

'Well done, Eddie.' Marsh had worked his way to where Marston sat watching the only snooker action.

'Cheers.'

'Which one would you prefer?'

'Paul, he's good at safety but not great at the long stuff. He'd be my best chance. Say, I've been thinking about your ex Major chap. Do you think the old dear made the whole thing up, or does she really know about something that's going on? I mean, orgies for the over seventies would be quite a story to investigate if you were a journalist.'

'Oh, knowing Flossy, she'll have made up the story based on something the ex Major said to her once. I have to say, though, some of these old folk are into some pretty strange things – if you believe even half of what you hear.. She does make up stories quite a lot, so no one takes any notice really. It's just attention seeking I think.'

Marston turned back to the game that was finishing, preparing himself for the last match of the evening – the final.

***

'Wow,' Karen said after they had been lying down for a few minutes, 'that was sensational. You can be so masterful when you want to be. You didn't mind, did you?'

'No. It was great to do something so different.' Palmer replied. 'I haven't actually done anything like that before. I guess that as I grew up with two sisters it's made me wary of things like that. I mean I used to hit my sisters when I was a kid, but not like that – and they were over five years older than me so it was all different.'

'I didn't know you had sisters.'

'Yeah, I've got two of them. Roxanne and Ophelia.'

'And where are they? Are you still in touch?'

'Sort of, Roxy's in Australia. She married some business tycoon and went to live out there. We write about three or four times a year.'

'What about Ophelia?'

'Oh, she's no longer with us. She got involved in the 'Peace For All' movement or something while she was at college. She started smoking weed and then moved on to harder stuff. Eventually she got involved on the game and you know how it goes. The men paid for the habit and the habit got worse. Then she got hold of some bad stuff, injected it, and was found on the banks of the river a couple of days later.'

'Damien, that's awful. Couldn't you have done something?'

'Well, we did try, Roxy and me. Trouble was, we didn't really know how bad it was until it was too late. Ophy basically did a disappearing act when she went on the game and it only took her about two weeks to OD. So we didn't have much time to find her again. Never did catch the bastard that sold her the dope and the cops weren't that interested in her due to her profession.'

'But that means there are other kids out there at this guy's mercy.'

'Yah, if he's still around. Don't forget this all happened about fifteen years ago.'

'I'm sorry Damien, I didn't mean to pry.' The woman lying naked next to the sleuth sounded close to tears.

'Don't worry,' he replied. 'Actually I don't think I've ever told anyone this before – it's just one of those things you don't talk about.'

'So, Damien, why tell me and tonight?'

'I don't know really, it just seemed okay to do it. I guess partly because it would have been Ophy's birthday tomorrow. Funny how these things stay with you through the years.'

Palmer reached over and placed an arm round the woman and they cuddled, not with any passion, but just for the warmth and friendship they offered each other. Slowly they drifted off to sleep and the stillness of the night overtook them.

Chapter Eight

The car remained parked in the road and the woman sat in the driver's seat listening to the radio. When she'd first arrived she'd read the notes that she'd brought with her. The contents of the few sheets of paper were familiar to her. She'd spent a good deal of time over the past few weeks reading them, soaking the words into her memory, encouraging her to almost live by what they said. Yet she still re-read them, absorbing the information she already knew. Finally, she sat back, turned on the radio and closed her eyes. As the music played softly around her she contemplated the changes to her life over the past few months. She had her friend to blame, or thank for those changes. Her involvement had only come about because of her friend, without her she would never have heard of the group nor met its leaders. There was security in friendship and she needed security. She was vulnerable and these people offered her security. They offered her companionship and so what if they were a bit quirky. Michelle Carranides had met many quirky people in her young life and quirky people hardly ever made her feel comfortable. These people did and that's why she was going to great lengths to do what they required of her. It was all a matter of friendship, friendship and trust.

So she sat in the car listening to the radio and keeping a half eye on the road, just in case the car she was watching moved. She kept her vigil until eleven o'clock. It was what she'd been instructed to do, sit and watch. She was cold for the heater in the car was old and didn't work properly. It was part of her test, part of what she had to do. She kept looking at her watch, waiting for the eleventh hour to materialise. As the evening wore on she watched the lights in the flats being turned on and off, leaving her to guess at which flat Palmer was visiting.

She wondered how her mentor had known where he would be that evening, though the fact he knew did not surprise her – he seemed to know most things. There it was again, one of their quirky habits, he was her "mentor" or, when they were all together, he was her "master".

She couldn't understand why she had to wait and watch other than it was a test, a test to see whether she was ready to be fully trusted, fully integrated into the body of people she longed to join.

The block of flats had been in darkness for nearly an hour when the watch finally indicated it was time to go. Quickly she restarted the car. She'd had the engine turning over periodically throughout the evening, trying to extract the barest of warmth from the heating system but to no avail. The radio programme had changed a couple of times and a late night chat programme was now in full swing. The topic did not interest her, she was just determined to get through this test and get accepted fully into the group of people she now called her friends. She had no notion that they were using her for their own ends, they were simply her friends. She ate with them, drank with them and joined in their quirky habits. On occasion, when she'd felt tired she'd even chill out and fall asleep while they were all together. It was what she liked to do, chill out.

With her teeth chattering from the cold, she started the engine for the final time that evening and pulled away from the kerb. She drove slowly, her mind and concentration numbed by the three hours in the car. She hoped her contact, her mentor, would be pleased with her loyalty to the cause. If he wasn't then she didn't know what else she would have to do to prove herself. She certainly didn't want to spend another freezing evening sat all alone in her car.

***

It was much later that night when an owl hooted noisily somewhere outside the flats. The couple lay on the bed still holding hands, still having not moved from the position they had lain in after their earlier exertions. Palmer lay there dreaming about his childhood. Perhaps it had been the activities earlier in the evening that had caused this particular dream but now, in the deep subconscious of his mind, he was reliving a particular day at school. He could clearly see the faces of the three bullies as they taunted him in the playground. The graze on his right knee and the dirt on his shorts were the results of one of the bullies pushing him over. He was about nine years old at the time, and it was only a few months after the unexpected death of his beloved father.

His father had not been ill. Indeed he was always a very fit, active person. Then the young

Damien had been sitting down to breakfast that fateful morning. The cereals were in the bowls and his father had started reading the newspaper that had been delivered a short while earlier. Suddenly he let out a low gurgling sound and slumped forward on the table. There had been no warning other than he'd taken a couple of paracetamol for a headache when he had got up that morning. Then at the breakfast table he had just slumped forward. The brain haemorrhage had been massive and instantly fatal.

Now, a few months later, Palmer was cut and bruised from the fall. As merciless as a nine-year-old thug can be, the brat with the glasses and oversized stomach had started to laugh at him and mock him for not having a father. The young Damien was sobbing and he knew the teacher was already walking across the hard play area, but the taunt from the bespectacled slob was the final straw. With an almost supernatural power, he lashed out. In his dream he remembered the full impact of his fist against the boy's face, and he could still see the look of total surprise on that face when a moment later the spectacles were flung into space and blood started dripping from his nose.

The teacher arrived and dragged Damien off to the head-teacher. It was the worst dressing down he had ever received. There was no mercy, for the school disliked bullies. Palmer was ordered to hold out his left hand and in an instant the searing pain of the principal's cane tore into the palm. Six times the cane landed before the boy was allowed to relax, his hand now a swollen, red, mass of tortured flesh. Even now, as he dreamed, Palmer winced at the pain. It was his first experience of punishment at the school, and it was not his last. As the cane landed the sixth time he moved on to dream about the sports car he had always wanted to drive.

As he dreamed, the woman beside him slept soundly, unaware of the graphic detail her lover was seeing in his slumber. Then, as the owl started to hoot, her eyelids began to flicker and her deep subconscious connected with a different plane. The pulses of energy reached deep into her being, and even beyond the physical. Suddenly she was back in her college bedroom. She recognised the dour walls with their magnolia covering. She recognised the board on the floor and the cup that stood inverted upon it. She even recognised the three people who were sat on the floor around it. From her perspective, high up on the ceiling, she could see every last detail as they touched the glass with light fingers and waited for it to move. It did so and in her dream Karen waited for it to repeat the message they had received on that night – a message she could still remember.

But now, in her dream, something was not the same for somehow the room was different. Now, instead of the planchet moving over the letters that would form the message, out of the top of the glass it seemed that tiny characters were rising. They were hooded characters that looked a bit like monks. The hoods flowed into the robes they were wearing, robes of crimson tied at the waist with a black cord. The figures grew as they rose from the glass until they were clearly visible, though their faces remained masked by the hoods. Then, out of the glass, came a young, blond haired girl. She looked to be no more than a teenager and dressed in a pure white gown she looked particularly vulnerable. Once the characters had arrived, they began to dance round the girl who twisted and turned as they pushed and jostled her. Then she fell to the ground, only to be rolled onto her back by two of the hooded people. A third grabbed her arms and stretched them above her head and a fourth untied the cord that fixed her robe to her waist.

This action complete, the first two men pulled back the robe to the sides. As they did so, the fifth man came from the background and stood over the girl. With a sharp dagger that had a glistening, gilded handle he stood poised above the young girl's chest. Viciously he plunged the knife downwards through the silken, white flesh. As he stood back, Karen saw the word etched on the girl's abdomen – EROS.

Finally the hooded figures began to disappear back into the glass and Karen woke in a cold sweat. Shaking with fear she nudged Palmer. Waking from his own slumber it took him some moments to realise that Karen was sitting up in bed shaking.

'What's up?' He finally managed to ask her.

'It was, it was, horrible.' She went on to describe the dream she'd had. As she told it a chill breeze floated through the bedroom and disappeared through the gap under the bedroom door. It was almost as if there had been something very real about this dream – as if some force or spirit not of the world was trying to convey a very important message.

Palmer listened to her as she spoke and held her close to himself, offering comfort. When she had finished he spoke.

'Do you think this was just a dream, or something else?'

'I don't know. It felt more than just a dream. I knew the scene and the people round the board and I still know what happened when we did it for real. This time it was so different, though equally horrible. I think it was a message for us – maybe for me or you, I don't know.'

As if noticing the temperature in the room for the first time, she started to shiver. Palmer felt her naked body and realised she was cold. Indeed, he felt unduly cold as well. It puzzled him, but his mind was preoccupied with her dream. Having experienced some of Karen's pictures and visions during their relationship, he had to accept the possibility that this might not just be a dream but something far more potent. For a logical man it was hard to even give her the benefit of the doubt but there was something nagging him, something that made him feel a degree of uneasiness about the pictures.

Finally, after five minutes, they lay back and pulled the duvet around them. It was several minutes before the woman fell back to sleep. Sleep did not return for Palmer that night for suddenly the word etched on the teenager's abdomen captured his imagination and because it was the same word that he'd pictured etched on a teenager's shoulder only the previous day, it burned in his mind until the first rays of the morning sun filtered into the bedroom. Then, dressing quietly, so as not to disturb his lover, he went into the lounge and sat there contemplating the case he was working on. He made a pot of tea and had just drained his first cup when she appeared at the door.

'Morning,' he said cheerfully, 'fancy a cup of tea?'

'Mmm, please.' Her voice was still groggy as if she was only half awake. In the dim light of the morning her bare flesh shimmered in the doorway. 'That was some dream, wasn't it?'

'Sure was. Anyway, it's over and done with. Now, I have to get a move on. Eddie's coming over first thing and I've got to get back to sort a few things out before he arrives. I don't know how you're fixed but I've got some surveillance to do tonight and you're welcome to come along if you want to.'

'That sounds fun. What is it?'

'Oh, just someone who wants her husband watched.' Palmer thought it best not to divulge too many details at this stage. He didn't want to scare Karen by telling her it was connected with the case he was working on.

'Okay, when and where?' Karen yawned as she finished speaking.

'Let's say we meet outside the pub on that big corner in Wimbledon Village at about seven. It's called 'The Fox' or something like that. It's close to where we're going and will give us time to get ready.'

'Okay, seven it is. Now, do you want breakfast?'

'No thanks, I'd best be going really. But before I do, thanks for last night.'

'It's I who should thank you.' Her eyes twinkled at him.

A few minutes later she closed the front door as Palmer began the journey back to his terraced house. It took him just under an hour to cover the distance, which was quite good considering the morning rush hour was underway. He opened his front door and went in. The house felt unduly cold and it sparked an alarm somewhere deep in the mind of the investigator.

He opened the study door and it was immediately apparent that something was wrong. Three shelves of books had been turned out onto the floor and his laptop computer was open and working. The top left drawer of his desk had been prised open and the contents turned onto the desktop.

With a thousand thoughts flashing through his mind Palmer reacted quickly. He ran into the other ground floor rooms. The dining room was untouched, but in the kitchen he found the reason why the house felt cold. The small window above the sink had been propped open by whoever had ventured into his house. It did not look like it had been forced and, without thinking, Palmer closed it.

Not stopping for a moment longer than necessary to work out that, apart from the forced window, nothing seemed to have been touched, he ran upstairs. Again the rooms were untouched.

'Strange,' he muttered to himself as he descended the stairs. 'Why would anyone break in here and then only go into the study? Why didn't they take anything, like the telly, video, hi-fi, or anything like that?'

He reached his study and for the first time saw the message that had been hastily scrawled on the blotter sheet:

'BURNSTON IS GUILTY – YOU WERE WARNED'.

It took Palmer a further ten seconds to note that the red light on the answerphone was flashing. He pressed the replay button and listened.

'You have one new message,' the electronically disembodied voice began. The introduction was followed by a bleep. 'Mr Palmer, by now you will have noticed that you have been visited. We have taken nothing this time, as you will see. Please do not think of tracing this call – it is a withheld number. Now, do I have your undivided attention? Good. You are working on the Burnston murder case and we know exactly what you are doing. For example, last evening you spent in Sutton at the home of your girlfriend. The guilty party is already in prison and there is nothing more for you to do. If you do not understand the meaning of what I am saying then we are quite happy to pay you another visit, one that will result in a considerable loss to yourself. I hope I am clear. You have had your final warning.'

The voice was male. It was a calm voice, even and with a slight Northern accent. Indeed, the voice was so dispassionate, Palmer thought, it could almost have been electronically created. Almost, but not quite, he finally decided. He played the message again and this time he recorded it onto his cassette machine. Having recorded it he picked the tomes up from the floor and lovingly placed them back on the shelves. Then he returned the contents of the drawer and carefully removed the sheet of blotting paper, mindful that it might be useful as evidence.

Chapter Nine

The doorbell sounded. Although the sound was familiar to the sleuth it made him start momentarily, as if he were coming back from a reverie. Cautiously he looked through the spy hole and saw the shorter man whom he knew. In a moment the door was open.

'Eddie,' he began, 'is that the time already? Come in.'

Marston waited until the door was open before he walked inside.

'Are you just back?' Marston sounded full of the joys of spring, but his exuberance became muted as he realised almost immediately that something was wrong. 'It's a bit chilly in here, isn't it? Is your heating not working?'

'No, Eddie, the heating is fine. It's just that I had a visitor last night while I was out and he left the window open. By the way, how did the snooker go?'

'You mean you had a burglar? Did he take anything? Not the laptop?' Marston now sounded concerned for his friend. 'I lost in the final, a fluke but that's how it goes.'

'No, nothing was taken. Whoever it was just left me a message and then phoned up at some point to drive the message home.'

'Have you reported this?'

'Not yet, and anyway what's the point? There's nothing to recover and I don't want any more visits.'

'What was the message?'

'Basically it told me to stay away from the Burnston case. There's somebody out there who is doing whatever they can to make sure she doesn't get out of prison, and I have no idea why. I'll tell you what, Eddie, this is beginning to worry me.'

'Have you still got the message?'

'Yeah, I taped it. Look, go on through and listen to it. I'm just making coffee.'

'Thanks.' Marston entered the study as Palmer returned to the kitchen. From the kitchen, as the percolator bubbled and hissed, he could hear Marston listening to the taped message. Five minutes later, Palmer took the tray of coffee into the study and sat it on the blotting paper in the centre of his desk.

'Right, Eddie, what have you got for me?' Palmer had now had time to compose himself.

'But the message – don't you think we should just drop the case?'

'Absolutely not, after all it's just what this person, whoever he is, wants us to do. That being the case he must have some damn good reason for wanting the woman locked up for the murder, and if that's the case, then it adds fuel to Manning's gut feeling that she isn't guilty. Moreover, I suspect that though we don't know it yet, we may have got unhealthily close to something while we were out and about yesterday. So I want to hear what you found out, from the top.' Palmer picked up a cup of the coffee and handed it to Marston before taking the second cup for himself. After sipping the steaming liquid, Marston began. It took him nearly twenty minutes to describe what he had done, the

120

questions he'd asked and the people he'd met. Palmer looked up approvingly when he described his observations on Palmer's own car. He looked up again with keen interest when Marston described following Rachel Connors after Palmer's visit.

'And,' said Marston finally, 'it's all there in the report, addresses, descriptions, names and so forth. Oh, and I've got this for you too.' He put his hand into his trouser pocket and withdrew the exposed reel of film. 'Took some snaps while I was at it too.'

Palmer took the film and placed it on the desk.

'Thanks, Eddie, that's good work. Now, apart from digging out a couple of sheets of paper from Burnston's attaché case, and frankly they don't make much sense, I did discover a couple of things. First off, there was no way anyone broke into the house. So, if Mrs Burnston didn't kill her husband, whoever did kill him must have had a key to the place. Also, I checked the picture out at the library. I've ordered a colour shot but the one printed in the paper clearly shows Mrs Burnston standing over the body and, as you said, there's very little blood on her. Which brings us to the question, if she didn't kill him, who did? Because if we can't come up with that person, then I don't think she's going to get off this. There's just too much circumstantial evidence for that, not to mention the fact she tried to escape from the scene.'

'Agreed, she's in a mess. Okay, so how do we find this other person, if they exist?'

'Oh, they exist, or at least he or she exists. The visit to my house makes me sure of that. What we need is some evidence, Eddie. Remember the three rules?'

'Motive, Means, and Opportunity.'

'That's it. Well we know the means. He was stabbed, several times, and quite forcefully.'

'We're looking for a man then.' Marston was trying to be helpful.

'Not necessarily. The knife was extremely sharp so a woman could have inflicted the wounds. Even the pathologist won't rule out a female hand, though he goes to great lengths to point out a number of the stab wounds were superficial injuries, little more than scratches.'

'Oh. Could they have been inflicted during some kind of fight?'

'The pathologist reckons Burnston tried to defend himself but was quickly floored. Also, there's no evidence to suggest the attack started outside the kitchen. Now, as a kitchen knife was used in the assault it looks as if the person who attacked him just picked it up and used it. It's as if this was an unpremeditated attack, or at least that's what the killer wants us to believe.'

'And that confusion simply adds to the list of questions concerning this case. So what are we going to concentrate on next?'

'Opportunity, I think. If Mrs Burnston has been telling her solicitor the truth we know he was alive when she went shopping at ten that morning, and that he was dead by the time the police arrived at 12:45. The police were called at 12:32 to say there was a commotion at the house, though both neighbours have been shown to be away that day. Also the pathologist put the time of death between 9:45 and 10:30 in the morning.'

'So it is possible Mrs B could have killed him. Afterwards she could have gone shopping and finally she was found as she started to clear up the mess.' Marston was again thinking out loud.

'It could be, but again we have to consider the point of the blood – she would have been covered in it.'

'She could have changed before she went out.' Marston protested.

'She could have done, but where were the blood soaked clothes when the police arrived? They searched the house from top to bottom and found nothing like that.'

'Including the roof?'

'I should think so, why?'

'Because they don't always do that, not if the suspect is found on the scene.'

'Fair enough, if you say so, but let's say she did kill him, took off her clothes, put them in a bag or something and then put them in the loft and they haven't been found. If we find them what will it prove?'

'That she really did kill her husband.' Marston sounded triumphant.

'No.' Palmer was still calm, still relaxed, and still thinking. 'It could mean somebody else put them up there to make it look like she did it. We're back to square one. Let's try a different angle.'

'Such as?' Marston sounded deflated that his theory had been rejected.

'Say for a moment that someone else had a key to the house and that person entered the house and killed the victim. That person could have changed and then disposed of any blood soaked clothes.

Then, knowing what time Mrs Burnston would return home, he or she could have anonymously called the police.'

'Sounds possible, but who else had a key?'

'Rachel Connors does for a start. She let me in yesterday.'

'You think she may have framed her own sister?' Marston finished his coffee.

'It's possible. Trouble is, we just don't know. The fact is that if Mrs Burnston is telling the truth and someone else does have a key to the house then that provides an opportunity. I'm not saying anything more, or anything less, but it is worth looking into. Also, when I get time, I think the loft might be worth a quick check. I'm doing a little job for Rachel Connors tonight as it happens and I'm probably going to see her tomorrow, so I'll try to get up in the loft then.'

'That leaves just one of the rules,' said Marston, recalling the start of the conversation.

'Motive,' Palmer spoke the word evenly and slowly. It was as if he were trying to conjure up the motive for the crime from simply speaking the word. He said the word again, equally slowly, 'Motive. Eddie, I have to confess that I haven't a clue if it's nothing to do with Mrs Burnston. If she is the killer then we'd have to follow the police theory that it's matrimonial. Personally, I suspect that the motive will come to us last in this case. Yes, it is the opportunity we must look for. The more we talk about it I'm convinced of that. The opportunity for this crime will lead us to the killer.'

'So how do you plan to go about that?'

'Well, let's go over what you've found out. She was in a stormy marriage – a number of people told you that. Also, she often carried some bruise marks on her face, which kind of indicates she was being smacked around a bit. We also know that John Burnston had had some problems with a drinking habit, and possibly he was involved in something a few years ago. Doesn't add up to much and I doubt it's enough for his wife to kill him over, but she might have done. So who else had opportunity?'

'Rachel Connors – you said that a few minutes ago. She had a key so she could have let herself in?'

'I suppose that's fair enough. What we need to find out now is what she was doing that morning. Leave that to me. What else can we do, Eddie?'

'Dunno. We could visit the area again. See if anything else comes up.'

'We could, but again we might arouse suspicion. I think we'll have to wait until I've seen Mrs Burnston this afternoon. Maybe she can throw some light on a few things.'

'Okay, anything you want me to do this morning?'

'Yeah, I had this call from a guy called Andy Fielding and I haven't had time to get back to him. He wants someone watched or found or something. Do you fancy having a chat with him and see what he wants – explain that you're a colleague. If you can, meet up with him and so on – you know the drill.'

'Sure.' Palmer handed him the message he had scrawled on a sheet of paper the previous evening. As he did so, Marston stood as if to leave.

'You can make the call from here if you want,' Palmer offered. 'I'm going to develop that film next, and it will take about half an hour. Make yourself at home.'

'Cheers.' Palmer stood up and walked round the desk, picked up the film and disappeared to the makeshift darkroom upstairs. Marston walked round, sat in the swivel chair, and picked up the phone.

***

It was an hour later, the film was developed, and Marston was on his way to meet with the anxious Andy Fielding. Palmer had placed the prints in the case file. They were mainly of buildings, a few of people, and the mysterious address that Marston had followed Rachel Connors to the previous afternoon. Palmer walked into the offices of Clarke and Manning.

'Mr Manning, please.' Palmer did not recognise the woman who was sitting at the receptionist's desk. She was dressed smartly, with her blond hair tied up in a bun. She wore thin-framed, silver-coloured spectacles. She was, Palmer concluded, quite pretty to look at, and for someone in her early to mid-twenties, quite mature. 'You're new here, aren't you?' Palmer's voice was friendly and disarming.

'Yes. I'm not a receptionist at all, really. She's on her break. Actually I've just joined the firm as a research assistant.'

'Oh, well I come here quite a lot so no doubt we'll meet again.' As he spoke, the door to the reception room opened.

'Mr Manning, it's nice to see you.' Palmer turned to greet the man. As he did so he mouthed the words 'don't mention my name' and slightly turned his head in the direction of the woman behind him.

'Thanks for coming,' Manning began, 'shall we go?'

'Yes.' The two men left the office and made their way to where Manning had parked his car.

'It's only a half hour away. You've met the research assistant then,' he sounded almost jovial.

'Yeah, only she doesn't know who I am.'

'Which was why you mouthed at me?'

'Look John, I don't know if she's involved in all this, but the address you gave me isn't where she is registered as living. Someone with a totally different name lives at that address. Also, my house got broken into last night and I was given another warning to drop the case.'

'Broken into?' the solicitor sounded concerned. 'Did much get stolen?'

'No, nothing, it was just done to scare me.'

'So, do you want to drop the case?'

'No. If anything it makes me more convinced that Mrs Burnston didn't kill her husband. But to be sure of that we've got to come up with either a cast iron alibi, or the person who did do it.'

'We can't give her a cast iron alibi, because the pathologist reckons death might have occurred anything up to fifteen minutes before she claims she left the house.'

'Okay, so we have to find the person that did kill her husband. This should be an interesting interview coming up.'

'Let's hope so, but I doubt you'll get anything more out of her than she's already told me.'

'Well, for her sake, I hope I do.'

Palmer sat back and closed his eyes. As Manning concentrated on the driving, Palmer focused his attention on the case that was beginning to unravel before him.

Chapter Ten

The interview room was cold and badly decorated. Palmer and Manning were seated on one side of the table when the woman was ushered into the room. She ,looked tired and drawn, pale and frightened.

'Thank you, officer.' Manning stood as she entered the room. 'Mrs Burnston, this is Mr Palmer. He has kindly agreed to assist us in this case.'

'Mr Palmer, I am very grateful.' She extended a hand in greeting and as Palmer shook it he noticed that it was painfully thin and bore the marks of faded bruises.

'Mrs Burnston, please do sit down,' Palmer smiled reassuringly. 'Mr Manning has told me a great deal about this case and I do not want to have to put you through it all again, you'll be relieved to hear.' He continued to smile as the woman took her seat, a smile that was meant to make her feel that he was on her side. It worked for she visibly relaxed, though she remained pale and drawn.

'So, Mr Palmer, how can I help you?'

'I'm hoping that it will be I who can help you, Mrs Burnston, but to do that I have a few questions I need to ask. You do know that I have only been working on the case for a little over twenty-four hours, don't you?'

The woman nodded and allowed the detective to continue.

'Although I have only just started to be involved in this matter, there are already some things I have discovered that I need to ask you about.'

'Please, go on.' The woman looked almost hopeful, and Palmer noticed her solicitor was also listening keenly.

'Firstly, Mrs Burnston, I have heard that your husband had a drink problem. Is that the case, or not?' Manning looked surprised at the revelation.

'I don't know who told you that, but yes it's true. He had been drinking quite heavily for a while and I suppose it had steadily become worse.'

'I see. Do you know why he had taken to drinking?'

'No, Mr Palmer, I do not.' She sounded tired.

'And is there any truth about the observation that he used to beat you?'

She hesitated a moment too long before answering. 'No, he was a sweet, sweet, man.'

'Are you sure, Mrs Burnston?' Palmer had detected the lie, as had the solicitor who now intervened.

'Mrs Burnston,' he said with a slow, even voice, 'it is most important you are perfectly frank with us. Protecting your husband will not help either him or you at this time.'

'Well,' she reflected, 'if he got very drunk then he'd shout at me and yes, there were a couple of times when he got so cross with me over silly things that he hit me – but I'm sure he didn't mean to hurt me.'

'And who else knew about this?' Palmer was becoming impatient.

'Well, I did tell my sister, Rachel, about it. She just laughed at me and said I shouldn't have got involved if I couldn't handle it.'

'Shouldn't have got involved in what, Mrs Burnston?'

'It's all very silly really and it goes back a long time. When I was sixteen, and Rachel would have been nineteen or thereabouts, she wanted to do a photo shoot. She had delusions of becoming a supermodel or something. Anyway she went along to this studio and did the poses – no clothes on, that kind of thing. A few weeks later she was called back to the studio and she did some more. That's when she met Warren. He was the photographer. He was also involved in some group called "Corpus Eros".'

Palmer froze momentarily but recovered before he was noticed.

'It was all very silly and Rachel got involved. Basically there was an initiation thing that meant the initiate had to strip bare and take part in some adult games as part of a group. It was all pretty harmless really and she thought it would help her career. Well it certainly got her close to Warren. After a couple of years, Rachel, who by this time was engaged, suggested I should join the group. I went along for a bit and went through the initiation ceremony. It had a name for it by then – something like the Rite of the First Hour.'

'And what does that involve, Mrs Burnston?' Palmer's voice carried a new degree of gravity.

'Is it relevant?' She sounded embarrassed by what she might have to reveal.

'I'm afraid it might be.' Palmer sounded almost apologetic.

'Well, all the members, men and women, dress up in cloaks and hoods and take the initiate out onto the Common in the dead of night. The initiate is wearing white. At about midnight the initiate is stripped bare and then it all turns into a bit of an orgy. That's all there is to it. I told you it was silly.'

'And are you still involved in the group?'

'No. John, my husband, was in the group and that was how we met. After we got married we carried on for a bit but then I dropped out – about three years ago now. John carried on for a bit but eventually he dropped out too. That's when he started drinking.'

'And is your sister still involved?'

'Oh yes. Warren, that's her husband, runs it now and I suppose she's his sort of High Priestess.'

'And do they still take on new initiates?'

'I really don't know, but I guess so if there are any who are suitable.'

'And what determines that?'

'I don't know really. In the early days it was down to taking on people who were willing, but I think more recently it's been down to Warren and Rachel.'

'That's interesting. Now, are you quite sure your husband was no longer involved?'

'Positive. It's a funny sort of group really – some funny rituals. For example, when I wanted to leave I was taken to a meeting of the six elders – they ran the group then. I was forced to strip totally naked and then I was bent over a table. Two of the elders then caned me six times – and it really hurt.

After that I was told to get out and I was promised that if I ever talked to anyone about the group I would be severely punished. I remember I couldn't sit down for three days after that caning – they weren't messing around. Basically I think they used me as a guinea-pig to try and discourage people from leaving.'

'And when your husband left?'

'He was one of the elders. I know he would have had to hand his cloak and hood back, as I had done. Other than that I don't know what else happened, and he never talked to me about it.'

'Now, Mrs Burnston, think very carefully. Of all the people in the group at the time you were in it, was there anyone you think might have wanted to kill your husband?'

'No, don't be absurd, we weren't into murder, just some harmless adult fun.'

'Wife swapping?' Palmer asked severely.

'Those that had partners, yes I suppose you could call it that, but there were single people involved too.'

'I see.' Palmer frowned slightly. 'Can you remember the people in the group when you were part of it?'

'Yes, Mr Palmer, I can.'

'Be so good as to write them down on this piece of paper.' Palmer shoved his notepad across the table together with the blue ball-pen.

'Is that really necessary?' The woman seemed more than necessarily agitated.

'Yes, Mrs Burnston, it is absolutely necessary. If you are not the killer of your husband then someone else is and, no matter how unlikely it may seem, it is just possible the killer has links to the group. I need to know the people's names and if possible their addresses so that they can be eliminated from the enquiry.'

Heather Burnston shrugged her shoulders and spent the next few minutes compiling a list of names and addresses. When she had finished there were four couples and four singles. Palmer noticed that the single entries were all female. Burnston pushed the pad of paper back towards Palmer.

'I see you have not included yourself or your husband on the list,' Palmer looked up enquiringly.

'There didn't seem to be much point in that.' The woman looked even more tired than she had done.

'I see, and you haven't forgotten anyone else?'

'No, Mr Palmer, those are the people in the group when I left it.'

'Tell me, Mrs Burnston, could whoever killed your husband have been protecting the group in some way?' The gravity in Palmer's voice had returned suddenly as if he were following a new thread in the case.

'Good God no, as I said, it was all a bit of fun, nothing that heavy.' The woman was adamant.

'And so far as you are aware your sister is still involved?'

'Yes I am, why?'

'It doesn't matter. Now, Mrs Burnston, this is very important. Apart from yourself and your husband, who has a key to your house?'

'Well, Rachel does.'

'I see. So your husband had a key, you have a key, and your sister has a key?'

'Yes, but why is it important?'

'Because whoever killed your husband didn't break into your house – which means they either had a key or your husband let them into the house. If he let them in then he must have known them because there was no sign of a struggle or anything until they were in the kitchen.' At this point Palmer scribbled a note on his pad of paper directly below the list of names she had written down for him.

'Now, Mrs Burnston, I have asked all the questions I have at this time. Is there anything else you think might help me?'

'No, I don't think so, Mr Palmer, but tell me, do you think I killed my husband?'

Palmer stood up and walked round to the woman. He stared at her face for a moment and then reached down to feel her arms. She shuddered as his hand touched her lower arm.

'Good day, Mrs Burnston,' he said as he transferred his hand into hers and shook it.

'Good day, Mr Palmer.' Her reply was weak and she looked paler than when they had first met.

'And for your information, no I don't believe you killed your husband.' He smiled at her as the female jailer opened the door to escort the prisoner back to her cell. 'We will come to see you again in a day or so,' Palmer concluded as she was led away.

'Well,' started Manning, 'what did you make of her?'

'It's exactly as you said, she isn't a murderer. She came across more as a victim, and there's so little strength in her arms that I doubt she could have inflicted half the injuries. Plus she was clearly telling us the truth though there are still things she has not told us yet. The problem we face is that from the authorities' point of view, this is a case full of circumstantial evidence and little else and we haven't got anything half as good for our case as the police do for theirs. It's going to take some effort to beat their 'caught on the scene with the weapon' allegations.'

'But, can you help us further?'

'Certainly, there are still the Connors' to tackle and with this sect thing it might throw up some more leads. Also there's this list of people to look into. Some of them are probably still involved and probably won't talk too much but we might get lucky. Look, we must get going. I've got things that need to be done today. We're finished here, aren't we?'

'Yes.' Manning placed the last few papers in his case and the two men made their exit from the prison interview room. Palmer breathed an almost audible sigh of relief when the final door was closed and they were once again standing in the land of the free.

Palmer returned to his terraced home a little after three thirty in the afternoon. He had never liked visiting clients in prison. The keys turning in the locks and the crashing of metal on metal as doors were shut behind him had always unnerved him. It mattered not who he was going to see, it was the claustrophobic effect of the metal doors shutting behind him. As he regained the comfort of his own home he noticed the light flashing on the answer-phone. He half-listened to the electronic voice stating that he had one message, and then there was the inevitable beep of the machine.

'You were warned to stay away from Burnston. You visited her this afternoon. If you go near her again there will be added trouble.' The message ended.

Palmer sat on his leather chair, stunned. The research assistant had not known who he was for the simple reason he had not given a name. Then, in his shocked state of mind, he began to think straight. Of course she knew who he was! It would have been written in Manning's diary that he was visiting the prison. He didn't need to state he was going with Palmer. Whoever was watching him already knew of his involvement in the case, and clearly anybody going with Manning to the prison would be the investigator. Palmer cursed his own stupidity for giving the game away so easily. He made a note on his pad of paper to make further investigations into the research assistant when he had time.

Having made his note he retrieved the case file from his briefcase. He pulled out the pictures that Marston had taken the previous day and scrutinised them. His attention finally focused on the house that Rachel Connors had gone to the previous day after her meeting with him. It was not her house, Palmer was sure, because his own enquiries had shown her to live a couple of streets further away. The registered dweller at the home that Connors had visited was one Julie Rawlings. It had taken Palmer less than ten minutes to locate that piece of information using a particular piece of software on his computer. What he didn't yet know was who Miss Rawlings was. He did not have time to find out now, but made a note that it needed to be checked out. In all probability she had no connection with the case he was handling, but he could not afford to write off the possibility.

Palmer turned on the computer and fetched coffee from the kitchen. When the machine was ready he started up one of his enquiry programs. He took the list that Burnston had given him and started tapping in the names one by one. It took nearly an hour and at the end of it Palmer was reasonably sure that the couples were still local as were two of the single members. One of the other single members had moved from the area a couple of years back and the other had died. Palmer noted this last detail and made further enquiries.

Half an hour later he had discovered the woman, who was in her early thirties at the time, had been the victim of a hit and run accident just outside her own home. A phone call had revealed there had been no witnesses to the accident and though the person who took the call was intrigued that Palmer was interested in it, he could offer little of any substance in the way of help. It had been just bad luck on the woman's part to step out into the road and get hit. Palmer terminated his enquiries and drew a big red circle round the name of the victim – Kelly Southbury.

The afternoon turned into evening and Palmer continued to pour over the various reports and notes he had collected on the case. As time passed he became progressively more convinced that something was missing, almost as if somewhere a false assumption had been made and it had tainted the angle taken on everything else that had followed. As the clock chimed six times, Palmer put the papers back into the drawer and locked it.

Unusually for him he removed the key and began to prepare for his meeting with Karen in Wimbledon Village an hour later.

**

After Marston left Palmer's house, he drove to the country home of Andrew Fielding. It was a cottage style building set in a quaint country lane in the middle of deepest Surrey. The cottage was one of four, identical, detached dwellings set in a neat row. The cottage he was visiting had a great ivy creeper growing round much of the front of the building, but in between the vines Marston could detect the crumbling white rendering that had been applied so many years earlier. He walked up the crazy-paving path that led to the solid wood door and rapped out three loud knocks using the wrought iron knocker that was situated plum in the middle of the door at head height. After a few seconds he heard the bolts being withdrawn on the inside and then in a moment his client was facing him.

'Mr Fielding, Eddie Marston.'

'Mr Marston, thank you for coming round so promptly. Do come in.'

Eddie noted his client was somewhere in his early fifties. He was short, shorter even than Marston. He wore spectacles, the kind of half glass spectacles that perch right on the end of the nose. His head was severely balding though he sported a full beard that had been trimmed to about an inch long. He was wearing typical country attire – a warm, check pullover and check sports trousers.

Marston followed him into the living room, a spacious room which boasted natural wood timbers that crossed the ceiling. A real log fire was burning gently in the large, central hearth. Pictures adorned the walls, and the shelves were covered in small wooden animals that represented dozens of species.

'Now, Mr Fielding, how can I help you?' Marston sat down on the ageing sofa and noted as he did so that a cloud of dust rose into the air.

'Well, Mr Marston, it's much as I explained to you over the phone. I have a daughter whom I haven't seen for maybe ten years now. I'm divorced from her mother and they just seem to have disappeared. It will be my daughter's twenty first in a couple of months and I'd like to be able to get her something.'

'I see, well that was exactly what you said over the phone. Your former wife has, presumably, stopped using your name?'

'I imagine so. It's a bit delicate you see, but our separation, well,' he paused as if worried about what to say, 'it wasn't very amicable. She'd met this other chap, about ten years younger than me and rather well off I think. She's actually six years younger than me in any event. Well, I caught them in bed one Saturday. That was nearly eleven years ago now, and Sonia, that's our daughter, was just ten. She was out with her friends for the day and I'd gone fishing early in the morning. My former wife,' he still sounded the polite country gentleman, 'thought I'd be gone all day – and so did I when I set out. But nothing was biting, well not on my stretch of the river, so I packed up and came home mid-afternoon. I opened the front door and heard a noise upstairs. Dropped the old tackle and padded up to the bedroom. I pushed the door open gently and there they were, both in their natural and him on top of her, banging away to his heart's content. I'll tell you, the tackle in the hall wasn't the only tackle that landed on the floor that afternoon. I caused one hell of a rumpus as I fairly kicked him out of the house. I never saw him again but a couple of months later she packed her bags, took Sonia, and disappeared.'

Marston had been listening carefully but was wondering just how long this interview might take.

'So, Mr Fielding, have you seen your wife since that day?'

'No, and I haven't seen Sonia either. The divorce was a quickie. It was uncontested by her and she accepted the half of the matrimonial home I offered her, and a nominal maintenance for Sonia. Everything was done through the solicitor. Afterwards I checked on the address she'd put on the affidavit and discovered it wasn't hers. It belonged, if I'm right, to some old girl who held the mail until she collected it from time to time. I wrote there a few times but I never got a reply.'

'I see.' Marston sat thoughtfully for a while. 'You don't happen to know this chap's name, the one she went off with, do you?'

'Sorry. I heard her call him Charles, but I never got to know his other name. I got his car registration number when he left, but that was eleven years ago so I doubt he'd still have it.'

'Maybe not, but it might give us a clue. You don't still have it, do you?'

'Yes, I do as it happens. Thought you might be interested in it so I wrote it down for you. Here,' he continued as he handed Marston a neatly folded piece of paper.

'Thanks. As you say, it was a long time ago, but it might be useful.'

'Now, I don't suppose you can remember where Sonia went to school do you?'

'Sort of, it was a private school. We lived in Sutton at the time and it was the big girl's school on the road between Sutton and Cheam. I can't remember the name of it and I imagine she would have left after we split up. It was quite expensive and I doubt my former wife could have afforded to keep her there, unless her lover shelled out for it.'

'Well, we'll still look into it. I'm sure we'll be able to find it from the location. There can't be too many of them in that road. Okay, unless you've got any pictures of your ex-wife I guess that's about it, unless you have anything else to add.'

Fielding frowned as if trying to recall something important, something that was just out of reach of his mind.

'No, I don't have any pictures of her. I burned them all after the divorce. I've got one of Sonia but I doubt that would be much use to you now – she was only nine at the time.'

'No, I don't think it would be of much use. Anyway, we've got a few leads to work on. I can't promise anything, Mr Fielding, we may get lucky, we may not. There isn't a lot to go on, so I don't want to raise your hopes too high, but we'll do all we can. Now, before I go, there is the matter of the cost of all this.'

'Yes, I thought you'd come to that sooner or later – you people always do.' Fielding did not sound cross at Marston's referral, but rather he sounded weary that everything eventually boiled down to money. 'What do you think this will cost me?'

'It's difficult to say off hand. I'd suggest the following. We do some initial enquiries round the school, registers, that sort of thing, and then get back to you. If we said a day's work for that lot we'd be talking less than two hundred quid. Does that seem fair?'

'Yes. But before you go any further I'd need to have a good idea what the rest might cost. Despite the old cottage and the location I have to say that I am not actually a well man and there isn't a huge amount of money just sitting round. That said I can afford a few hundred, but if it goes a lot higher there would be a problem.'

'Don't worry, Mr Fielding, we'll keep you informed all the way. I would guess we'll get back in touch with you in a couple of days, a week at most.'

'That's good. If there are any other questions, just give me a ring. I'm usually here these days.'

Marston had already stood up and was edging towards the door.

'Thanks, we will. Anyway I must get going, I have another appointment in,' and Marston glanced at his watch, 'just over half an hour, and it's a good drive from here. I'll be in touch, Mr Fielding.' Marston had opened the front door and was standing on the path the led to the gate at the bottom of the front garden. He walked quickly away from

143

the cottage as if he was in a hurry. He wasn't, but he had plans for the evening, plans involving a particular redhead who worked in a bank just down the road from where he lived. As he turned away from the cottage so his focus of attention turned to his date for the evening.

Chapter Eleven

As Marston prepared for his evening, Palmer was driving towards Wimbledon Village. It was quarter to seven when he arrived. With fifteen minutes to wait he parked up and walked casually over the grass towards the large oval pond that occupies the centre of the open area at the village end of the Common. He found a bench and sat down, looking out at the ripples that endlessly washed up on the banks of the pond, driven there by the light evening breeze. There were two young children playing by the bank with their mother watching their game from a short distance away. The older of the children threw a small stick out onto the water. His younger sister then followed his actions, trying to out throw him. She failed but seemed happy with her effort. The mother smiled warmly at her daughter's antics.

It was beginning to get dark now and the evening air was becoming decidedly cool. Palmer sat on the bench watching the children at play, thinking back to his own childhood and the seemingly endless days of bullying and strict discipline. How he hated those middle days of his childhood and he still carried the scars that bore testimony as to just how cruel they had been. There were, of course, the physical scars, the deep imperfections in the skin of his body that bore testimony to the playground incidents, the bullying, and ultimately the canings that had followed when he had taken matters into his own hands. Those scars remained, but they no longer inflicted the pain that their formation had brought him.

Then there were the mental scars, the scars that never healed, the damage that continued to occasionally rear its ugly head. Those scars, inflicted by the sudden death of his father, the bullying, and the unfair discipline he had endured for several years, still remained. They remained as a reminder to him that the world was a very unfair place. They remained as the source of his single-mindedness, and they remained as the focal point of his empathy towards others that were suffering unnecessarily as a result of injustice. Into this last category he firmly placed the thin, miserable, pathetic, figure of Heather Burnston. As he looked out at the children playing he pictured this poor woman languishing in her cell in her own state of misery and her eventual release from it entirely dependent on Palmer's own abilities. This responsibility did not worry him, he was too single-minded for that and, after all, it was not his freedom that was in jeopardy.

The younger child took another step closer towards the pond and was pulled back by its mother. They were clearly preparing to go home. No, it was not the responsibility that worried him, though Palmer was worried and nervous about this case. If it was not the responsibility that was troubling him, he reasoned as he sat watching the children walk away with their mother, it was fear. Yes, that was it, fear, and a totally rational fear – a fear of failure. Palmer reasoned he had no doubt the woman was totally innocent of the crime with which she had been charged, yet the circumstantial evidence against her was almost overwhelming. There was something else that concerned him, something about what she hadn't yet divulge and of that he was certain – there was something she was holding onto, some secret that might make all the difference to the likely outcome of her trial. Palmer puzzled at her reasons for keeping the secret and he was sure she had done so.

Even without the added hindrance of the secret, it was almost as if the system was so geared up against the innocent victim that it would take a mighty force to break the wall down. That would be something, to break down that impenetrable barrier – the wall of injustice.

There seemed to Palmer to be just a few too many 'almosts' in this case. He was almost sure he knew who had killed John Burnston, and that was out of reasoned logic. Only one other person had a key to the house, the woman he had met there the previous day. And Palmer had little doubt that the murderer had used a key – there was absolutely no sign of any break-in. Likewise, and with an even greater degree of certainty, he was almost sure that Heather Burnston was innocent. So, yet again, he was almost sure, but there was something more, something as yet intangible, and it was this thing that made Palmer nervous of failure. It was a last lingering doubt, a doubt brought on by something Heather Burnston had said that afternoon – something about Corpus Eros, and how she had been punished when she had left the group. Perhaps, just perhaps, Burnston's murder was his punishment for leaving. If it were, then it opened up even greater avenues of investigation, areas which the organisation called Expert Investigations had not even touched on. Those investigations, Palmer figured, would have to begin with the list of people Heather Burnston had given him earlier that afternoon.

Palmer glanced at his watch, stood up and began to walk in the direction of the pub and his rendezvous with his lover. Karen was waiting for him outside the pub when he strolled up.

'You're late, Damien! Had a bad day?' She kissed him, a mere peck on the cheek.

'Yeah, it's not been that good, how about you?'

'So so, I guess. Anyway, have we got time for a drink?'

'Not really, but I've got some things in the car. It's just down the road.'

They walked down the road to where Palmer had parked his car earlier then, before driving off, Palmer handed the woman an envelope.

'The guy we're watching is in there, together with a few details. I don't know for sure that he's home at the moment and I can't phone his wife to find out. But she assured me he's going out at eight, which means we need to be in place at least half an hour before then. You'll see the guy drives a dark blue BMW and the index number is in there somewhere. Not that we'll probably see him on foot but he's 43 years old, tall and thin. By tall I mean he's over six feet three. Apparently he's got a slightly greying, full-face beard, though he hasn't in the picture, and he's starting to recede on top.'

'So, what are we going to do?'

'Well, first off, we'll just take a quick look to see if the car's in the driveway or in the road, and then we'll see where we can park. It's only a short distance away.' With that Palmer started the engine. As he pulled out into the traffic and headed into the village the woman beside him scanned the few pages of information that were contained in the envelope. The traffic through the main village street was heavy, a combination of commuters making their way home and early restaurant goers making navigation through the narrow street something of an art. It took over five minutes before Palmer could turn right at the roundabout that signalled the start of the drop into the main shopping area of Wimbledon.

Once he had completed the right turn the traffic was much lighter and Palmer soon located the road in which Warren and Rachel Connors lived. As he drove carefully down the road looking for the right house the woman beside him spotted the car parked in the road.

'That's it,' she said, pointing at the blue BMW ahead of them. A moment later they were passing the driveway of the house, a driveway that was empty.

'Curious that,' said Palmer, his attention once more on the road.

'What is?'

'Well, why park a decent car like that in the road when you have an empty drive? It doesn't make sense.'

'Well, perhaps it wasn't empty when he got home.'

'Possible, but I'm sure Mrs Connors said she'd be in all afternoon. Oh well, I suppose that if he's going out in it later on it doesn't really matter. Let's find somewhere to park.'

With that, Palmer stopped, reversed the car into the shingled drive that he had just passed and began a slow crawl back towards the house they were about to place under surveillance. Some fifty yards before the driveway there was a space and Palmer skilfully drove his vehicle into it so that he was parked parallel to the badly pot-holed pavement. Having applied the hand-brake and disengaged gear, he turned off the engine and sat back.

'So what do we do now?' This was Karen's first tour of duty with the sleuth and she had no idea what would happen next.

'Now, we wait.'

'You mean we just sit here?'

'Exactly, we just sit here, and we watch.'

'What until he comes out? But how do you know which way he's going to go?'

'I don't. But the Beamer is pointing up the road away from us, so either he'll go that way, or we'll have plenty of time to watch him turn round. My guess is he'll head for the common.'

'What if he doesn't show?'

'We charge the client for a couple of hours of work and go and have a bite to eat.'

'How long do we give it then?'

'Questions, questions,' Palmer laughed. 'He's due out at eight according to Mrs. Connors, so I'd say we sit tight until nine and then call it a night.'

'An hour and a half in this thing!' Now it was the woman's turn to smile. 'Oh well, we'll have to find something to do I guess.'

'Just keep your eyes on that driveway. Take note of anyone that walks down the road and anything else you can think of. It all goes in the report. It all shows that we've been observant – and it's what the client is paying us for.'

Their banter continued as they watched three pedestrians walk down the road. As the first one passed the car Karen shrank back into her seat as if trying to become invisible. The pedestrian continued walking, either oblivious to the couple in the car or totally disinterested in their presence. After the first pedestrian had passed them and disappeared Palmer asked a simple question.

'Okay, here's a poser for you. Describe that woman who just walked down the street.'

'I wasn't really paying much attention, Damien. I guess I felt awkward.'

'So you can't describe her?'

'Well I can, a bit. She was about five two, dark hair that was cut fairly short, had a dark blue jacket on. I didn't register much else.'

'Not bad for a beginner. You missed the short wool skirt and the dark brown club shoes. I think she had a gold bracelet on her left wrist – it might have been a watch. Oh, and most importantly you missed the fact she was wearing spectacles.'

For a moment the woman looked surprised but then she re-joined the conversation.

'Yeah, and she had Chanel No. 5 on too.'

'How did you know that?' Palmer had fallen into the trap before he realised it. When he saw the joke he laughed and Karen joined him. 'Okay, so you caught me out. But it really is important to stay awake and observant. After all, she just might have been his bit on the side.'

'She was at least sixty, if not older,' Karen responded.

'So you were watching?'

'Yes to a certain degree.'

The next five minutes passed by interminably until the second pedestrian, a young fair-haired lad, passed the car. As he passed them he spat something onto the pavement.

'Charming,' was the only word Palmer uttered.

'Yeah,' the woman replied.

The third pedestrian passed them a few minutes later. This time it was a middle-aged city gent, complete with pin-stripe suit and attaché case. Palmer was just about to speak when he noticed something ahead of them.

'We're on the move.' He spoke softly now as he attracted his companion's attention.

'That's him, is it, are you sure?'

'Positive, I've seen the picture. That is definitely him.'

'So what do we do now?'

'We see what he does.'

It took the tall, thin, man several seconds to walk to where his BMW was parked. It took Palmer a few more seconds to realise what was happening.

'Damn, he's going on foot.' The man had walked past his car and was continuing his journey up the road, away from where Palmer and Shaw were sitting.

'So what do we do now?' The woman's voice was calm though it contained a note of resignation, as if she already knew what the answer would be.

'We follow him. Let's go.' Palmer picked up his brown top-opening attaché case from the rear seat and rummaged inside it for a moment. He pulled out the portable cassette recorder and his camera. A moment later he had the driver's door open, just as Karen opened her own door. In less than thirty seconds they were walking up the road, hand in hand, to all intents and purposes a couple walking back home. They passed the driveway of the Connors' house. As they did so Palmer noticed the thick green vine that was climbing up and along the front wall of the building. He also noticed the hanging baskets either side of the storm porch. It was clearly a well-looked-after home, and its owners were obviously proud of it.

'Where do you think he's going?' Shaw was still holding Palmer's hand as she raised the question.

'No idea, but he could be going to the bus stop.'

'Or perhaps he's just going to walk to where ever he's going.' As she spoke she withdrew her hand from Palmer's and placed it in the pocket of her coat. After a moment she withdrew it, holding a tissue which she then proceeded to wipe her nose with.

'He could be. That would be interesting if he does. Now, he hasn't looked back yet so I reckon he's fairly confident he's not being followed, but we won't get too close, just in case.' They saw the man ahead of them reach the end of the road. He crossed over and continued walking, straight towards the Common. Palmer and Shaw followed him, keeping some distance behind him.

At the next junction and with the Common directly ahead of him, the man stopped. He looked down the road in both directions and then turned to look back down the road he had just walked. He saw the man and woman some distance behind him but they did not concern him. He was simply checking that there was no traffic coming from any direction and when satisfied it was safe to do so he continued his walk by crossing the road and stepping onto the Common land.

As Palmer and Shaw also reached the junction they noticed that the man had now walked several yards across the Common.

'He's taking a cut across the grass. You saw him look round at the junction so he must have seen us, but judging by the way he's walking I don't think he's suspicious.' Palmer and his companion had now stopped at the junction.

'So?' her voice was enquiring with a hint that she was somewhat tired.

'So, if we just walk over there and he turns round again he's bound to suspect something. If we walk round the side for a bit then he won't think he's being followed. But we'll have to walk fairly quickly or we'll lose him.'

'Okay by me, but how do you know where he's going?'

'I don't, but I reckon he's going to pick up that little dirt track over there,' and Palmer gesticulated in the general direction of the man they were following, 'and that goes off up to the memorial. So I suggest we aim for that.'

'Fine, but we'd better get moving.' As she spoke the couple set off to the right and started a brisk walk. Five minutes later, and having crossed several minor roads they were facing the war memorial. The grey symbol of remembrance stood before them as they walked towards it. The man they were following was already over a hundred yards further on, heading up the main road that leads from Wimbledon Village towards Putney.

Concentrating on not losing their target, Palmer failed to look behind him. Had he done so he would have noticed the small car that followed them up the road from Connors' house. He might also, if he'd been very lucky, have recognised the woman behind the steering wheel. Palmer and Shaw were already walking towards the memorial when she pulled up at the end of the junction. She stopped and picked up her mobile phone that had been lying on the passenger seat. She dialled a number and waited.

'They're following you,' she said quite simply. 'No, there's no doubt about it. They got out of the car just as soon as you'd walked off up the road and they're now heading off towards the memorial. What do you want me to do?'

She waited while the man walking across the Common gave her instructions.

'See you a bit later on,' she said and switched the mobile off. She pulled out onto the main road and passed the couple walking on the pavement before they had covered a hundred yards from the junction.

As Palmer and Shaw walked towards the memorial stone their sight of the man was obscured for a few moments. Palmer breathed a sigh of relief when they had passed the memorial and regained sight of their target.

'It can't be much further,' Palmer commented. The road they were walking along was a major vehicular artery. To their left was the Common, the playful variations of spring green foliage a delight to the urban-weary traveller. On the far side of the road were the large houses of the rich, and occasionally famous. These houses, almost without exception, were shielded from the casual onlooker by high walls constructed from brick. As if their owners valued their anonymity most of the drives to the houses were protected by wrought-iron gates. Such was the situation at the driveway where the tall, thin, man now stood. As Palmer and Shaw continued walking he pushed open the tall wrought-iron gateway and disappeared from sight.

It took the couple only a minute to walk the remaining distance to the same gate. Palmer made a mental note of the address.

'That's a strange name,' the woman beside him observed. The single word "CUPROSSERO" was burned into the slice of log that was attached to the front wall of the house. 'That's a very strange name.'

'Yeah, it might be Italian or something. Perhaps it's something significant to do with the guy who lives there.' At that moment Palmer became conscious they were not alone in the road. 'Keep walking.' He gently reached out and grabbed the woman's hand as he continued to walk down the road. 'There's a couple coming up behind us.'

'Oh,' she said and made as if to look behind her.

'Not now, we'll walk on for a few yards and then cross over onto the common. There are some trees there that will give us some cover.'

'They're not in leaf yet,' she protested.

'I know, but it's getting pretty dark now. It must be half eight, and if we can avoid the street lights it will be difficult for anyone to spot us.'

'Okay, if you say so. But what are we going to do?'

'Watch, and see what happens.' They stopped and crossed the main road, quickly gaining the relative safety of the trees that line the Common. Turning, Palmer noticed that the couple behind them had just closed the wrought iron gate.

'That's interesting. There must be some sort of party going on, only we're not invited.' Palmer was already looking at the cover afforded by the trees. 'We need to move into the rough a bit more. We're too visible just standing here.'

'I told you we would be.' The woman was now sounding very tired, and Palmer knew she was not used to this sort of adventure.

The couple walked behind the second line of trees just in time to see a car pull up at the gateway. Two young looking girls alighted from the back of the car and pushed the gate open, closing it behind them again as they approached the house. Palmer was ready with his camera and reeled off three shots.

'Isn't it too dark for that?'

'No,' he replied, 'there's still enough light from the streetlight over there to get a reasonable shot.' Two more people walked down the road to the wrought iron gate a few minutes later and again they were captured on camera.

Half an hour later, and with no further activity in the direction of the house they were watching Palmer decided it was time to pay the property a closer visit.

'Stay here and keep an eye out. I'm going to nip across and see if I can spot anything,' he whispered, though the muted tone was unnecessary. They were quite alone on that particular stretch of the Common.

'Okay, but what do I do if anyone comes by?'

'They won't, but if they do, just stay here. If I'm not back in ten minutes then you'd better contact Eddie and get him out here.'

'Okay.' The whispered nature of the conversation had become infectious.

Palmer stood up and clambered through the bracken that had afforded them protection against observation. In less than a minute he was standing by the wrought iron gates and in a few more seconds had closed them behind him. Sticking to the shadows he almost crawled his way round to the living room windows. The light was on and the curtains were open. Clearly the occupants were aware that the brick wall surrounding the gates meant no observer could watch them from the road. However, from his vantage point Palmer could see everything quite clearly.

The man he recognised as Connors was sitting in a big armchair facing sideways to the window. Behind him stood four adults. They were dressed casually and it was clear that the assembled group were involved in some kind of ritual for kneeling in front of Connors were the two young girls that Palmer had seen alight from the car earlier. As he saw them now from his shadowy refuge he realised they were not quite as young as he had imagined. The blond haired girl, the one who had hair reaching halfway down her back, Palmer estimated, in her early twenties, and he vaguely recognised her from somewhere. From his sideways view he could see that the girl was attractive as she knelt before Connors, her breasts jutting out from underneath the skimpy black sweater that she wore. Next to her and slightly shorter than the first girl was a second. She had darker hair and it was cut in a short style. She looked somewhat younger than the other girl and Palmer noticed she had a sweet smile.

Connors handed the two girls something that Palmer could not quite see. As they ate it Connors placed a hand on each head. As he did so the four adults changed positions. They walked round the chair and two stood behind and to the side of each of the girls. After a moment they each offered an arm to their charge and the girls stood up, using the arms for support. Connors clapped his hands twice, though to Palmer there was no sound through the closed and double-glazed window. As he did so the adults moved forward slightly. Palmer noticed at this point that both of the girls at the centre of the gathering were wearing identical clothing. The skimpy black tops gave way to short skirts and what looked like black tights. As he noticed this, the two adults standing by each girl unfastened the girl's skirt and let it fall to the ground. Palmer noticed now that the girls were in fact wearing black stockings.

As this happened Connors leaned forward. He smiled at what he saw. He beckoned to the blond girl who stepped out of her fallen skirt and took one step closer. Connors reached out and touched her. The girl offered no resistance to his ministrations. Palmer could not see exactly what was going on but after a few moments the girl started to sway as he continued to caress her. Then, and quite suddenly she noticeably trembled before collapsing on the floor. As she fell to the ground she twisted round slightly and Palmer noticed that she was wearing no underclothes. The two adults who had been standing beside her reached out and slowed her collapse so that she landed gracefully on the carpet. After she had fallen the two adults straightened her body so that she was lying on her back, her legs together.

By the time she was lying on her back Connors had turned his attention to the other girl. Again he beckoned and she stepped towards him. Again he touched her. This time Palmer was better able to see what was happening. He could see the way in which Connors touched her. She was totally yielding, totally obedient. Then, after a minute Palmer saw her move her feet apart slightly. As she did so Connors' hand moved to her most intimate area. In moments she was standing on tiptoe as if trying to move away from his touch. Then, like the other girl she was shuddering and trembling. Finally, she yielded to the attentions of the man and collapsed on the floor. Like the first girl she was laid out on her back with her legs together.

Palmer looked at his watch and realised that his ten minutes were nearly up. As he had been watching so his camera had been busy. He had no idea if the pictures would develop but the light from the room was quite good and Palmer hoped that the film would not be wasted. As he stood to leave his hiding place he noticed that the four adults had started ministering their own attentions on the hapless, yielding girls.

With some regret Palmer slipped out of the wrought iron gates and made his way back to the place on the Common where Karen Shaw was waiting for him.

'You took your time,' she started. 'I was about to call Eddie. What happened?'

'Well, there's some kind of ritual act or something going on over there. You know those two girls we saw getting out of the car, well they look like the victims, or sacrifices, or something. It's really weird.'

'And our man?' Shaw sounded somewhat miffed that she had missed out on the action.

'He looks like the ringleader, or whatever you want to call him.'

'High priest – remember my dream Damien? Remember the five men in hoods?'

'Well, as you happen to mention it, there are four other people beside Connors in there, and judging from what I saw they're only just getting started so I think they'll be some time yet.'

'Oh no, not another wait, I'm getting cold out here. Do we have to stay?'

'I don't think so. We know where he went and I've seen who's there. Chances are he'll just go home from here, seeing as he's on foot.'

'Good. Are you coming back to my place tonight, it's closer than yours?' As she made the suggestion Palmer realised what she was offering him, and the scenes across the road had already aroused him.

'I don't think so, not tonight, but I wouldn't mind a kiss before we go our own separate ways.' He leant in towards her and pulled her to him. She offered no resistance and an open mouth as he sought out hers. Their lips met and their tongues began to play with each other. As they did so Palmer recalled the scenes across the road.

Their act of lovemaking was brief and for a moment they seemed to ignore the coldness of the night air. It was as spontaneous and as physical as it could be and as their act of lovemaking drew to an end, Palmer realised they were both breathing heavily from their exertions.

'Better get dressed,' he said after a minute or so as their breath returned. 'You okay?'

'Yes darling, and you?'

'Great. Don't know what happened to trigger that but it just seemed right somehow.'

'I know what you mean.' She was trying to replace her skirt.

'Did I hurt you with the tree?' Palmer sounded concerned and he affectionately put an arm round the woman's shoulders.

'No, I don't think so. A few scratches that's all. God that was good. Talk about having your breath taken away. My legs still feel like jelly. It's a good

162

job my car's only just down the road. Can I give you a lift back to the Connors' place?'

'No, it's all right. I could do with a walk. I'll see you back to your car first though.'

'Are you sure you don't want to come back with me?'

'I'd love to, but there are things I must do, both tonight and early tomorrow, and I know you've got an early start too.'

'Yeah, fair enough.' They were walking back to Karen Shaw's car and Palmer still had his arm over her shoulders. After a few minutes they reached the car and stood there like teenage lovers as they kissed each other goodnight. Finally, after about five minutes, the woman started the car and began her journey back to her flat in Sutton. It was nearly ten o'clock now and the traffic was light. As she set off, Palmer crossed the road and for the second time that evening made his way to the wooden bench that conveniently waited for him at the side of the pond.

He sat there for several moments reflecting on the day's events. The visit to Heather Burnston, the message on his answer-phone, the weird goings on at the house they had just been watching and then the spontaneous session he had just enjoyed with Karen. It had, he concluded, been a most interesting day. Palmer sat on the bench looking out over the cold, dark, water of the pond. He sat that way for several minutes chewing over the case. There were certainly more loose ends to tie up than he had first expected and he now had to hope that one of those loose ends would be helpful to him. As he sat there with his mind drifting over the various aspects of the case, he began to worry over the loose end that was Rachel Connors. She, after all, was a key holder. Finally he decided it was time to collect his car and he wandered off in the direction of the Connors' home.

He was walking past the Connors' driveway when he noticed the dark green Fiat. He knew it was not Rachel Connors' car, nor her husband's, and it intrigued him that the woman had a visitor while her husband was out. Curiosity ensured that Palmer stepped into the driveway and made a cursory examination of the vehicle. He noted the index number and checked out its contents. The light was on in the front room, and the curtains were drawn. Palmer noticed a chink of light coming from the side of the bay window. He padded over to the place where the light was coming from and as he cautiously looked in he could just see three women. Two of them were sat on the settee. In front of him was an armchair and he could see the head of the person sitting there. He guessed this was Rachel Connors. Certainly the hair colouring was correct. One of the other women he recognised as the woman Rachel Connors had visited the previous day. He could not tell who the third woman was, but she looked somewhat younger than Connors and the other woman. It seemed an innocent enough gathering and Palmer mentally noted a few details concerning the unknown woman.

Having completed his observations he returned to his own car and began his journey home. It was now late evening and the traffic heading towards Putney from Wimbledon was light. The bistros and cafes that occupy much of the central part of the

Village were empty though the public houses were still alive.

Palmer picked up the main road from the Village and skirted the boundary of the Common, passing the house that they had been watching sometime earlier. As he passed it he wondered what activities might still be taking place behind the safety of the wrought iron gates. He was still musing on the thought as he passed the turn off to the historic windmill, the restored building and museum that nestles into the edge of the Common's golf courses. His journey continued to Tibbets corner, the almost infamous roundabout that provides access to the A3. He approached the roundabout with caution though he was virtually alone on the road that evening. Taking the turn that headed for Putney the scenery soon changed. Leaving behind the opulent and grand buildings that front the Common and the beauty of the Common itself, Palmer was soon driving through the urban dwellings and buildings that signalled the approach to Putney itself. It was here that he made the turn that took him to his own home. Finally, having parked with some degree of difficulty, he reached the blue front door of his house, the sixth in the terrace. It had been a long day and Palmer took little time in retiring for the night.

Chapter Twelve

The following morning dawned with a clear sky and confirmed the risk of frost had finally passed. The sun was not particularly warm as the weak rays penetrated Palmer's bedroom. He rose early and while the percolator was still filling with the freshly brewed coffee, Palmer turned his attentions to the third bedroom of his house. Several years earlier he had converted it into a makeshift darkroom and now he began the process of developing the film of the previous evening's surveillance. It was a process he had grown accustomed to and with his growing proficiency the whole task took him just over half an hour.

Palmer left the room with the developed negatives in his hand. He rarely printed the pictures unless they were to be sent to a client, and for now the pictures of the submissive girls did not warrant being printed.

He took the negatives to his study and, after a visit to the kitchen, sat on his leather swivel chair sipping the fresh brew. Casually he looked at the negatives as he held them up to the window. They were surprisingly good and Palmer made a few notes of the descriptions of the two girls on the pad of paper that sat on his desk.

Having done this, he unlocked his desk drawer and pulled out the file of information he was accumulating. He looked once again at the pathologist's report and the other documents Manning had given him a few days previously. It still seemed to Palmer that the logical decision any jury would reach was Heather Burnston had murdered her husband. There was just something that prevented Palmer from believing it and it had something to do with his meeting with the woman the previous day. The hit and run case also intrigued him though it was surely a coincidence.

Palmer continued to ponder the case until the clock in the hall sounded nine o'clock. As it did so he picked up the telephone and dialled the number he had written on the top of the pad of paper.

'Mrs Connors?' His question was framed politely.

'Yes,' he heard the woman's reply.

'Hello, it's Damien Palmer. Can you speak freely at the moment?'

'Not very easily I'm afraid.'

'In which case, can I meet you later on?'

'That should be okay.'

'Excellent. I have something for you, and also I'd like to examine something at your sister's house. Could we meet there at about twelve?'

'That would be fine.'

'I'll talk to you then. Goodbye.' Palmer replaced the receiver and set about the task of writing up his report of the previous evening's surveillance. It took him nearly an hour to complete. He chose to describe the way he had followed her husband, and where he had walked. He omitted the graphic details of what he'd seen through the windows, but he did describe the fact that various other people had arrived at the house about the same time as Connors. As it was evident this was not a meeting between Connors and one other person,

Palmer had seen little point in waiting for long. It was a short, succinct report and stated exactly what Palmer wanted his client to know. After all, apart from her sister, Rachel Connors appeared to be the only other living key holder to the Burnston home. If Palmer were to believe in Heather Burnston's innocence of the murder then it cast a shadow of suspicion on her sister, a fact which Palmer figured should make him wary of Rachel Connors.

There was a second reason why the report was short, and that was quite simply because Palmer did not intend to charge the full rate for the work he had done. When the report was complete he quickly made up an invoice and put it and the report in a brown envelope. The morning was passing and Palmer took a look at the notes he had scrawled while talking to Heather Burnston the previous day. He also looked again at the list of group members she had given him somewhat reluctantly. It certainly seemed that Warren Connors was still involved in the group and Palmer decided if that were the case then in all probability his wife was too. Palmer also considered the likelihood that if Heather Burnston had been punished when she had decided to leave the group, and she was but a member, then when her husband left his punishment would surely have been greater. Yet there was no indication from the woman that her husband had been punished, unless of course his punishment was death, but that seemed to be somewhat extreme. Palmer had to admit that such an event was not impossible. The next course of action, he decided, was to find out a little more about Corpus Eros and its members.

The clock in the hall sounded the eleventh hour and Palmer began his journey to Wimbledon, to the desirable, but not overly ostentatious house where John Burnston had met with his death. At a few minutes to mid-day he arrived, parked the car and purposefully strode up the garden path. He had barely reached the door when it was opened for him.

'Mr Palmer, bang on time,' Rachel Connors smiled at the sleuth as he approached her.

'I try to be punctual. How are you today?'

'Oh, not so bad though I think I might be getting a cold. Anyway, do come in and tell me what Warren got up to last night – I'm dying to know.' She closed the door behind them and they entered the lounge.

'Not a lot actually. It's all there in my report.' Palmer handed her the envelope as he carried on talking. 'Actually, there are a couple of things I'd like to look at while I'm here, if you don't mind.'

'No, not at all, help yourself. I'll just read this while you poke around.' Her voice sounded interested in what she hoped to read and Palmer felt sorry she was going to be disappointed.

'Well, I'd just like to take a quick look in the loft. Probably nothing up there, but I forgot the other day.'

'It should be easy enough to get into. There's a proper loft ladder, or so Heather once told me.'

'In that case I won't be more than five minutes.' Palmer stood up and left the room. As he did so, the woman slit open the envelope. Palmer walked up the staircase and pushed on the loft hatch. As he had guessed, it was spring loaded. It opened easily at his touch and the ladder came into view. In seconds, Palmer was reaching up into the loft, trying to locate the light switch. He found it and a moment later the loft was bathed in soft yellow light. There was little to see. A rolled up scrap of carpet occupied one side of the loft area, and in front of it was an old, battered, suitcase. Palmer walked over to the suitcase and found that it was not locked.

Inside he found what he was looking for. The brown cloak had an attached hood, a bit like a monk's habit. A length of cord lay under the garment. Also in the case was a black facemask with two slits for the eyes and another for the mouth. Palmer picked up the cloak and beneath it was a small, black diary. Palmer picked up the diary and skimmed through the pages. There was a lot of writing and some addresses and Palmer knew immediately he hadn't got time to study the little black book whilst crouched in the loft. He slipped the book into his own jacket pocket and replaced the cloak.

Palmer debated with himself what to do next. To remove the garments from the house would be tricky without arousing the suspicion of the woman who at that moment was reading his report. Palmer decided to close the case and leave the contents where they were, keeping the diary in his own pocket. It had evidently been overlooked beforehand and as such it was unlikely anybody would notice it had been removed now.

In less than the promised five minutes he was back in the lounge.

'As I suspected, it was a waste of time. There's just a rolled up carpet end and a battered old suitcase with what looks like some old clothes in it. Nothing of any interest whatsoever,' he lied. 'Still it shows I've been thorough.'

'Yes, I suppose it does. So dear old Warren wasn't naughty last night?'

'I doubt it, not with half a dozen people or so in the house.'

'You didn't mention the house's name or number?'

'Didn't I? Oh it was a weird name as I recall. Something along the lines of "CUPROSSERO". Must be Italian I should think.' Palmer noticed that the woman went a slightly paler shade of colour at the mention of the name. 'Does that name mean anything to you?' He enquired, feigning he had not noticed her change.

'It should do, it's where I first met Warren. It's where we did the first photo shoot.'

'But I thought that was at his studios from what you said the other day.'

'No. I didn't meet him at the studios for the first shoot I did. It was only when I arranged to do some more, slightly more adult shots, we met, and that was at that house.'

'So, what do you think he was doing there?' Palmer detected that the woman wasn't telling him the whole truth.

'Dunno,' she said but her face had started to redden with the deception. 'Perhaps he was talking to someone about some pictures. It is his line of business.'

'Yes, you're probably right. Now, unless you want me to follow him again I don't think there is much more I can do for you. It looks like you were mistaken.'

'I guess so, but I'll keep your number in case I need you again in the future.'

'Well, I suppose that about covers it. Oh yes, there was one other tiny matter.' Palmer paused for effect, a pause that was designed to fully attract the woman's attention. 'I went to see your sister yesterday. She mentioned something about some Rite of The First Hour or something. I wasn't really paying much attention at the time, as she wasn't making much sense. I don't suppose it means anything to you, does it?' It was as if Palmer had spoken five magic words for Rachel Connors shuffled uneasily on the sofa and her face went crimson.

'Yes, it does mean something to me, but why Heather would want to bring it up I have no idea. She is no longer involved, as doubtless she told you, and frankly my private life has little, if anything, to do with this case.'

'But it would have something to do with it if her husband had been involved.'

'I don't see how. Now, unless you have any other questions to ask I must be getting home.' It was evident from her manner that Palmer was not going to elicit any further information from the woman, but he gave it one last try.

'So there is no truth in the rumour that John's death had anything to do with something called Corpus Eros?' As he spoke the words he watched closely for the tell-tale sign he was looking for. He spotted the sign just before the woman spoke.

'Of course it didn't!' She was trying too hard. 'Look, if you really want to know the truth I'll tell you.' Palmer sat back in the armchair and waited as the woman composed herself. Palmer watched her closely as she began to tell her story.

'It all started when I was eighteen. I was, if you'll forgive the expression, a stunner in those days, and a number of my friends had suggested I tried modelling. Well, after my A levels were over, I did. I found a photographic studio in Putney that did me a shoot – nothing too hot, but I tried to show myself off to the best. The photographer, he was called Gary, had contacts and it wasn't long before I got asked to do another shoot. The contract wasn't that good, but it paid some money. This time, though, they wanted something steamier and I was sent to a private address for the shoot. That's where I met Warren, at CUPROSSERO. He was a gentleman and a real professional photographer. I was naked in front of him and he didn't try to touch me once. I got talking to him and we met up a few times and got to know each other. After a few months I met John and they told me about Corpus Eros, which I take it you have heard about.' Palmer nodded but remained silent. 'Well, it all seemed a bit of a laugh at the time and I went along with what Warren wanted, after all he was quite attractive and I'm not a prude. So I got involved and really began to enjoy our little secret meetings. For a laugh the two guys invented some initiation rite that had to be performed at the first hour on the night of the full moon out on the Common. It was a scream and being out in the open at that time of night was highly erotic for me. I had both Warren and John that night and a couple of other blokes. It was just one of those things.' She paused for effect before continuing.

'Anyway Heather, who is three years younger than me, started to badger me about it so I suggested she came along too. She was seventeen at the time. She got involved and went through the same ritual that I did. She didn't seem to enjoy it so much but she met John and they started dating each other. Of course there were other people joining all the time, and it got to the point where we must have had about twenty people involved. After a bit I married Warren and Heather married John. It wasn't long after they married that Heather wanted to leave the group. We'd sort of always expected people to stay members forever so when she wanted to leave we had to invent a rite for that. Warren devised it and by now he'd got John and five others, including me, as his elders. We sat like a jury while he tried poor old Heather. Her sentence for leaving was to be caned by two of us and to vow never to tell anyone about the group. She signed a confession and promise document and then took her punishment, and that was that.' Palmer was watching her intently, waiting for her face to show she was lying.

'About a year after that Warren seemed to go off me, and I started to suspect he was with another woman.' She bit her lip as if realising something for the first time but continued. 'It got to the point where I couldn't face being in the group with him anymore so I decided to leave as well. I'll tell you, my punishment was four times as bad as Heather's.

I couldn't sit down for a week afterwards, and to make matters worse it didn't bring Warren and I closer together. Actually I think he liked delivering the cane to my rear end, it gave him some sort of power over me. And then John got killed. I suspected it was because Heather found out he was still in the group even though he'd told her he'd left.'

'Sorry,' Palmer interjected, 'John was still in the group?'

'Oh yes, he and Warren ran it together. He was in it right up to his death, no question about it. You might as well know it now, as you're sure to find out. John had been unfaithful to Heather for about as long as they were married – it came with being in the group, just like Warren has always been unfaithful to me. The difference is I don't mind, whereas Heather did.'

'Hmm, and do you think she killed her husband?'

'No, I don't. Actually it was much more likely she would have filed for divorce.'

'I see, and had she?'

'Not that I'm aware of but then, when she found out John was still in the group, she didn't have much time before his death.'

'She found out! How do you know?' Palmer was becoming intrigued at the woman's story, intrigued as to how much was fiction.

'Oh, she told me about a week before his death. She was furious about it. Apparently he'd come home one evening, quite the worse for drink and totally incompetent in the male department. Heather was in the right mood for making love and wanted

175

him badly. When he couldn't perform she started quizzing him. In his drunken state he told her exactly what he'd been up to that evening, and it transpired his flaccid condition wasn't just down to the drink.'

'He'd been to a group meeting and had another woman?'

'Yeah. They're getting a couple of young women ready for their initiation at the moment. Warren told me a few weeks ago. I guess he had one of them. These initiation things take a few months to prepare for and they have to wait for the full moon and it has to be fine and so on. So even a few months ago these kids would have been getting ready for their big night.'

'And do you think that's what your husband was doing last night?'

'Probably, but like I said, I only care about the fact he isn't getting serious with another woman. This group thing is all just for fun – something to satisfy his urges.'

'But don't you do that?' It was Palmer's turn to take the initiative.

'Yes, I used to, but his needs have grown beyond what I can offer him.'

'I see. Well that does put a different light on things. I've just had a thought. You have a key to the Burnston house. Do you know if anyone else does?'

'I don't think so, why do you ask?'

'Oh, it's just that when Heather goes down for this the authorities will want to know who the key holders are – security reasons I believe.' Palmer lied, but he was fairly sure she had told him the truth. 'Well, Mrs Connors, time is getting on and I have lots to do. Thank you for being so frank with me. You know that I will do all I can to keep your information in confidence. I doubt it has anything to do with John's death anyway.' Palmer stood up and in a few minutes had said his farewells to the woman and walked back down the path to the pavement.

It was nearly one o'clock and Palmer decided to have lunch sitting on the Common. He drove the short distance to the village, parked and located the sandwich shop he had patronised on a number of occasions. The spring day had turned out fine and warm and Palmer took his purchase and once again found the bench that overlooked the pond. There were people walking round the banks of the pond, people enjoying the warmth and freshness of the early afternoon, people like Palmer taking their concerns for a lunchtime airing.

He chewed the sandwich carefully as he weighed up the conversation he had just held. In some ways it was what he had expected - the husband cheating on his wife and carrying on behind her back. Perhaps he was surprised at Rachel Connors' own confession and the way she reacted to her husband's own affairs, but then again she was an unpredictable person, so maybe her reaction could have been expected.

Palmer fished inside his jacket pocket and withdrew the small, black diary he'd taken earlier. He started to thumb through the pages. It was a diary for the previous year and checking through the address section, Palmer noticed it contained an entry for Kelly Southbury. From the address section he flipped to the start of the year and idly thumbed through the diary section. He found entries relating to various appointments where the only identity to the appointee was his or her initials. Palmer was looking for a specific connection and in February he found it. The initials "K S" appeared on several days with mostly evening appointment times.

Palmer extracted the list of names Heather Burnston had given him and on which he had recorded the date of Kelly Southbury's demise – it was 4th April.

'What if she knew what he was up to?' Palmer muttered to himself almost without realising it.

Whatever the situation it certainly gave Heather Burnston more of a motive for murder. If the authorities knew about the diary then they would have an even stronger case. However, Palmer had to consider the fact that the authorities did not know about the diary. He also had to consider the possibility that anyone wanting to set Heather Burnston up for the murder of her husband could also have been the killer of Kelly Southbury. It was a big "if" that Palmer posed himself next – the whole of his thought chain was based on the unproven premise that the death of John Burnston had any connection to his involvement with Corpus Eros. If it didn't then Palmer knew he was no nearer to finding out whether Heather Burnston really was the murderer she had been accused of being.

Palmer knew Rachel Connors was a key holder – she had admitted the fact. As he chewed over the facts as he knew them, Palmer became intrigued by the possibility Rachel Connors just might have killed her sister's husband to get her sister framed for the crime. It seemed callous and without reason unless, and the thought hit Palmer quite forcefully, unless Heather was having an affair with Warren Connors, and Rachel Connors had found out. Palmer's eyes lit up at the suggestion and he finished the sandwich.

He took the newspaper out of his case and sat there scanning the back pages. He found what he was looking for, the little chart showing the phases of the moon. There were just two days to the next full moon, and with the weather chart indicating a settled and warm period Palmer began to formulate a plan of action, a plan he hoped would unveil the secrets of the Rite of The First Hour.

**

The journey back to his terraced house took a little over half an hour. The traffic was unusually heavy and by the time he had shut the front door behind him the clock in the hallway was chiming for the half hour. Palmer fetched himself coffee from the kitchen and sat at his desk. Quickly he scribbled a few notes, the bare bones of his scheme. Then, under the notes, he drew a very large question mark. It was the missing piece of the jigsaw puzzle he was assembling, the missing clue that would enable him to resolve the whole case and prove once and for all whether Heather Burnston was the murderer.

He was still looking at his notes as he reached out for the telephone. He pressed some number and waited for the person on the other end of the line to respond. He did not have to wait long.

'Eddie, how are you?'

'Not so bad. How are you?'

'Okay. I'm glad I caught you in, are you busy this evening?'

'Why, have you got something for me to do?'

'Us actually, but I need some of your skills if you get my meaning.'

'I get your meaning, and you know I don't do that stuff anymore.'

'Yeah, well you may not have to, but I need some help with something. Are you up for it?'

'Is it something to do with the Burnston case?'

'Yes. I need to get some pictures taken and it might be a bit tricky doing it on my own. Can I pick you up at about nine?'

'Sure. Where are we going?'

'Putney. Look I'll pick you up later and fill you in on a few things.'

'Okay, Damien, by the way how did it go last night?'

'Pretty good, I'll tell you about it later. How did your evening go?'

'Very nice, we went to that restaurant you told us about and then she took me back to her flat. You know I love a redhead, and Bryony was really good fun to be with. She's got such a dry sense of humour.'

'Yeah, like you. Anyway, I'm glad it worked out for you. You can tell me more later on. I've got some things to sort out this afternoon which might give you a bit more work to do. Do you think your lady friend would be into surveillance – with you I mean?' The question was friendly though Palmer had an ulterior motive for asking it.

180

'She might be. It depends what it is.'

'What I have in mind is watching a house tomorrow evening. Probably nothing will happen, but I have a hunch.'

'Do you have any particular house in mind?' Marston was already sure where the conversation was leading.

'Yes, the Burnston's.'

'But there's no-one living there!' Marston's exclamation of surprise made Palmer move the earpiece further away from his face.

'I know, but I suspect someone has a key to the place and I think they'll be going in there either tonight or tomorrow.'

'And what if it's tonight?'

'I still have to get that one covered. But don't worry about that. Are you up for tomorrow?'

'Probably, but I'll have to let you know later on.'

'Okay Eddie, now I'll pick you up at nine sharp. See you then.'

'Okay, bye.'

'Bye.' Palmer replaced his handset and ticked one of the lines of comments he had scrawled on the pad of paper.

His second call left him speaking to a receptionist.

'Good afternoon, can I speak to Karen Shaw, please?' His voice was neutral and polite.

'One moment sir, I'll put you through.' The sound of canned music momentarily grated in Palmer's ear before the familiar voice of the woman intervened.

'Karen Shaw, how can I help you?'

'Something along the lines of what we did last night lover! It's me, Damien. How are you?'

'Actually I'm busy, and you?'

'Busy. Look, what are you doing this evening?'

'I had planned to do my hair, some washing and have a long, hot, bath.'

'Sounds nice, do you fancy doing something for me instead?'

'What are you after Palmer? Wasn't last night good enough for you?'

'I didn't mean that. I've got a house I need watching and nobody to watch it. I was only asking if you were willing.'

'Oh I see. Well, what does it entail?'

'Not a lot, you've just got to sit outside it and if anyone comes out you follow them as best you can.'

'And how long will it take?'

'That's difficult to say. But you don't need to get there until it has got dark, and I think you can call it a night at midnight.'

'Christ, that's four hours.'

'Yeah I know. Do you want me to find somebody else?'

'No, I'll do it. What's the address?'

'Thanks darling – I owe you one.' Palmer proceeded to read out the address of the Burnston house though he didn't tell the woman whose house it was.

'Okay Damien I've got that. Now I have to go. I'll talk to you tomorrow.'

'Thanks Karen, see you soon.' With that Palmer terminated the conversation and ticked a second line of comments on the pad of paper.

Palmer turned his attentions to his laptop computer. It sprang to life as he pressed the power button and in a few minutes he was searching through a database of names and addresses. He searched for the owner of the house he had watched the previous evening, and was intrigued when the search drew a blank. He repeated the search on the road and came up with a whole list of addresses and names. He whistled softly to himself as he located the house he wanted. It was an easy mistake to have made. All the houses that fronted the Common had nameplates and it had not occurred to him that in an official listing they might still be numbered. However, the name he found was what he had expected though he had no idea who Major C Hempleworth was. Perhaps he was one of the other men Palmer had observed the previous evening. Palmer made some further enquiries and a few notes though the next half hour did not reveal anything that seemed remotely useful to the case. Finally he gave up and turned his attention to the file of papers that he had so far amassed. He spent the next hour revisiting the various documents that had been presented to him, though his perusal failed to shed more light on the matter.

Then he picked up the letter that had arrived in the post on the morning he had taken the case. It still intrigued him that someone had tried to warn him off the case before he had even been told about it. Presumably that same person had trashed his study and also left the message on his answerphone. Perhaps that same person was the one who'd arranged for someone to follow him.

If that were the case, Palmer conjectured, the voice on the answerphone suggested the person was a man and that ruled out Manning's research assistant. He'd met her when he'd gone to meet Manning to go for the visit to the prison. She'd looked a bit plain, prim and proper, but not a blackmailer or thug. So who was responsible for the threats? Who wanted to have Heather Burnston locked up so badly? What did she know that she wasn't telling? The questions filled the sleuth's mind as he sat there with the threatening letter still held in his hand.

Palmer played the tape of the message again, though he could clearly remember its contents. The voice was still unfamiliar, though Palmer did pick out the references to 'we'. It could have been bluff, but if it wasn't then it signified more than one person was involved - but the research assistant? It seemed unlikely and too great a coincidence that she just happened to be working for the right solicitor at the right time. There had to be another explanation, though for the moment it eluded Palmer. There was, though, something chilling about the note he was still holding. There was also something else, something that Palmer had been told and it had to do with the way Manning had become involved in the case, but like the explanation it eluded Palmer.

Finally Palmer gave up trying to solve the mystery of the threatening note and decided to take a short walk over the grassy area in front of his house.

Chapter Thirteen

It was much later that evening when Palmer set out to pick up Eddie Marston. The warmth of the day had passed and because the sky was clear it had once again turned cold. Palmer had spent some time preparing for the evening's adventure and the pockets of his coat contained the equipment he would need. The flashlight, cassette recorder and camera had been thoroughly checked before he left home, and new batteries ensured they would work properly. Now the coat lay on the back seat as he made the journey to the drab block of flats where Marston lived. The radio was playing some music though the sound was turned down low and it was barely audible above the engine noise. Palmer seemed not to notice the music was playing as he concentrated on the roads.

He had scarcely pulled up outside Marston's block of flats when the somewhat short, slightly stocky, bespectacled Marston pushed open the front door. His cheery smile and somewhat ruddy complexion belied the fact that he was a man who had suffered much. Palmer realised, as Marston walked towards the car, that although he knew quite a lot about his recent years, the near fatal stabbing and the disastrous relationship that had led up to that incident, the snooker halls and the drink, that he knew very little about what had made Marston the person he was. Palmer made a mental note to ask him sometime. As the car door opened and Eddie Marston slid into the passenger seat, Palmer also recalled the sensitivity of the man next to him when it came to dealing with young folk, in particular teenagers in trouble. It was a quality Palmer admired and one which had encouraged him to include Marston on the evening's adventure.

'On time as usual,' Marston quipped as Palmer began the drive to their destination.

'Part of my nature, I guess.' Palmer started the car and pulled out. Behind him, about fifty yards down the road a dirty, white Fiesta also pulled out into the road. 'I don't want to worry you, Eddie, but I'm pretty sure we're being followed.'

'How come?' Eddie sounded less than anxious.

'Oh, a small, white car followed me here. I let it. If it gives the person a thrill, then so be it. The thing is I don't want it to follow me now, so if you'll give me a few minutes I'll try to lose it.'

'Sure. Is it the car about fifty yards behind you?'

'Yeah, hang on.' Palmer had a clear road ahead and floored the accelerator. The turning to the right was fast approaching and with a clear exit he slammed on the brakes and spun the steering wheel. The car slid into the side road and the accelerator pedal was back down on the floor. Palmer roared the engine as he crashed up through the gears, his advanced motoring skills coming into their own though any onlooker would say he was being reckless. Approaching the next junction he slammed on the brakes and changed straight down to first, the engine whining with a high-pitched scream as it struggled to cooperate with the demands the driver was placing on it. He was gaining ground and knew the driver in the following car was more cautious than himself. He smiled slowly as the distance between the two vehicles grew.

Palmer repeated the actions down the next four side roads before he was sure he'd lost the tail.

'So where are we going?' Marston had waited until the avoidance measures were complete and Palmer had started driving with greater consideration for other road users and pedestrians.

'The Studio, it's called. It's in the back streets of Putney and I want to take a look round.'

'Why?'

'It's the place where Warren Connors and a chap called James work – actually they own it. Only I think there's more to The Studio than meets the eye.'

'So, what are we looking for?'

'Pictures probably, but really Eddie, I'm not sure.'

'And you expect this place to be open this time of night?' Marston was clearly fishing for information, concerned at what he might be told.

'No. At least I hope not, and that is why I need your assistance.'

'You know I gave up the entering business years ago, and I don't have the gear anymore.'

'Yeah, I know, but this is a bit different.'

'How on earth do you work that one out?'

'Okay, I'll tell you. If I'm right then in a few days from now a couple of girls, late teens or early twenties, are going to be put through an experience they are going to regret for the rest of their lives. I can't prove it yet, but I think the place we're going to holds the proof we need. Now I really need your help, Eddie. I have got to take a look inside.'

'Okay, but how do you know all this?'

'Because last night I saw the owner of this place acting like some kind of High Priest of a sect in a house that's owned by an ex-army Major, and because that sect, or group, or whatever you want to call them, are waiting for a full moon to carry out some kind of ritualistic orgy, and there's a full moon the day after tomorrow. That means we don't have much time. And from what I saw yesterday I don't think the two girls I saw are in any way expecting what's going to happen to them, and that's based on conversations I've had with the Burnston woman and her sister. They were involved in this group some years back and there's no doubt in my mind that it's gone from being a sort of orgy thing, which was just for fun, to something a damn sight more sinister, and there are people starting to get hurt now.'

'Christ, you have been uncovering things.'

'Yeah, but some of it is speculative. All I need is the proof that I'm right, then we can do something about it.'

'Okay, so I'll help you. You know I can't stand seeing kids getting messed up with things.'

'Thanks Eddie, look we're almost there now. I suggest we park up and walk the last bit. Give us a chance to get round the back and see if there's an easy way in.'

The car was parked and the two men walked up the street as if they were going to the local pub. They passed the façade of 'The Studio', its single window and glass panelled door protected by a roll-up metal mesh. The street was empty as they turned sharply into the side alley that led round to the back of the small parade of shops. Palmer counted the four shops back to The Studio and pushed open the wooden gate that led to the back of the premises. The gate gave way easily under his pressure and in a moment they were standing in the concrete courtyard that was the back garden to the shop. The courtyard was empty save for a black plastic bin. The building ahead of them was three storeys high. The lights inside had all been turned off and the building was shrouded in darkness. On the ground floor was a small extension. It looked as if at some point an outside toilet or boiler room had been integrated into the main building. Apart from that there was a single window and a door that led onto the courtyard. Palmer tested the door with his gloved hand. He was not surprised to find it locked. The window also looked secure so Palmer turned his attentions to the extension. Set into the wall was a double window with a fanlight window above it. He smiled when he saw the fanlight was ajar.

Nudging Marston, he pointed to the open window. Not a word had been spoken since they had entered the yard. A combination of stealth and the surge of adrenalin at the thought of being discovered had made the two men extremely cautious. Even as Palmer pointed at the window Marston indicated what he needed. Palmer cupped his hands and hoisted the shorter man to a position where he could reach the catch. In a moment the window was wide open and Marston reached inside. It took him a few seconds to loop the length of wire he had taken from his pocket around the lower window catch, but his practice over the bygone years had not been in vain. In less than two minutes after entering the courtyard the main window was open. In less than another minute both men entered the building and the window was closed.

The room they had gained entry to was clearly a small kitchenette. The sink, a shelf-top fridge, and a wall-hung cupboard took up most of the space. The door immediately opposite the window was not locked and Palmer gently opened it. This was the moment when any alarm bells would ring, he had figured, but as the door opened there was no sound. Slowly, Palmer walked into what was a small hallway. To the right hand side was a staircase that led to a higher floor. In front of him the hallway gave way to a room. It was not a particularly large room but boasted maybe a half-dozen comfortable chairs and a coffee table on which had been placed numerous magazines. Palmer played the light from his torch around the room, careful that the light did not shine near to the window fronting the street.

'Waiting room, I would guess.' He spoke softly into the tie clip microphone that was attached to the cassette recorder in his pocket.

'Yes.' Marston was close behind him. 'That must be the reception desk through that door.'

'Probably.' Palmer moved over to the door that was near the window and pushed it open. Marston's suspicions were correct. The reception desk occupied much of the front entrance to the building. Behind it was a single chair. The telephone sat neatly on the far side and next to it was a directory. Palmer passed quietly into the reception area and tested the desk drawers. They were locked.

'Locked,' he muttered as he returned to the waiting room. 'Let's try upstairs.'

He returned to the narrow staircase and quickly climbed the steps to the first floor landing. Two doors opened off the square landing and a further staircase led to the top floor. Palmer opened the door to the room that faced the main street. Blinds were already drawn across the sash window. It was clearly the office. The two desks sat back to back in the middle of the room and two typist chairs had been pulled in close to the desks. There was a filing cabinet in one corner that occupied Palmer's attention for a moment. He pulled open the top compartment and rifled the contents. It looked as if the contents were contracts of some kind or another. He closed the drawer and opened the lower one. In this sat a kettle, various cups, tea caddy, and a jar of coffee. There was also a half empty packet of chocolate digestive biscuits. Palmer closed the drawer carefully.

On each of the desks was a computer, though both were turned off. A printer sat on a side table and under the table sat a couple of boxes of paper. Palmer concluded his examination and left the room. He turned and opened the door opposite. The room was clearly the studio. A chair and selection of backgrounds occupied one corner. There were the usual lights and canopies that one would expect of such a room, and very little else.

'Okay, we have an office and a studio on the first floor. Let's try the top floor.' They had been in the building barely five minutes when Palmer reached the top floor. The square landing again had two doors that led onto rooms either side of the building, though this time there was no staircase leading upwards.

'You try in there,' Palmer pointed to the door on the right, 'and I'll look in here. Be with you in a minute.'

Palmer opened his door at the same time as Marston opened his and slipped inside. The room faced the road but, as Palmer had noticed earlier when they'd walked up the road, the windows had been boarded over from the inside. The reason was now obvious for this room was a den. Clearly rigged for photographic purposes it was a fairly large room and clearly intended for the production of adult material. A horse, similar to the one Palmer remembered being in the school gymnasium, was sat in the middle of the room, though this particular species was somewhat strange to look at. For a start it was not symmetrical, one side had a much gentler slope than the other. Also, near the base of the legs were metal hoops. The horse itself was well padded. On the wall was hanging a riding crop. It seemed incongruous in such a place, but it made Palmer understand the strange shape of the wooden contraption. This was an instrument of punishment and Palmer had little doubt that it was well used. He shuddered as he recalled the punishments he had received at school.

Along the far wall of the room was a couch – almost the same size as a single bed, its white cover was clearly picked out by Palmer's torchlight. The floorboards were bare, though polished. Palmer concluded his examination and went to find Marston.

Marston spent the first few minutes in the final room of the building with his eyes open wide taking in the scene. Reels of film hung from hooks and clips. He examined a few of the shots. Most of them were of young looking women, though a few were male. Most of them were what could be described as legitimate portrait poses. He was examining the tenth such string of negatives when Palmer entered the room.

'What have you found?' Palmer asked in a voice that was barely above a whisper.

'Photographs, and lots of them. This must be the darkroom. There's dozens of reels of the stuff. What I've seen so far looks pretty normal – kids doing poses, that sort of thing.'

'Damn, well I suppose it was too much to expect. Have you checked that cupboard over there?'

'Not yet.'

Silently Palmer walked over to the metal cupboard and pulled the doors open.

'This is what we came for, I think!' Palmer's voice rose slightly at his find. In the bottom of the cupboard were large bottles of chemicals used for the developing process. Higher up were more reels of film hanging by clips on a rail. Palmer unclipped one film and looked at it. 'This is exactly what we came for.'

He held the film up and looked at it under the torchlight. The girl was naked and lying on a couch while a hooded person wearing some kind of cloak stood over her. 'We need some prints of this stuff.'

'Of course and how are we going to do that?' Marston sounded confused. Film processing was definitely not one of his skills.

'It's actually quite simple, just watch.' Palmer took the reel of film over to the printing table and in a few minutes had worked out how to operate the machine. In less than ten minutes he had printed the negative he wanted.

'Okay,' he said, 'let's see what else we have here.' He replaced the strip of negatives and took out another. He repeated the procedure, this time selecting two negatives to be printed. He repeated the process with the remaining strips of negatives until he had accumulated a dozen pictures, then he turned the machine off.

'Right, time to go, and make sure you leave everything as you found it.'

'Don't worry, I will.' They left the room and carefully closed the door. Two minutes later they had left the building as they had entered it. They walked out of the courtyard, and back down the street looking like two friends walking home from the pub. In his coat pocket, Palmer held onto the prints he had made.

'There's something about this kind of activity that makes me thirsty,' Palmer said as they sat in his car.

'Yeah, it does leave a sort of dry feeling in your throat. Do you fancy a pint?'

'Why not! If we go back to your place we can use your local. That way I only have to drive home afterwards. Sound reasonable to you?'

'The Crown it is then. They do a reasonable bitter in there – just what I need right now. And to think I used to do this thing for real – I must be getting old.'

'We all are mate. I haven't done that sort of thing for some time either. I'll just put the pictures in my case. Don't want them falling out in the pub, eh!"

'No,' Marston grinned, 'it might create a reaction.'

'Very, very likely I would say. Especially that one with the girl paying homage, or at least I suppose you'd call it that.'

'That's a nice way of putting it. Most people that read the stuff those pictures belong in would call it something else.'

'I suppose they would but what with the monks gear and all that, I thought homage sounded nicer.' They were driving back to Marston's now. 'It makes you wonder what else this Connors chap is into.'

'It makes you wonder how he gets the girls into it all.' Marston sounded somewhat hurt.

'That's easy. Money I should think, and probably plenty of it, at least to start with.'

'Yes, until he's got them hooked on his little group. Then of course, the emphasis changes.'

'You're learning fast. That's exactly what it is. He lures them in, pays them for a start, gets them involved in Corpus Eros, or whatever he calls it, and then he gets them buying from him, so he recoups his outlay. You know, that's very clever.'

'Yeah, but what's he selling them?' Marston began to sound angry.

'Drugs, and that's what the two girls I saw yesterday were taking. That's why they were so compliant. It all begins to make sense now.' Palmer looked intently out of the window as he drove and Marston could sense he was thinking. They journeyed in silence for a few minutes until Palmer spoke once again.

'Those two girls are in deep trouble. He's getting them hooked on something. Heroin or Coke I should think, and I'll bet he's selling the pictures he takes. Not only that, but over the years since his wife and our client joined it has all taken a very sinister turn. I have a strong suspicion that what started out as some silly ritual, Rite of the First Hour or whatever they call it, is very soon going to turn into something terrible, because that's where Connors is headed with this stuff. It's only a matter of time, and I think from these pictures we've got, the time is near, possibly very near.'

'And why do you think that?'

'Because Connors is dangerous, he's lost the control he once had. Now anything goes and one day it will just go too far. He's got to be stopped and soon.'

'But surely you don't think he could have killed Burnston, do you?'

'No, but I think he's very happy to have him out of the way and for our client to be facing life in prison.'

'Why?'

'Because John Burnston probably wouldn't have wanted to take things as far as Connors does, and Heather Burnston knows too damned much. She probably knows enough to get a number of people sent down for a large number of years, which is why someone is going to great lengths to have her locked up.'

'What if she talks?'

'She won't, if only because her sister is involved in the group, and there's a certain bond between siblings that makes it difficult to grass the other one up. Heather Burnston won't grass on the group even if she gets locked up. Probably they are all relying on something to come up that shows she isn't the murderer and then everyone is back to square one with the group intact and she gets some kind of reward. I'm only guessing but it's beginning to sound the likely scenario.'

'So, how do you plan to stop Connors?'

'I have no idea yet. Right, shall we have that pint?'

'Okay.'

Chapter Fourteen

The next morning was typically spring-like. The weather forecast in the paper seemed as though it was wrong, for the forecast had been for dry weather with sunny spells. At the early hour when Palmer stirred, a fine rain was falling lightly on the world outside his terraced house. He stirred early that morning because he had much on his mind. The pictures he had retrieved the previous evening had remained in his coat pocket, and throughout the night they had been much on his mind. Palmer slept for barely one hour and when the first rays of light penetrated his bedroom at just after six o'clock he saw no point in remaining in bed any longer. He was, habitually, a light sleeper in any event and the early morning light only served to make the task of getting to sleep a virtual non-starter.

So it was, with the house shrouded in the gloom of the drizzly start to the day, that Palmer sat in his lounge sipping the cup of freshly brewed coffee. On the coffee table in front of him sat the pile of pictures he had printed the previous evening. Slowly he began to look at each one. It took him only a few minutes to count the six girls that were pictured in his collection. Admittedly the one that was stretched out over the strange gymnasium horse-like object couldn't be seen, well not her face at any rate, and so she could have been a seventh candidate. Having identified the number of girls involved he spent more time examining each print in detail. Several, he observed, related to staged scenes in the room where the gymnasium horse belonged, but there were half a dozen that were clearly taken in another building.

His examination complete, Palmer wandered into his office and picked up the strip of negatives from the film he had taken just two nights previously. He scrutinised them carefully and selected one frame which he held carefully between his thumb and index finger. Holding it this way he made for his darkroom, to return to the lounge barely ten minutes later holding another print in his hand. He added the print to the collection on the table and identified the two girls. Curiously they had posed both in the gymnasium and also in the unidentified room. One of the pictures in the unidentified room had another figure in it, the figure of a human dressed like a monk with a hood over his face. He was sitting astride the naked girl who was lying on some sort of couch. There was no further clue as to the identity of the hooded person. It was fairly evident that the hooded figure was involved in a sexual act with the girl, who looked like she was in her late teens. As Palmer looked at the picture, his attention was drawn to the girl's face. She had a glazed look in her eyes and the picture suggested she was lying quite limp on the couch.

This observation made Palmer look more closely at the other pictures. After a few minutes he had to concede that it was speculation, but in most of the pictures the girls seemed to have the same glazed expressions, as if they were somehow not aware of what was happening.

Having gleaned as much information as possible from the pictures, Palmer read the report that Marston had given him the previous evening – the report concerning his interview with Mr Fielding. Missing daughter, now about twenty-one years old, wife left eleven years previously, no contact for some time, whereabouts unknown. It was the kind of case Palmer loved.

He took the report into his office and turned on the computer. As it completed the start-up procedures, Palmer made himself a second mug of coffee. It was still early and his body was craving even more caffeine than usual. Finally the machine was ready and Palmer dialled a number. It took only a few seconds to connect and immediately a window opened up on the screen. He typed in his user identity and a password and waited for the screen to change. The enquiry was simple. He typed in the name Fielding's former wife – Julie Anne Fielding. She had to be in the system somewhere.

He waited patiently as the machine he had connected to performed its search. His patience was rewarded for the search produced the details of the marriage certificate. This in turn identified Julie Fielding as having been born Julie Anne Rawlings. There was no other indication from the search as to what had happened to Julie Fielding, other than the mention of her divorce from Andrew Archibald Fielding nearly nine years previously. It was information Palmer already knew, but he was pleased to find her maiden name. Without thinking, he typed the new name into the search engine and waited for the results. This time he was provided with details of the woman's birth though there was no indication as to whether she had died. There was one final entry, her daughter Sonia, and that was nearly twenty-one years ago. Again it was information Marston had already been told.

Palmer closed the enquiry and inserted a CD into the relevant slot in the side of the computer. In a few moments a new search screen appeared. Palmer typed in the name Fielding. He was quickly presented with a list of several hundred names, far too many to be of use to him. To his initial search he added the name Julie. The list was swiftly reduced to no more than twenty entries, still a large number if he were to investigate each one. Palmer decided to try a different approach. He was halfway through typing in the name Rawlings when the penny finally dropped.

He retrieved the Burnston case folder and flicked through the top few pages. He came to the page of writing he had added only a few days ago – the house Rachel Connors had visited after his first look round the Burnston home was registered to someone called Rawlings, though it must be a coincidence. Palmer finished typing the name and waited for the results of the search to be displayed. Again he was presented with a list in excess of a couple of hundred entries, so again he added the name Julie which in turn cut the list down to a dozen entries, one of which related to the house Rachel Connors had visited. Moreover it was the only house in the southern part of England.

Of course it was only guesswork, after all Julie Anne Fielding could easily have remarried in the preceding nine years and her name might be quite different now, though it had not registered as such in his earlier enquiries.

Palmer changed the first name in the search to Sonia and waited. The screen found no matches which intrigued Palmer until he realised that in all probability she would have retained her father's name, Fielding. Accordingly, Palmer changed the surname and waited again. This time he was presented with five matches, one in each of Wales, Northern Ireland and Scotland, the fourth was in Birmingham and the final entry was in Morden. It was this final entry that interested the sleuth, for Morden was only a short distance from the South Eastern entry for Rawlings. With Morden nestled between Wimbledon and Sutton it was an address he could check out quite easily. He clicked on the entry and noted the full address details on his notepad.

His enquiries complete, Palmer exited the program he had been running and instructed the computer to shut down. As it did so he went upstairs and dressed. It was now nearly seven o'clock. Ten minutes later, and armed with a road map of Surrey, he left the house. It was still early but he knew the rush hour traffic would soon build and he wanted to get through to Morden before the traffic became too heavy.

He soon left the urbanity of Putney behind him and passed along the familiar Common that led into Wimbledon Village. Passing through the Village, he dived down the hill into the centre of Wimbledon. Almost without realising it, he passed the old library building on his left at the bottom of the hill, and immediately he was occupied with the double set of traffic lights. He had long since discovered the absolute importance of getting his vehicle in the right lane at these lights. On his left was the revamped old town hall. No longer used for that purpose it had, several years earlier, been converted into what was grandly called the Centre Court Shopping mall. His focus on the growing volume of traffic precluded him from even noticing the mixture of old and modern in the structure of the shopping centre. Now, with the speed restriction down to just twenty miles per hour, he followed the queue of traffic through the one-way part of the system that controls the traffic through the heart of Wimbledon.

A minute later and leaving the town centre behind him, he passed first the cinema complex on his right, and then the YMCA where he had once stayed a few nights. The traffic was still moving freely as he crossed the traffic lights at South Wimbledon tube station. He drove carefully, the map open on the passenger seat. Morden lay ahead of him, an outgrown village that now boasted its own one-way system for traffic control purposes. He joined the system and followed it round to the turn-off towards Raynes Park. The traffic was noticeably heavier now and the digital clock in his car showed the time was now nearly quarter to eight. With his speed of progress reduced, Palmer looked at the open map beside him and made a mental note of the last part of his journey. Suddenly the road he was looking for appeared on his left. From there it was a couple more turns in side roads and Palmer located the address where a certain

Sonia Fielding was registered. He pulled over to the side of the road and waited.

After fifteen minutes the front door to the house he was watching opened. A young man in a pin-stripe suit closed the door behind him and walked away from where Palmer sat in his car. Palmer cursed himself for not having checked who else lived at the house – it would have been easy to do. Fortunately he looked the right sort of age for someone who might be attached to a twenty year old.

The next half hour passed very slowly for Palmer. There was little activity in the road and he was becoming frustrated the person he had hoped to see had not appeared. Then, after those thirty minutes, his luck changed. It was nearly half past eight when the front door opened again. The child appeared first. Palmer guessed the young girl was about four years old. She skipped onto the pavement and then looked back at the front door, waiting. The pushchair appeared next, and finally the woman. Palmer looked intently at her as she pushed the buggy down the short path that led from the front door to the pavement. He need not have done so for she turned and walked towards him. It was evident now that she was not the Sonia Fielding he was looking for. Palmer guessed she was at least thirty years old. Disappointed that his search had proved fruitless, he decided to call on the woman Rachel Connors had visited a few days earlier.

He started the car and joined the heavy flow of rush hour traffic that led from Morden back to Wimbledon. In contrast to his outward journey, it now took him over half an hour to travel back to

Wimbledon Village. As he had been driving in the endless queues of traffic, Palmer had devised a plan, a plan which would make his early visit to the woman seem quite natural.

Once he had reached the top of the hill that led from the centre of Wimbledon up to the Village itself, Palmer turned left. The school outfitters and toy shop on his right were familiar buildings to him. He found the newsagents Marston had visited on the first day of this case and then he passed the road that led to the Burnston's house. He travelled a short distance further until he found the road name included in Marston's report. It tallied with the details he had noted from his enquiry into the property Marston had traced Rachel Connors to. In less than three minutes Palmer had parked his car and was standing at the glass-fronted porch door of the house in question. The buzzer was still echoing inside the building when Palmer spotted the figure of a woman approach the door. The glass panel was frosted for privacy reasons but it still allowed a silhouette shape to be recognisable. The woman opened the inner door and then the porch door.

'Yes?' She enquired, and Palmer figured she was somewhat flustered at having been distracted from whatever she had been doing.

'Sorry to trouble you, madam. My name is Andrew Clarke,' Palmer lied. It was an alias that he had now used on a number of occasions. 'I'm an investigator. Here is my card.' He offered the small, white, business card to the woman.

'So, Mr Clarke, why are you knocking on my door at this hour of the day?' The woman sounded wary, though not hostile.

'It's rather a delicate matter actually, madam. My organisation has been asked by a firm of solicitors to locate a young lady and well, after making some enquiries we have narrowed our search down to a few possibilities. Basically I'm standing here because you are one of those possibilities.'

'And what does that firm of solicitors want?'

'I'm afraid I don't know, madam. They just asked us to locate this young lady. Usually these things have to do with a legacy or something like that. We get quite a lot of those kinds of enquiries.'

'I see.' The woman paused and clearly the mention of the word legacy had changed her attitude somewhat. 'Well,' she said after due consideration, 'perhaps you'd better come in and I'll see if I can help you. Mr Clarke, wasn't it.'

'That's correct, madam.' Palmer stepped over the threshold as she stood back to allow him entry. The woman showed him into the front room and invited him to sit down.

'Now, Mr Clarke, what can I do for you?' She was sitting on the settee as Palmer sat in the somewhat battered green armchair. As Palmer had walked up the pathway that led to this house he had recalled the picture that Fielding had given Marston a few days ago and as a result had immediately recognised the woman when she had opened the door.

'Well, I first need to check your name. It is Mrs Rawlings, isn't it? Mrs Julie Anne Rawlings?'

'Well, it's Miss actually. I got divorced about nine years ago and reverted to my maiden name.'

Palmer let his head drop as if he were about to be the bearer of bad news.

'I see, and your married name was …?' he paused to allow the woman to finish the sentence.

'Fielding.'

'Excellent.' Palmer now had her undivided attention. 'That is precisely what my enquiries have shown to be the case, but you can't be too careful in these situations. I hope you appreciate that.'

'Of course, Mr Clarke, but what is this all about?'

'Well, this is rather delicate. You see, Miss Rawlings, it is not you whom I am trying to locate.' Palmer paused as if thinking, though his plan had been thought out several minutes earlier as he had sat in the queues of traffic. 'Do you have a child from that marriage?'

'Oh,' she exclaimed, 'so that's it. The old bugger has finally died and left everything to her. Didn't give a toss about her in life but now he's dead he wants to show he had some feelings for her.'

'Sorry? So there is a child?'

'Oh yes. Ten years it's been since the old sod gave her so much as a penny. He left me all on my own to bring her up. Well, I don't see why she shouldn't have what's hers by rights. How much is it?'

'I'm sorry Miss Rawlings, but I really have no idea. I don't even know if this is a legacy case.'

'But you said it usually is in these situations.' Her voice was sounding indignant.

'I know, but it could be for other reasons. All I have been asked to do is locate the child and provide the firm of solicitors with the evidence they require.'

'Well, Sonia is nearly twenty-one now. She will be in a couple of weeks. She's out at work now but she'll be home this evening. You could come and talk to her then.'

'I don't need to do that, Miss Rawlings. You are her mother and presumably you have pictures of her as a child?'

'What if I do?'

'Well, in these cases, the child is usually confirmed by a childhood picture. In fact that is precisely what I have been asked to provide as evidence. A childhood picture,' Palmer paused as he was looking round the room. He found what he was hoping to see and continued. 'And a more up to date picture, if you have one.' His cursory look around the room had gone unnoticed.

'Yes, I have them, but I'll want them back.'

'There's no need for me to even take them, Miss Rawlings. I'll just place them beside each other and take a couple of pictures. I then swear a document called an affidavit. That makes the pictures admissible evidence, so it will be good enough for the solicitors and there should be no need to trouble you further.'

'Well in that case, if you'll give me two minutes?'

'Certainly.' Palmer stood as the woman left the room. The moment she had departed he went and more closely examined the picture of the blond haired girl in the picture that had attracted his attention. She was dressed in school uniform and the winning smile showed she was delighted at

208

having received the 'A' level results which she was holding in her hand. Palmer was sitting in the chair once again when the woman returned.

'I've got these from when she was about ten or eleven, and there's that school picture over there if they are any good.'

'Excellent. And if you could write down the contact details for your daughter for the daytime, in case the solicitors want to contact her quickly, that would be really helpful.'

'Okay, anything else?'

'I don't think so.' Palmer retrieved the school portrait and lay it beside the arrangement of other pictures he'd placed on the coffee table. He reeled off half a dozen shots to be sure and thanked the woman. It had been incredibly easy to do, far easier than Palmer had expected, but then the thought of an inheritance often appealed to a person's greed.

Palmer stood at the front door and thanked the woman again before returning to his car. He had taken the folded slip of paper with Sonia Fielding's employer's details on it and slipped it into his coat pocket. Having regained the relative safety of his car he examined the piece of paper and felt the surge of adrenaline as it shot through his body making his nerve endings tingle.

'So the little madam is using a false name,' he muttered to himself. 'That makes a whole big piece of this jigsaw a lot easier to understand.' He refolded the piece of paper and pocketed it carefully. The clock on the dashboard sprang to life as he started the car. It was now just after ten o'clock and the rush hour traffic had subsided sufficiently to allow Palmer to drive home in less than twenty minutes. As he drove, Palmer wondered what connection there might be between Rachel Connors and Julie Rawlings. They seemed an incongruous pair. This puzzle stayed with Palmer all the way home. Finally he had to admit he could not think of a logical link between the two women, and yet it seemed particularly strange that Rachel Connors had gone to visit the woman immediately after he had been to the Burnston house.

Palmer made his habitual mug of coffee and took the recently exposed film to his darkroom. He spent half an hour in the darkness first developing the negatives and then printing the pictures themselves. They would, he thought, now serve a double purpose, though he did not know how he was going to approach Andy Fielding with his discovery. As he developed the negatives and placed them carefully in the fixing solution, Palmer considered that his report to Andy Fielding should wait a few days until he had completed the Burnston case. After all, Heather Burnston was in more urgent need of his skills than was Andy Fielding.

The developing process complete, Palmer took the prints down to his office for further scrutiny. In particular, the school portrait attracted his attention – there was something familiar about the blond-haired and blue-eyed girl. Palmer was sure he'd seen her in another picture. He sifted through the case file and found the set of prints he'd taken from the negatives at The Studio. He flicked through these until one particular shot captured his attention. He held it next to the school picture and smiled. The girl from The Studio was clearly the same as the one who had earned her 'A' level grades.

Then Palmer turned his attention to the pictures he had taken of the two girls in the house a couple of nights earlier. Again he smiled for clearly the girl nearest the window was the same as in the other two pictures.

'So, you're into Corpus Eros. I wonder who the other girl is, and I wonder if your mother knows?' He placed the photographs back in the case folder and began to pace up and down the room. He paced slowly as his mind cogitated the findings of the morning.

Palmer decided it was time to call the solicitor handling the case and in less than two minutes the receptionist had connected him with John Manning. Palmer had been glad the research assistant had not answered the telephone.

'John, this is Damien Palmer. Good morning, how are you?' Palmer sounded cheerful.

'I'm not so bad, and yourself?'

'Fairly good actually, and it seems like we're making some progress.'

'That's good. When do you expect to get a result?'

'Oh, any day now I should think. There are a few loose ends that need to be tied up before we can be sure. Do you think it would be possible to see our client again – perhaps this afternoon?'

'Well, I'm tied up until three but we could go after that.'

'Excellent. Can I leave you to make the arrangements and I'll pop by at three?'

'Of course. See you then, and keep up the good work.'

'Thanks, John, oh by the way don't tell anyone what you're doing this afternoon, and don't write it in your diary. I'll tell you why later.'

'If you say so, Damien. I'll see you later.'

'Cheers, bye.' Palmer terminated the call and dialled a second number.

'Karen Shaw, please.' His voice sounded urgent.

'I'm just putting you through now sir.' The receptionist's voice was momentarily replaced by the canned music.

'Karen Shaw, how can I help you?'

'Karen, hi it's Damien. How are you?'

'Bored and fed up. How are you?'

'Busy. Would you like to come over this evening for a meal?'

'I'd love to, just so long as we don't have to sit outside a boring old house afterwards.'

'We won't, I promise. I take it that nothing happened then?'

'You're dead right, nothing. The house was dark when I got there and nobody came or left. I got there just on eight and stayed until midnight. Glad I had a book to read.'

'Okay, well it was something that had to be done, and thanks. Look, say you get over here for about eight, would that be okay?'

'Yeah, that'll be fine. I'd best go. The boss has just come through the doors at the far end. I'd best pretend I'm busy.'

'Okay, darling, see you later on then.'

'Yes. Bye now.' And with those final words Palmer heard the line go dead. He replaced his receiver carefully. It was just after half past eleven and Palmer had three hours before he needed to go to Manning's office. Without talking to his client again and without someone going into the Burnston's house there was little more he could do on the case at this precise moment. Palmer found these situations perplexing. He hated the lull moments, even if they only lasted for a few hours. There was still much to do on the case but for now he needed an indicator as to what might happen next. That indicator, he hoped, would come from Heather Burnston herself.

Palmer looked again at the pictures he had taken at the house opposite Wimbledon Common. There was no doubt Warren Connors was the person sat in the chair, his face was clearly visible. Equally visible were the two adult males that stood behind the girl furthest from the window, the girl who Palmer now knew to be Sonia Fielding. Even one of the people standing behind the girl nearest to the window, the girl who as yet remained unidentified, was definitely male, but the person closest to the window was not so easy to identify. This person's back was turned to the camera and Palmer had originally assumed it was a male. Now as he looked at the pictures he could not be sure. Actually the more he looked at it the more convinced he became that the short, dark hair and the shape of the person could have been a woman. Not a young woman but one in middle age. The general fuzziness of the picture in the foreground made it very difficult to form an opinion. One thing Palmer could be sure about though – it was not Rachel Connors. Also, as he thought back to the evening, he was sure he had counted more people enter the building than were in camera. That meant other activities were taking place elsewhere in the house. Perhaps, he thought, these four were Connors' henchmen, and possibly woman.

The possibility of there being a woman did not go away and Palmer strained to glean more information from the pictures. There were four of them where the person was in camera, but each time the person appeared as a somewhat fuzzy shape, as the camera had focused on a brighter object in the middle of the room. There was, thought Palmer as he recalled the evening, something in the way the person had helped the young girl fall to the floor – something not quite masculine, and something maternal. The idea made him focus hard on the best of the pictures.

'It could be,' he muttered. He picked up the photograph that Marston had borrowed from Fielding and looked at it intently until in his vision it too became out of focus. 'Good God, it just could be!' His exclamation reverberated off the wall and he seemed surprised at his outburst. 'A mother and daughter ensemble, well that changes things a bit, and that's for sure!' He took another look at the two pictures, holding them at arm's length. 'Yep, it just could be. Shame I didn't get a picture of her this morning.'

Palmer sat at his desk, writing down the names of the various people he now knew were involved in the case. He drew lines that linked the various names and spent the next hour filling in the various links with comments. The definite links he wrote in blue, the guesses he wrote in red. When he had finished it was one o'clock and he sat back and said just two words:

'I wonder.'

Chapter Fifteen

At exactly twenty to three Palmer closed the front door of his house and began the short walk to the offices of Clarke and Manning. He was not in a hurry so walked slowly, his coat unbuttoned as the afternoon sun was still reasonably warm. He strolled nonchalantly, with the beginnings of a self-satisfied smile on his face. Although he knew there was one obstacle to overcome in the next five minutes he did not seem concerned, for life was looking up at this particular point in time. As he strolled, Palmer extracted the mobile phone from his pocket and dialled a number.

'John Manning, please,' he said in a somewhat deeper than usual voice.

'One moment, sir, may I ask who it is?'

'It's personal.'

'I see sir, in that case hold the line please.' The voice was not familiar to him, meaning it was not the usual receptionist.

'John Manning, can I help you?' The voice of the man was familiar.

'John, its Damien Palmer.'

'Hi, Damien, where are you, you're supposed to meet me here in five minutes?'

'I know. I'm standing just down the road from you. I wanted to check whether your research assistant was around first. I guess that was her who answered the phone.'

'It was. What's this all about Damien?'

'I'll tell you when we meet. Can you come out in a few minutes and walk down the road – I'm just outside the dry cleaners.'

'Yeah, no problem, I'm parked down that way in any case. See you in a couple of minutes.'

'Thanks, John.' Palmer terminated the call and replaced the mobile in his coat pocket. He had with him his battered, brown, top-opening brief case. Inside it he was carrying the case notes and the pictures he had taken over the past few days. It was beginning to look like an impressive bundle of documents. He stood waiting on the pavement until the man with the slight limp came out of the solicitor's offices and walked towards him. They shook hands and continued to walk away from the offices.

'The car's down the next side road. It will have to be a quick visit, less than half an hour. That's all I could get out of the authorities there.'

'That will be fine. It's good of you to arrange it all at such short notice.'

'So, just how far have you got with the case then?' Manning sounded interested as they turned the corner.

'We're doing quite well. We've got a lot of openings and possibilities, but nothing yet that firmly shows our client didn't kill her husband. Actually, John, I need to level with you on that. Her sister thinks she did kill him and my guess is if you put her in the witness stand she'll say just that. I don't know why she'll say it, I just think she will.'

'So what has she told you?'

'Apparently the deceased was tied up in some group or other and was carrying on behind his wife's back. When she found out, according to Rachel Connors and I quote, "she was bloody furious". So there is added credence to the police evidence I'm afraid.'

'And what do you think? Here it is.' Manning stopped at the car and opened the passenger door for Palmer. When Manning had set the car in motion Palmer responded.

'What do I think? Well, I don't think she's the killer but frankly, unless the Connors woman can be shown to have been in the house on the day, I don't know who else it could be.'

'Why her?'

'Because she's the only person apart from our client and the deceased who I know has a key to the place.'

'And why is that important?'

'Because the house wasn't broken into – the double-glazing and door frames are good quality and I'd bet my career they haven't been tampered with. Whoever killed the deceased either had a key to let him or her into the house, or Burnston let the killer in. If he'd let the person in, he must have known who it was, and the police have been down that route and so have I and we've both drawn a blank on a suspect. So it looks to me that it's either our client or her sister or someone else we haven't located yet.'

'But you can't prove it's the sister, can you?'

'Not yet, but I'm working on it. There's a full moon tomorrow night and I think it may play a part in this little adventure. Don't ask me how because it would just take too long to go into it. What I can say though is the deceased was into something which is still alive and kicking today – and of that I'm one hundred percent certain.'

'You're saying this might all get resolved because of a full moon?'

'Yeah, I know it sounds crazy, but I actually think the full moon could do our client a big favour. I'll know later on tonight. Now, I want to talk to you about your research assistant. How long has she been with you?'

'About two months or so I should think. She's training to be a lawyer and has taken a year out to get some practice. She came to us highly recommended.'

'Hmm. Those details you gave me the other day, you know they're false, don't you? She doesn't live at the address you gave me. Actually she doesn't live in Putney at all. She lives with her mother in Wimbledon Village. She isn't even called Sonia Rickman, her real name is Sonia Fielding.'

'Good God, but how come all her references and everything worked out okay?'

'Who were her referees?'

'College lecturer, name of Brown and some Major something or other.'

'Not Hempleworth by any chance?'

'Come to think of it, I think you're right. How did you guess?'

'Call it insight.' Palmer smiled to himself. The jigsaw was definitely falling into place. There were now just a few loose ends to tidy up. 'I think it's time to see our client.'

Manning parked the car and a few minutes later Palmer was inwardly grimacing as the metal doors of the prison were banged shut and locked behind him.

They occupied the same badly decorated, drab little interview room that they had sat in a few days previously. Their client was escorted to the room and Manning dismissed the escort.

'Mrs Burnston, how are you keeping?' It was Palmer who asked the question. He noticed that there was a bruise on the woman's face, a bruise that had not been there a few days earlier.

'I'm bearing up, just about, thank you Mr Palmer. How are you getting on?' Her question sounded tired and amply reflected the pallid, tired, look on her face.

'It's all beginning to take shape. I just have a few questions to ask you, if that's all right.'

'Go ahead, though I think I've told you all I know.'

'You probably have, but there are a few things I need to check.' Palmer decided to test the consistency of her evidence with what she had stated at their first meeting. 'Firstly there is the matter of the key holders. You have a key, and obviously your husband has a key, and so does your sister, but is there anyone else who holds a key to your house?'

'No Mr Palmer, there isn't. Actually Rachel has my keys at the moment. Mr Manning gave them to her when I was locked up in here. Only John and I have keys to our house. Why would we want anyone else to have a set?'

'Well, just in case you got locked out or lost a set, perhaps.'

'No, there was no other set of keys.'

220

'I see, well then I must ask you a delicate question. Have you ever had an affair with your sister's husband?'

'Absolutely not! We did have something once, but that was before we all settled down. It was all to do with the silly group. But once we settled down I never touched another man.'

'Very well, and do you know whether your late husband had ever been unfaithful to you?'

'Of course he hadn't. From the outset I made it quite clear that if the roving eye didn't stop, and that meant he had to leave the group if necessary, then I'd file for divorce. I wanted him and only him, Mr Palmer.'

'I see. So he was not part of the group after you got married then?'

'He was for a while but the temptation of having another young girl was too much so after I left he decided to as well.'

'And so far as you are aware that was an end to it all, so far as the group was concerned?'

'Definitely. He couldn't have deceived me if he'd tried. John was hopeless at that, and a hopeless liar.'

'I see. Now, Mrs Burnston, what do you know of someone called Kelly Southbury?' Palmer smiled reassuringly, disarmingly so.

'Not a lot, Mr Palmer. She was in Corpus Eros when I was in it. I imagine she still would be if she hadn't died last year.'

'You know she's dead?' Palmer sounded surprised.

'Of course, Rachel told me all about it. Some hit and run accident wasn't it, if I remember correctly.'

'Yes, you are correct. Do you think it was anything to do with the group, her death I mean?'

'I would doubt it, Mr Palmer. Accidents do happen, you know.'

'Quite so, now one final question, Mrs Burnston. Are you sure your sister is still in the group with her husband?'

'Oh yes, she keeps telling me about it. Boasts about her conquests – it's all got very hedonistic I think. Warren, that's her husband, has taken things way beyond what we used to get up to, but as I'm not in the group any more I don't get told any details. All I get to hear about are Rachel's boasts about the men she has slept with.'

As the woman spoke, Palmer reflected back to his first encounter with Rachel Connors, and he remembered how close she had come to seducing him. He had to admit she was good at it – and he could well imagine many younger men falling for her charms.

'I see. Now do you have any questions for me?' Palmer was sitting in front of the woman at this point and Manning had, during the course of the questions chosen to stand and walk behind her, so whereas Palmer could see him, the woman could not. Even as he framed the final question he spotted Manning shake his head slowly but deliberately. But Manning's actions were too late for the question was out.

'Well, I would like to know where you are with your investigations?' the woman sounded remarkably composed to Palmer.

'Well, Mrs Burnston, you knew from the outset that the police had a lot of circumstantial evidence against you.' He paused for a second too long.

'But I'm not the killer, you have to believe me.' Her voice was raised and she was becoming agitated.

'It's not me you have to convince, Mrs Burnston, it's the jury. And don't expect to be given an easy time by the prosecution's barrister because you won't. If you want to convince them that you are not the killer of your husband then you had better start to tell the truth, and now, while there is still time to do something about it.'

Palmer's voice had remained quite calm though he had moved in closer on the woman until she could smell his breath as he spoke. He looked closely into her wide, frightened, eyes.

'But I've told you the truth, I am not the killer.'

'That is as maybe, but you have not told me one thing to help you. All the way through my enquiries I have come up against discrepancies, threats, and even lies. And the biggest lie was perpetrated in this room earlier this week.' Palmer moved in a further few inches until he could hardly focus on the woman's eyes. 'Why did you tell me your husband had left the group when you knew he had not?' The effect was dramatic as tears started to pour down the woman's face. Palmer withdrew.

'Because,' she sobbed, 'because he had left the group. He told me he had.'

'But others in the group say he was in it right up to the point of his death. They are saying that when you found out you went mad, that you killed him in a pique of revenge. Is that not the truth Mrs Burnston?' With the final flurry of the question, Palmer's voice became raised by a fraction.

'No, no, no.'

'Mr Palmer that is quite enough.' Manning intervened.

'I totally agree,' said Palmer smiling, his voice returning to normal. 'Sorry about that, Mrs Burnston, but you can expect something similar from their barrister. You see, there are people out there who want you put away for this crime, and I don't know why. It's just that when we get to court, if their side is half as good as me, they will call these people to give evidence against you. We have to be prepared for that. Now, one final time, is there anything else you haven't told me?'

'No, Mr Palmer, I've told you everything. I don't know who killed John, but it wasn't me. You have to believe me.'

Palmer looked across the table at the sobbing, pathetic woman. He looked intently and decided she wasn't acting.

'I believe you, Mrs Burnston, but I don't know if a jury will. It seems I must explore other avenues in this enquiry. Now, I must get on. I'm sorry for putting you through what has just happened, but I had to be sure. I hope to have some better news for you in a few days.'

Manning called the prison officer back into the room and Heather Burnston, complete with her tear-stained cheeks, was escorted back into the very heart of the prison. As she was escorted inwards, so Palmer and Manning were escorted to the outer door, the metal doors clanging shut behind them as they made good their exit.

'Did you have to be so tough on her?' Manning asked once they were walking back to his car.

'No, probably not, but it proved a point.'

'It did?' His question was one of surprise.

'Certainly. Either she is a very good actress, or she is telling the truth.'

'And which is it?'

'Well, I still think she knows more than she's letting on, and that makes her a good actress. On the other hand, I don't think she killed her husband. It's a dilemma, and I don't know if I can prove it one way or the other.'

'Why do you think she's holding back on something?'

'Because I'm more or less certain the deceased was involved in this Corpus Eros thing until the day he died. And if that is the case, I can hardly believe that his wife didn't know about it – especially as she had been involved at one time.'

The conversation paused as they took their seats in Manning's car and he began the drive away from the prison.

'So,' said Manning when he'd joined the main flow of early rush hour traffic, 'what next?'

'Well, there are some loose ends I have to tie up this evening. Also I have a feeling that this whole thing is going to come to a head fairly soon, probably in the next day or so. There's also something else that's bothering me.'

'And what's that?'

'Well, it has to do with dates really. Rachel Connors was nineteen when she first met the person who is now her husband. At that time our client would have been sixteen, pushing seventeen. Okay, after a while our client gets involved in the group. At best I reckon that makes her eighteen, and within a couple of years she's married. She's now twenty six, and we know they were married for just over five years. If she left the group straight after they got married then two things come to mind.'

'And they are?' Manning was listening though concentrating on the slow-moving traffic.

'Well, firstly, how come her husband managed to carry on behind her back for most of that time without her suspecting anything?'

'Perhaps his job let him?' Manning did not sound convincing.

'I don't think so and anyway, what young wife wouldn't miss her husband on the nights when these early morning rituals were taking place? No, she knew her man was still involved. The second question is who is she protecting?'

'It could be a false sense of loyalty to someone perhaps, but whom?'

'Well she can't protect her husband now he's dead, but by saying she didn't know he was still involved, and I think she's lying, she must be protecting someone.'

'It's a thought, but have you got any idea why she'd do that?'

'No, it's purely guesswork at the moment, but mark my words carefully, John, your client knew her husband was involved and she also probably knows other things she isn't prepared to divulge.'

'But the whipping she endured when she left the group, and her general demeanour – why does she want to perpetuate the suffering with a prison sentence?' Manning was, thought Palmer, quite a good lateral thinker.

'We only have her word for the thrashing though in all probability something like that did happen – from what I've found out about the group it's the sort of bizarre thing they'd do. But there is something deeper that I do not understand yet. There is something at the very heart of this group that makes it dangerous, even sinister. It is this thing, whatever it is, that is making our client tell us only partial truths.'

'But why go down for something she didn't do?'

Palmer sat and pondered for a moment before responding.

'I've got it John. She's waiting for something to happen. I don't know what, but it's the only logical answer, unless she's mad, which she isn't. She is waiting for an event to take place.'

Manning momentarily took his attention from the road but recovered quickly. 'You mean she's playing games with us?'

'I don't know. Let's say for the moment that she is waiting for something to happen. When it does, and it must be before her trial, she'll either,' Palmer paused and bit his lip and then slapped the dashboard with his left hand. 'I've got it, she must be being bribed to take the heat for now.'

'How on earth did you come to that notion?'

'Simple. I've been warned off the case, had my house broken into, and received a second threat of dire retribution if I carry on. Someone knows I'm getting close to finding out the truth on this case, and whatever that person wants to do they need to have our client behind bars at the moment, if only so she has an alibi for something.' Palmer paused long enough to let the solicitor respond.

'Okay, I'll grant you that it has possibilities, Damien, but why is she keeping quiet to the extent that she could go to prison for a crime she didn't commit?'

'I don't know. Maybe it's because she knows she won't end up going to prison. I know it sounds odd but it is possible, especially if she is involved in whatever is afoot.'

'In which case, what are we going to do next?' Manning had pulled up outside the detective's home.

'We, John, are doing nothing. You have your job to do, and I'd appreciate it if for the next couple of days you'd keep a close eye on your young research assistant and tell her nothing. That is of paramount importance. She must see no case file, no communications, and hear no conversation about this case. If I am right about her then the less she knows the better and with luck it might stir something up. While you are doing that I am going to be following up a few leads that I have not yet explored.'

'Fair enough, but why have you got it in for my research assistant? Okay she gave me a false name and address, but she might have her reasons for that.'

'Oh she does, John.' The car door was open and Palmer turned to look at the solicitor. As he spoke his face adopted a grave expression. 'Didn't I tell you? Your young Sonia Fielding is one of the initiates in Corpus Eros at the moment.'

Manning, momentarily looked shocked. 'How do you know?'

'I've seen her at one of their meetings.'

'But she might have been doing some research on this case?' Manning's protestation was far too weak.

'Sorry, John, but according to Rachel Connors the current initiates have been involved since before the beginning of the year, and that's at least three months before she joined you. Do you understand what I'm saying?'

Manning nodded sadly. 'Yes, but what about her referees?'

'Well, the lecturer I don't know about, but the good old Major, who claims he is a family friend, I do know something of. Let's say he's also involved in the Corpus Eros family.'

'Oh God, this is awful. I should get rid of her.'

'It is awful, and you can fire her soon, but not until we solve this case, please John?' Palmer was not quite pleading, because he knew his request would make sense to the solicitor. 'It is vital that she does not suspect we know who she is.'

'Okay, but as soon as this case is over I am having her in my office for words.'

'After this case you can do as you see fit. Now, I have to go, because I am expecting a visitor shortly and there are things to do first.'

'Well, your work has been very different from the Expert Investigations approach. I'll say that for you. When will I hear from you?' Manning still sounded shocked and somewhat bemused at the way this case was progressing.

'Soon, John, it will be a couple of days at most and possibly less. Now I must go, and thanks for the lift.' Palmer alighted from the vehicle and banged the door firmly shut. He walked up the short pathway to his blue front door and heard the solicitor engage gear and pull away behind him. It was now nearly six o'clock and Palmer had two hours to prepare for the evening he was looking forward to. A few miles away, Marston was preparing for his own evening, an evening with his girlfriend of a few weeks, an evening with her and a house to watch.

Chapter Sixteen

The power of the water from the shower pressed millions of tiny water droplets into the back of his neck, each microscopic bubble creating a tiny prickling sensation that usually brought Palmer a degree of relaxation. It was relaxation his body was craving but his mind was too preoccupied with the case to take advantage of the therapeutic effects of the water. He washed carefully as his mind considered the various aspects of the case. There was, of course, the possibility that Heather Burnston was indeed the killer and all of his investigations were a futile waste of time. That was option number one and it was the case that would currently have to be presented at the trial in a little over a week.

The second option was the possibility that Rachel Connors was the killer. She would have had the opportunity if it could be proven that she had access to keys to the house. Her motive was weak, though it had to be considered there was more to the love triangles surrounding Corpus Eros than met the eye. Given time, Palmer did not doubt that he could find a motive.

Then there was the research assistant. Was she seriously a third option? Okay, her presence at the solicitor's was suspicious, but other than her links to Corpus Eros there was nothing that linked her to the Burnstons. Number four was Warren Connors. He was, Palmer considered, at least a possible candidate. Somewhere, he recalled, he had been given the notion that Connors had been having an affair with Heather Burnston and wanted her for himself. That idea had surely been pure conjecture, or was there more truth to the sentiment than Palmer had realised at the time?

There were, of course, other members of Corpus Eros, people Palmer had not even begun to investigate. There were nameless people he had seen a few evenings ago, and doubtless there would be others besides. As he washed, Palmer continued his brain storming session. Finally, he admitted to himself, the police were probably right and they already had the killer under lock and key – only something didn't quite add up.

He was dressing for the evening when he remembered Karen's dream the first night he had mentioned the case. It was an unsettling and strange dream, but now as the investigation continued it seemed relevant. It was, he reflected, a shame that the concluding part of the dream had been lost as she had awoken in a cold sweat.

He could already smell the food cooking in the kitchen, the various aromas of the curry bubbling in the pan wafting up through the house. He hurried to complete his preparations for the evening and had just returned to the hall when the telephone rang.

'Hello, could I speak to Andrew Clarke please?' The woman's voice was vaguely familiar to Palmer and it helped to reduce the shock of hearing his alias name being used at this time of the evening.

'Hello, it's Andrew Clarke speaking.'

'Oh, Mr Clarke, it's Julie Rawlings. You called round earlier.'

'Miss Rawlings, what can I do for you?'

'I don't know, Mr Clarke, but I've just been going through my daughter's room sorting out some clothes for washing and I've come across something that bothers me.'

'I see, so how can I help you?'

'Well, I'm worried what she might be getting into. I was wondering if I could employ you to follow her for a few days and see what comes up. Do you do that sort of thing?'

'I have done, but as I said this morning, most of my expertise is in locating missing people.' Palmer lied, but was now intrigued. 'What exactly is bothering you?'

'Well, under her bed I found a few sheets of folded up paper. The heading on the first of these says, "Preparation and Procedure for the Rite of the First Hour". Then there's a whole list of things which are, to put it mildly, perverted. There are three sheets of closely typed instructions. I don't know what it's all about but it worries me. Then, as if that weren't bad enough, behind them is a page of handwriting. Neatly written at the top of this page are the words "Preparation and Procedure for the Rite of Death". It looks like notes that have taken at a lecture. Mr Clarke it's this page that worries me, as it looks like instructions for an execution.'

'And have you talked to your daughter about it?'

'I did try but she just accused me of spying and stormed out of the house saying it was time to find somewhere else to live. I think she's probably gone round to her boyfriend's place.'

'Well, I could come and talk to you about it tomorrow morning if you wanted, only I am busy this evening.'

'That would be very kind of you. Shall we say about ten, Sonia will be at work by then?'

'Ten it is, Miss Rawlings.' Palmer replaced the receiver and rubbed his hands as he smiled. 'That's a turn up for the books,' he spoke out loud though no one else was within earshot.

Palmer had barely put the receiver down when the doorbell chimed in his ear. Carefully he peered out through the spy hole and then opened the door.

'Karen, you're early!' His exclamation was one of pure surprise for the time was not yet half past seven.

'I know. I left work early tonight and thought I'd come over and see if I could lend a hand with anything.'

'Well, I've started a curry – hope that's okay with you, and other than boiling some rice I don't think there's much to do. Come in, we'll go through to the lounge and have a drink.'

As ever, Karen Shaw was dressed for the evening. Her long, sandy hair swirled about her body as she took her coat off to reveal her dress. It was a new one to Palmer and he commented on it.

'Is that new – I don't recall seeing you wear it before?'

'Yes. I popped into Sutton at lunchtime and found it just begging for me to buy it.'

'And by the looks of it, it doesn't come from a chain store either.'

'No, it came from a little boutique that's just opened in the St. Nicholas Centre. They had a sort of opening promotion so I treated myself.'

The mid blue dress was, Palmer decided, quite figure hugging and showed his girlfriend off to her best. He loved it when she dressed sexily for him, and this dress, with its upper mid-thigh length skirt was perfect, the kind of dress a woman like Karen could wear out for a meal, the kind of dress that was almost bound to attract attention. As she turned to walk into the lounge Palmer noticed the low back and admired the lightly tanned flesh that was visible between the wafer thin straps. He had already surmised it was not the kind of dress which required the woman to wear any form of bra, and this only added to the seductive quality of the garment. He could not resist giving her an affectionate pat on the bottom as she passed him.

Flattered by his approval she stopped and turned to kiss him, a kiss that lasted fully five seconds.

'I'm thirsty,' she said, leading the way to the lounge.

'Fancy your usual?'

'Yes – whisky and dry ginger. Only you'd better take it easy on the spirit – I've got to drive back.'

'You could stay over if you want to.' Palmer's suggestion was expected by the woman and her response was immediate.

'I'd love to darling, only I don't have anything to wear tonight, or tomorrow at work for that matter.'

'Well, you needn't worry about tonight so far as I'm concerned and you could always pop in at home on your way to work to change, if you wanted.'

'Or I could just take the day off sick.'

'That sounds like someone who's fed up again. What's the matter now?'

'The usual, I'm just not allowed to use my creative talents, and then my fucking boss goes and takes all the credit for a project I've worked on for two months. She hasn't lifted a bloody finger to help the team but she didn't even have the decency to say thanks. Oh, sod it, go easy on the dry ginger and fill the glass with whisky – we only live once.'

The woman flopped onto the sofa and watched her lover as he prepared the drinks.

'Christ, I didn't mean it to be neat,' she complained when she'd taken a sip.

'Is it too strong for you? Here have mine,' Palmer reached out his glass as an offering. She declined the offer.

'It's all right I've just had a bad day. How's yours been?'

'I've still not cracked the Burnston case. Eddie's watching the house tonight, just in case. Went back to see the client today, and you know how much I like visiting prisons. Though there was a phone call with a bit of news just before you arrived, but I'll have to wait until tomorrow to find out if it's important. I'm probably following another blind alley but you never know. The thing is, this Corpus Eros lot are actually pretty clever and, if you want my opinion, they've been one stage ahead of us from even before Burnston got killed. It even makes you wonder whether his wife did kill him and we're just being led a right song and dance.'

'So your day has been a bit rough too. What time will dinner be ready?' As she asked she placed her drink on the coffee table and shuffled along the sofa until she was only a few inches away from Palmer. She put an affectionate arm round his shoulder and drew him towards her.

'Half eight,' was all he managed to say before her mouth had covered his. He responded to her affections and enjoyed the attention she was giving him. As she kissed him her fingers found out his neck and began to massage it in the way he liked, the way that instantly began to arouse him. In response he reached round and began to rub her neck, lifting her long, sandy, hair with his fingers as he did so. He knew that this was something that always turned her on. The effect was swift and predictable. He heard her murmur as her tongue explored his dental work, and he sensed her breathing become faster and deeper. Their caressing lasted for perhaps five minutes before she pulled away from him.

'You definitely have the knack,' she murmured seductively, and Palmer noticed she was slightly breathless. 'I'll be back in a moment.' She left the room and Palmer heard her climb the stairs. As she did so, he went into the kitchen and checked the meal that was simmering on the hob. He tasted it and adjusted the flavour by adding a sprinkling of powder from one of his spice jars. He returned to the lounge and heard her descending the staircase.

She entered the room and mouthed two words silently to her lover: 'Fuck me'.

Palmer was used to this from Karen. It was something he had discovered about the woman that she would have a bad day at work and in some peculiar way it had the effect of arousing her. It had been a bad day, and Palmer was sure she'd spent some time working herself up as she'd got ready for the evening. She had become aroused by his touch just a little too quickly but it had flattered him that she had done so. Then, and it was again her custom, she always had to leave the scene just before their lovemaking. It didn't annoy him, but rather was like an early warning for him. He knew from her demeanour that she needed him now. As he reached her he turned her round and whispered in her ear,

'Not in here.'

***

It was over half an hour later when they came back down the stairs. Palmer gestured towards the lounge.

'Give me five minutes and I'll bring dinner through to the lounge.'

Palmer adjusted his hastily replaced attire and set about the kitchen while she walked unsteadily back to the lounge.

The meal was good. Actually Palmer was an accomplished cook, and the curry was a quick meal for him to prepare. Nonetheless it was tasty and earned him appreciative comments from the woman who was still glowing from their lovemaking. As their meal finished so she turned the conversation back to the case Palmer was working on.

'You know I had that dream the other night we spent together? That dream about the hooded men and the young girl coming out of the Ouija board and what the hooded men did?'

'Yes.' Palmer's mouth was half full of curry and he was hardly able to speak.

'Well, I had some thoughts last night when I was stuck outside that house. I think that it was a picture of something that has happened, not that will happen as we thought the other night. I think it was a picture of what has taken place – a hapless young woman, or girl, being molested by this group of men. I don't know why I think it – I just do.'

'Well, if that's the case then it isn't a warning.'

'Exactly, it's more like information. Look this isn't an exact science and I don't understand why it happens to me the way it does, but I've just got this feeling it is something that we needed to know, not something we need to be wary of.'

'Well, your instincts have been right a few times before, so if we go on that basis what else did you get to thinking?' Palmer's mouth was momentarily empty and he took a bite from his Naan bread as she replied.

'Well, if it's something that has already happened, and if it's relevant to this case then I had an idea. What if one of the hooded men was the dead guy? What if some time ago a girl got badly injured by him and some of his friends and what if she is now out for revenge?'

Palmer stopped chewing and thought for a moment.

239

'Well?' She questioned him when he had not replied as quickly as she would have liked. Palmer swallowed hard before replying.

'If that is the case then who are we looking for? Heather Burnston, the wife, claims she was caned by the elders when she left. If you're right, then who's to say she isn't out for revenge? Also I've found out one other member of the group died last year, someone by the name of Kelly Southbury. She was involved in a hit and run. It's probably just a coincidence but what if her death was part of this revenge thing? We'd either be looking for a double murderer or two murderers.'

'Look, Damien, it may have escaped your notice but loads of women like being dominated and even spanked. I do with the right guy, but it doesn't mean I'm going to kill the guys who do it to me. If you ask me, from what you've said about the Burnston woman I wouldn't mind betting she's a closet submissive. No, she wouldn't kill her husband because he was part of a group that caned her. She knew the score when she joined the group, and she probably joined because she enjoys being dominated – it sounds that kind of group. And so when she left she just took her punishment. Again, if she is the killer, why wait until now to get rid of him, why not do it at the time? Also, if she killed this Kelly woman, why wait several months before killing again?'

'But if it wasn't her, then who?'

'Could it have been the research assistant?'

'Not on that basis – she's only an initiate so she hasn't really had a chance to experience too much of the group yet.'

'Her sister?' Shaw looked directly into Palmer's face as she spoke.

'It's possible, but I doubt it. She's more likely to have killed her sister if she'd been having a fling with her husband.'

'So it must be someone else in the group.'

'Maybe, but I'm beginning to wonder if we're trying too hard. After all, the evidence points to Mrs Burnston, so perhaps it was her after all.'

'What about my dream?' Karen was looking intently at Palmer as he struggled to finish his meal.

'Perhaps that was just what it was, a dream. Perhaps there's more to it, I just don't know.' Palmer sounded almost defeated.

'And that phone call tonight? What was that about?' Karen was not about to give up.

'Oh that was the mother of the research assistant. Found the initiation stuff in her bedroom and wants me to follow her daughter.'

'That's a bit risky seeing as the girl knows you.'

'Yeah, I hadn't thought of that. But there is a bit more. Apparently she found another page which looks like it is more to do with an execution than an initiation. I'll find out more in the morning.'

'And I'm coming too, if you'll let me.'

'What about work?'

'I'll take a sicky, one day won't matter, and we're not busy at the moment. I've just got a feeling that you're going to need a woman's intuition on this one – and don't forget I have a psychology diploma to go with the computing and business management degrees.'

'Okay, okay, you can come tomorrow.'

'I hoped you say that. Now, I think we should have an early night, don't you?'

'But it's only half nine. It's too early to go to sleep yet.'

'Who said anything about sleep? I'll stack the dishwasher and you can tidy up here.'

'If you say so,' Palmer's attempt at a protest went unnoticed. Typical of his nature, the kitchen boasted many labour saving devices. Although not excessively lavish, the kitchen clearly showed Palmer enjoyed his culinary adventures, and the full range of major appliances, including the dishwasher and microwave were in regular use.

It took the woman less than five minutes to clear away the remaining dishes and to set the dishwasher going. As she emerged from the kitchen she called out to her lover,

'Are you coming up?'

By way of reply Palmer opened the lounge door and went upstairs with the woman. His earlier passion had done little to diminish his desire for this woman and it was not long before they were engaging in some intimate contact under the duvet. It was the kind of contact that was intended to provide both of the lovers with epicurean delight and the moans of pleasure as fingers gently raked over tingling flesh indicated they were both enjoying the sensations.

Outside, the night air grew colder as the clear skies persisted. The almost full moon rose slowly to its highest point in the arc of its orbit. The man and woman lay on their backs holding hands while their peaceful, sated bodies relaxed and the throes of slumber engulfed them.

Chapter Seventeen

The evening began for Marston by him picking up the redhead he had been dating for a little over three weeks. Susan was a few years younger than Marston and almost the same height. She was attractive to look at and about the same age as him. They drove to the house in Wimbledon, stopping off at a fish and chip shop to purchase their meal.

'So, Eddie, how long have yer been doin' this then?' She asked him as they were driving to the fish shop. Her voice was somewhat more East London than was Marston's.

'About three years, on and off. You sure you don't mind sitting with me?'

'No, love. I always wondered what them investigators do, now I'll find out.'

'As I said on the phone Sue, it will probably be a waste of time, and nothing will happen.'

'Yeah, but leastwise I'm with you.' She smiled at him though he failed to notice the uneven row of somewhat yellowing teeth. 'You mind if I light up?'

'No. Just open the window and leave the ash outside.'

'Okay, dear. Now, that fish shop I was telling you about is right round this corner. If you pull over I'll get the nosh. Cod you wanted, wasn't it?'

'Are you sure Sue? Yes it was cod.'

'Course I'm sure – you paid the other night.' Marston stopped the car and in a moment the woman was standing at the counter ordering their supper. A few minutes later Marston was picking up the traffic at the Tibbets roundabout before turning towards Wimbledon Village. It was early, only a few minutes after seven and Marston decided to turn right into the Windmill car park. The museum underneath the ruins of what had once been a fine windmill was closed. Even the café that nestled at the rear of the museum was closed and the car park that doubled up as the golf club car park was virtually deserted. Marston drove to the far end and parked so that they were looking out over the common land.

'Nice up here, isn't it?' The woman was already unwrapping the first dinner.

'Yes.' Marston took the meal from her and waited while she unwrapped her own parcel. 'Oh yeah, this is nice,' he commented after the first taste of the fish. 'You brought along something to read as I suggested?'

'Yeah, a detective novel. I thought it would be appropriate, somehow.'

The incongruous couple sat eating their supper, watching out over the now empty space of common. When the meal was over Marston looked at his watch. There was still half an hour to go before Palmer had told him to be at the house, but there was something worrying him.

'I think we'd better drive round there now, we don't want to be late.' He made up his mind as he screwed up the remains of the supper in the newspaper wrapper.

'But you said eight and we've got half an hour. Can't we have a little stroll first?'

'Later, maybe. I don't intend to sit there for more than a couple of hours, so we can get a drink and have a walk later.'

'If you say so.' The woman sounded relieved.

Marston turned the ignition key and in a moment had reversed the car to continue with the journey. It took him five minutes to reach the house they were going to watch and immediately he knew his instincts were right. It was not yet dark, though a little gloomy, but as they approached the house he could see that the porch light was on.

'Curious,' he said.

'What is?'

'Well the porch light is on, which means someone has been inside.'

'It could be on a timer?' The woman was attempting to be helpful.

'Not that light, it goes straight through to the main circuit, so Damien says. I reckon someone's gone in there and hit the wrong light switch by mistake.' The car had now pulled up so that the couple had a perfect view of the house.

'So what do we do now?' The woman spoke more for the sake of conversation than any question as to what was on the agenda.

'We wait, and with a bit of luck, not for long.' Marston had barely finished the sentence when the front door opened. 'Quick Sue, I need my camera from the glove compartment. The person was already standing outside the front door. She looked round, made a gesture to herself and stepped back indoors. In a moment the outside light was extinguished and she reappeared. She closed the door and appeared to lock it.

Even as she began to walk towards Marston's car he was fumbling with the camera case. Finally he had it off and pointed the camera in the woman's direction. He reeled off four shots as she approached him. Then, the panic of the moment past, Marston reached over and gave the woman in the passenger seat a kiss. As he did so it looked to the woman outside like two lovers having a farewell hug but to Marston his almost photographic memory was absorbing as much detail as he could, including the bulge in the plastic carrier bag she was carrying. As the woman walked past the vehicle, Marston straightened up and was about to phone Palmer when he remembered he had left instructions not to be disturbed that evening. Marston replaced the mobile phone in the bin attached to the driver's door.

They waited until the woman had cleared the top of the road before Marston started the engine.

'What are we doing?' The woman sounded surprised by Marston's action. 'I thought we were supposed to be watching the house.'

'There's no point. Our target has been and gone, and I don't think she'll be coming back, not tonight at least. Clever old Damien, I wonder how he knew?'

'You wonder how he knew what, precisely?'

'How there was another key holder.'

'Oh. Did you recognise who she was?'

'Nope, but that's not my problem. Just glad we got here early. Now it's down to Damien when I visit him tomorrow. Fancy a drink?'

'Why not, but don't you want to know where she lives? I mean she's on foot – it can't be too difficult to follow her.'

'Okay then, it would be interesting to know where she lives. Let's drive up the road to catch up a bit and then we'll follow on foot.'

Marston drove the short distance to the top of the road and looked around. There was no sign of the woman carrying the bag.

'Damn, she must have already gone down another side road. Oh well, we know she lives pretty close then. Damien can sort it out in the morning. Now, let's find a pub.'

'There's that one in the village on the corner that's quite nice.'

'Yeah, only that's the one I end up in every time I come to this place. Let's drive the long way round the common and see if we can find another. Marston turned left at the top of the road. A hundred yards down the road and opposite the rather posh, public school for boys that boasted the name feared by many a sporting institution, he found what he was after. Across the road from the school were two public houses. As he parked the car and escorted the woman across the road it occurred to Marston it was awfully convenient for two such places to co-exist barely a stone's throw from the school. It was as if fate had lent a hand of kindness to the older pupils, a hand that allowed them to frequent one hostelry while those that educated them patronised the other. Perhaps, he questioned himself, such fine schools even had unwritten rules as to who went where? It was probably part of the inherited tradition, he concluded.

The public house they selected was almost empty. A couple sat nervously at one table and an old timer with his walking sticks sat at another. Apart from them the pub was empty. The old timer stood and with the aid of his sticks tottered over to the bar.

'A pint of bitter, barman, please.' His voice carried a certain quality of strength, and an air of authority that sent a shiver of fear down Marston's back. He was not a man to be frightened easily, but there was something about the voice that made him feel he had been put in his place.

'Certainly, sir, won't keep you a minute,' the barman called out as he walked the length of the bar to where the old timer was standing. 'On your own tonight?'

'If you mean I am without company then yes, only of course that is a subjective observation, seeing as there is no-one with me.'

'You haven't changed a bit, have you, sir? You don't recognise me, do you?'

'No, young man I can't say that I do. Please elucidate for me.'

'Sixth form, ten years ago, sir. You taught me Physics. I wasn't quite so fat then of course and my hair hadn't started to recede.'

'Tomlinson-Smythe isn't it?' The old timer's face lit up. 'I never forget a face.'

'That's right, sir, and I never forgot your voice. I was out back when you ordered your first pint. I heard your voice and I thought "it can't be" but it is. How are you, sir?'

'Well the hips are mostly gone now but the brain is still razor sharp. So how come you have ended up here Tomlinson-Smythe? I had higher, much higher hopes for you.'

'Oh no, sir, I got my Chemistry degree and all that and then I went to work in the family business. We own the brewery, and about twenty pubs, in the South of England. I'm filling in for the manager while he's on holiday.'

'I see, but you could have done better with the brain you had.'

'I don't think so sir. With respect, when father pops it I'll inherit the whole lot which will be worth a tidy sum. Tell you what, sir, have this one on me for old time's sake.'

'Well, thank you very much, Tomlinson-Smythe. That is most kind.' The old timer replaced the coins in his pocket.

'You go and sit down sir and I'll bring it over. James, could you serve please?' The younger fresh-faced twenty-year-old appeared from somewhere and took Marston's order. As the effusive Tomlinson-Smythe continued his conversation with the ex-Physics master of his school, Marston sat with the woman who was accompanying him that evening, sipping his bitter in almost unbroken silence.

'Well,' she said after she had downed the better part of the pint, 'after this shall we go for a stroll over the common?'

'We could do. Strangely quiet in here, don't you think?'

'Yeah,' the woman lowered her voice, 'but if he comes in here on a regular basis it probably drives folk away.' As she spoke she jerked her head in the vague direction of where the retired Physics

249

master was loudly continuing his conversation with his ex-pupil, though the subject matter had changed a number of times in the intervening minutes. 'It sounds like he could literally talk the hind legs off a donkey.'

'Yeah, he is a bit loud isn't he? Okay, let's finish these and then we'll go for that walk.' And so it was that a few minutes later and holding hands the couple strolled out over the open space of common land. As Palmer had often done before, they found the bench by the pond and sat down, cuddling each other. It was a pleasant evening for the time of year, not too cold, and they held each other out of affection for some minutes. As they did so, Marston began to wonder as to the reason for the woman's presence at the Burnston house earlier that evening. What, he kept asking himself, was she doing there? The second question that kept filling his mind was who she was. Palmer had described the research assistant, Sonia Fielding, to him in some detail and he was reasonably certain the person he'd seen at the house was not her, though Palmer had made it plain that she was the person he was anticipating would turn up. Of course, Palmer had given no reasons why that should be the case, it was just a hunch, so he'd said. As Marston held the woman beside him his mind was far away from romance. Something, somewhere, was niggling at the edges of his conscious thoughts.

***

It was late when Marston finally reached the drab block of flats where he lived. He arrived home alone having first taken Sue back to her equally squalid bed-sit. Marston set the alarm clock and in less than five minutes was asleep, his mind still clearly focused on the mysterious woman who had visited the Burnston house that evening.

A few miles away, her body sated from sexual activity, Karen Shaw lay naked beside her lover. Palmer was snoring gently as he lay on his back. Sometime during the night the duvet had become dislodged and they were both exposed to the cool night air. Palmer was dreaming and as he did so he became enchanted by the music that filled the auditorium where he was sitting. It was a strange auditorium, almost an open-air amphitheatre, and the orchestra was also not quite human. This detail had eluded the investigator, for his dream was taken up with the soothing, relaxing, music that filled his head. Beside him his lover was also dreaming. As was often the nature of her dreams, this particular dream was violent. It started with a furious row between a man and a woman, a row where he slapped her hard across the face with the back of his hand. The scene changed to some countryside. Here the woman was running towards the man with what looked like a kitchen knife in her hand. He turned to her and she lunged forward, the knife plunging deep into the man's chest. She thrust again wildly, stabbing his body until he fell to the ground, blood pouring from him, covering him completely. She was dressed in jogging pants and a tracksuit top and now, as she stood triumphantly over his body, her clothes were soaked with his blood. She laughed at his pathetic, limp, body, laughed, laughed, laughed. In her dream, Karen noticed the clothes, and the

251

woman's short dark hair. The laugh was becoming infectious, not because it was the kind of laugh that followed a joke or a comic sketch, but because it was more the kind of cackle made by a witch. As its intensity grew Karen became alarmed by her dream and suddenly opened her eyes.

'Oh God,' she said as she sat bolt upright in the bed.

'Huh. What did you say?' Palmer rolled onto his side but did not open his eyes.

'Oh God,' Karen was clearly disturbed and in his semi-conscious state of mind, Palmer reacted slowly.

'Bad dream, was it?' he still sounded disinterested, though his mind was beginning to wake up.

'Yeah, it was awful.' The woman went on to describe what she'd seen. By the end of it Palmer was sitting beside her and had his arm round her shoulders.

'It's okay,' he said, 'it was only a dream.'

'God, it seemed like more than that, it was all so real. And that man, I'm sure I've seen him before, one of the pictures you showed me perhaps.' She paused as if thinking. 'No, I know who it was. It was that chap we followed the other night.'

'Are you sure?' Palmer was now fully awake.

'Positive.'

'And what about the woman, what did she look like?'

'Not that tall, dressed in jogging pants and tracksuit top, short dark hair. I don't remember much else.' Karen was still trembling from the memories of the dream.

'Well, that's not his wife, so you must have been putting bits together in some way. Dreams do that you know.'

'Yes, I know, but this wasn't a dream, Damien, it was too vivid, believe me.'

'You think it was more than that? Like the dream you had the other night about the hooded men?'

'Yeah, there's just a certain quality to them that unnerves me.'

'Okay but if you're right why wasn't his wife in the dream? She looks completely different to the woman you saw.'

'I know, and I don't have the answer to that, unless of course he's involved with someone else.'

'He might be, I don't know. The thing is to put it out of your mind now – we both need to get some sleep.'

'Okay, baby, I'll try. You go back to sleep and I'll try to. I'll be okay.' She sounded vulnerable, more vulnerable than she had done so before. Palmer lay back down and closed his eyes. As he did so he thoughtfully placed a reassuring hand on her leg. In minutes the sound of his gentle snoring once again filled the bedroom and the woman beside him lay down and closed her eyes, though she would not sleep again that night.

Chapter Eighteen

The morning dawned grey and damp. Palmer woke at seven o'clock.

'Did you sleep okay after the dream?' He asked as he nuzzled into her.

'Not a wink.' She resisted his advances though not out of any animosity but because she was preoccupied.

'You mean you've been awake all night?'

'Yes, nearly all night. Look, I've been thinking.'

'That's dangerous.' Palmer meant it as a joke but he had missed the gravity in the tone of her voice.

'I'm serious, Damien. There is something absolutely awful about to happen to that guy we followed the other night. I don't care if you don't believe me, but it's going to happen.'

'I believe you. So apart from the death scene, have you had any more thoughts?'

'Plenty. From what you say he runs a photographic studio that has a dubious nature about it. Okay, he is also into the Corpus Eros thing, and I've spent half the night in your study reading the notes on the case so I know it all. There's some weird kind of initiation rite to get you into the group and from what you saw the other evening it looks awfully like there's two girls about to go through it, only they need a full moon which happens to be tonight. Right, so I think there will be some sort of ceremony type thing happen tonight.' She paused for breath and to check she had Palmer's undivided attention. She did, so she continued.

'Okay, we know Burnston was involved in the group at some point. Some say he left it, others that he was still involved. His wife was in it, but we know she left. Her sister was in it, and she says she's left, but there's no corroborating evidence for that. Next we've got the solicitor's research assistant who has been identified as one of the initiates, and there's some scrawl on the final page that you're seeing her mother this morning about some procedure and preparation thing. I couldn't read the rest.'

'Yeah, there's something to do with a couple of Rites that she had written down.'

'Fair enough. This talk of Rites and what have you fits in perfectly with my first dream a few nights ago. What has been bugging me is the person I saw stabbing Connors to death. She doesn't fit in unless she's the other girl you saw a couple of nights ago. I don't know but if she is then there must be some connection, and I can't think of one.'

'Good grief, your mind has been working overtime. No wonder you look so tired.'

'Thanks, Damien, but the full moon is tonight, not next week, tonight. So what are we going to do?'

'Okay, I'll tell you over coffee. Now, are you going to the office today?'

'I don't think so. I'll phone in when it's time. Do you want me to help you with anything?'

'Yes if you want. You can come with me to see the very interesting Miss Rawlings, and we can have lunch in the Village. Now, give me five minutes to get up and put the coffee on and I'll tell you what we're going to do tonight.'

Palmer washed, shaved and dressed as quickly as he could. While the percolator was filling with fresh coffee he sat at his desk in the office writing short notes on the pad of paper. Upstairs he could hear the water draining from the bath while Karen towelled herself dry. One thing was certain, it was going to be a busy day and having a second pair of hands around, as well as a brain that had digested the details of the case overnight, would prove useful. Finally, Palmer poured the coffee and piled the hot toast on a plate before taking the breakfast tray through to the sitting room. As the couple sat on the settee eating the breakfast Palmer explained what his plans were for the day and then the evening that lay ahead of them.

'And,' he said in conclusion, 'I haven't a clue what will happen, or if anything will happen, but it's the best shot we've got, do you agree?'

'Yes, darling, it's the best shot. Let's hope for Heather's sake that it works out.'

'I think it will. Now, we have an hour before Eddie is due to turn up. He said he'd be here at nine sharp. Let's hope he is and let's hope something happened last night.'

'Okay, so what do we do for an hour?'

'Well, I have some household chores to do. You can watch television if you want to?'

'Okay. Do you want a hand with anything?'

'No need, unless you want to empty the dishwasher.'

'Okay. I guess I'll find where things go.'

'Yeah, it's easy. There are only three cupboards nearest to the machine that you need to look in.'

The woman set about the task she had volunteered for and Palmer busied himself upstairs. It was nearly an hour later, and Karen was watching the television when the doorbell rang. She stood up, turned off the television and went to answer the door.

'Eddie, it's nice to see you. How are you today?' She smiled at the shorter, somewhat chubby faced man as he stood on the doorstep.

'Pretty good, and you?'

'Oh, not so bad. Damien's upstairs, he'll be down in a moment. Come in.'

Marston crossed the threshold and the woman shut the door.

'Eddie's here,' she called up the stairs.

By way of reply Marston heard a movement on the landing a moment before Palmer appeared and began descending the stairs.

'Eddie, good morning, how are you?' The woman looked at Palmer as though he was somewhat dusty, which he was.

'What the hell have you been doing?' She asked.

'Oh, been up in the loft looking for something, but I couldn't find it. I'll have another look later on. Not important. Coffee anyone?' She thought Palmer sounded unnecessarily ebullient, a tone of voice he used when he was up to something and usually when he was up to no good.

Marston and Shaw confirmed they would love a cup of coffee and the woman went off to the kitchen whilst the two men went into the study.

'So, Eddie, did anything happen last night? With the surveillance I mean.'

'It sure did.' It was Marston's turn to sound pleased with himself. 'Got there at half seven, just in time to see this woman come out of the house.'

'The research assistant, I knew it!' Palmer sounded almost triumphant.

'I don't think so, not unless she's cut her hair short and died it a dark brown. I got some pictures. The film and my report are in here.' He handed the envelope over to Palmer who extracted the contents and read the single sheet report with interest.

'Any idea as to who she might be?' Palmer asked his colleague as he put the report down on his desk. 'Ah, coffee, thanks Karen.'

'No, none, but I reckon she lives fairly close by, because she was on foot and she didn't go to the bus stop.'

'That's a good deduction and one which only leaves us with about a hundred or so homes to look into.'

'Do you know who she is?' Marston asked hopefully.

'I'll develop the film first and take a look. I have an idea but it doesn't make any sense.'

'And what is that idea?' Karen had been reading the report and now looked up at her lover.

'Well, the other girl at the house we watched might fit the description, but I'll have to develop the film first. If she does, we may have a problem, because I have no idea who she is.'

'You could always ask Manning's research assistant.' Karen was sitting forward in her chair, eager to contribute to the discussion.

'Maybe, but then again maybe not. There might be another possibility. We'll find out when we visit Rawlings in a few minutes. First though, I want to get this film developed.'

Palmer spent twenty minutes in the darkroom and when he returned he held the four prints he'd made.

'Good work, Eddie,' he began as he opened the case folder. He held up one of the prints against one of the pictures he'd taken a couple of evenings previously. 'Very good work but with her face so covered up I can't be sure that our mysterious visitor to the Burnston house is the other initiate. The hair is similar but I don't think it's the same person.'

'So, who is she?' Marston queried the sleuth.

'No idea, but Karen and I have an appointment to keep in Wimbledon in half an hour and we're running late. Eddie, can you do me a favour?'

'Sure.'

'Go back to that photographic studio we went to the other night, make some enquiries on some pretext about having some adult shots done of a girlfriend or something and see what comes to light. Anything might be useful, but most importantly I want to know that Connors is there. Then, after your visit, hang around and follow him if he comes out. You have your mobile with you?

'Sure.' Marston stood to leave as Palmer and Shaw prepared for their appointment in Wimbledon Village.

Five minutes later they were on the road, Palmer driving with his usual lack of concern for other road users.

'Damien, a thought,' Karen spoke as he drove.

'Yeah, what is it?'

'This Rawlings woman, you said you'd seen her at the house in Wimbledon with the two girls.'

'Yeah.'

'Well that makes her part of the group, so why would she alert us to some preparation and procedure document and show concern for her daughter joining the group, or for that matter confront her daughter about it?'

'Well spotted, and that is exactly why I am so interested to talk to our Miss Rawlings. Either we are being set up, or there is some other explanation. I don't think it is a set up. I have a good idea who warned me off the case, and I presume some other group members visited my house, so why would the group now let on about one of their secret practices? That's nonsensical. No, there is another explanation. And if the moron in the red Fiesta would actually find the gas pedal we might get to hear it.' At that precise moment Palmer had to brake sharply as he drove up behind the red Fiesta, whose driver was merely following the thirty miles per hour speed limit.

'Okay, calm down, we'll get there, and if we're a few minutes late it won't matter.'

Palmer continued driving, forced now to comply with the speed limit. Finally the Fiesta turned off the road and he completed the journey in his usual style of driving.

'Miss Rawlings,' he said as the woman answered the door, 'Andrew Clarke.'

'I remember, Mr Clarke, do come in.'

'Oh, I should introduce you to my colleague, 'Helen Brown. I hope you don't mind if she joins us, only she is more, how shall we say it, experienced, in these matters than I am.

'Miss Brown, nice to meet you. Do come in.'

Palmer and Shaw were shown into the living room and offered tea which they accepted. Finally, Palmer was able to begin the discussion.

'Now Miss Rawlings, has your daughter contacted you since yesterday evening?'

'No, but her boyfriend phoned last night to say she was okay. I guess she just needs some time to sort things out for herself.'

'At least she has a boyfriend.'

'Yes, she's known Michael for about a year now. They are pretty close. He has a flat somewhere over Southfields way – do you know the area?'

'Not really, but isn't that just past the tennis club, by the park?'

'Yes, I think I know where you mean. Anyway, he's quite a nice chap, and a lot more thoughtful than Sonia. Now, this is what I found.' The woman handed Palmer four sheets of paper. Palmer read them closely and handed them onto Shaw with a look that indicated she was not to react in any way to what she was going to read. As he passed her the sheets of paper she nodded slightly.

'So, Mr Clarke, what do you think of it then?'

'Well, it looks like your daughter is involved in some group or other. Either that or it is something she is studying.'

'Well, she isn't studying – not that kind of thing anyway. She's working as some office temp or something, so she tells me.'

'In that case I would say this Rite of the First Hour is an initiation ceremony into some group or other. As for the Rite of Death, that is a different matter. Seeing as it is handwritten it suggests it is the author's own ideas.'

'I see. You are clever, go on.'

'Well, on the face of it is a ritual for an execution, and a quite horrific one.' Karen had just finished reading the documents and Palmer noticed that her face had turned a pale colour.

'That is what I thought. Have you any idea what she might be involved in?'

'Not really, but we did a bit of investigating before we came here this morning.' Palmer was watching Rawlings closely now. 'We did come across one group that operates in this area – it's called Corpus Eros. Have you heard of it?'

The woman was either an extremely accomplished actress, or she had never heard of it for her expression did not change.

'I can't say that I have. Is it one of those dangerous groups, like the one in America where all the members killed themselves a few years ago?'

'I have no idea, Miss Rawlings. Probably the Rite of the First Hour is little more than some kind of perverted and silly ritual, but it's the other one that I am worried about. I take it that the writing is your daughter's.'

'No, Mr Clarke, it isn't. I don't recognise the writing.'

'It's written by a left handed person,' Karen chose to join the discussion.

'Are you sure?' Palmer asked her.

'Oh yes, the letter formation and slope is classically left-handed. No doubt about it.'

'Well it can't be Sonia then, she's right handed.' Rawlings sounded almost relieved.

'So, could it be a friend?'

'Sonia doesn't have many friends. Let me think. Tania and Catherine are both right-handed. Michelle is left-handed I think, but she's a really nice girl. I can't imagine her ever getting involved in a cult or sect. Of her male friends I think there are only four and to be honest I don't think any of them are left-handed.'

'You don't have any pictures of her friends do you?' Palmer's question was more a stab in the dark rather than one that carried any real expectation of a positive response.

'No I don't think so. Having said that, I might have one of Michelle from three years ago. We went on holiday with my twin sister and her family and I think Michelle came too. Hang on a minute and I'll get the album.'

The two words, twin sister, reverberated through Palmer's mind as he waited for the woman to return. She was gone for less than a minute and returned holding a large brown, vinyl-backed, photograph album. She flicked through the pages until she found the point in the family history she was looking for.

'That's her, the one with the short hair.' She spun the album round so Palmer could have a look and pointed at the girl in the picture.

'You said your twin sister. Are you identical, or just similar?' Shaw was picking up on the observation she had mentioned to Palmer while the woman was out of the room.

'Oh, identical, we look totally alike to anyone who doesn't know us. The only difference is I have a mole under my left cheek, my sister doesn't. Of course that's where the similarities end, in our looks I mean.'

'And why is that, if you don't mind me asking?' Karen was continuing the discourse.

'Well, I have a responsible job, a wayward daughter, and a fairly non-existent social life apart from my church friends. Frances on the hand is more of a free spirit – loves parties, a bit of a swinger, and has two idyllic offspring who have joined in the Kosovo rescue mission or something. In fact, if I didn't know better, I'd say Frances was just the kind of person to get involved in one of these cults or sects or whatever you want to call them.'

'And how do you know she isn't?' Palmer asked the question while Shaw was still formulating her own.

'Because she's too old to be bothered with it these days, and as she's my identical twin I think I'd know if anything like that was going on.'

'One final thought, does your sister live near here?'

'About two miles away – she also happens to live in the Southfields area. Why?'

'Oh, no reason. Now, to go back to these documents, I wonder if your daughter could have taken them home for her friend. What was her name?'

'Michelle. It's possible.' Rawlings sounded somewhat relieved.

'Perhaps it is Michelle who is involved and not Sonia, in which case you really have nothing to worry about. Now, if I can turn to your request on the phone last night. We could do some more investigating if you want, and we could follow your daughter, but that would hardly help your relationship if she suspected anything. Also, it could cost you quite a lot of money. But it's your call Miss Rawlings.' Palmer sounded firm but friendly.

'I see. Well it hadn't occurred to me that it might be her friend's stuff. I suppose you are right. Perhaps that's what it is. Perhaps I should wait and see if anything else turns up.'

'That might be best, though before I go it might be worthwhile having a quick look at your daughter's room, if that's okay with you, just in case.' Palmer sounded reassuring. As he had been speaking, Karen had been writing notes from the four documents that she had now read at least three times.

'I suppose it might be worth a look. It's up the stairs and first door on the left. You don't want me to come up with you do you, only I really do need to attend to some washing in the kitchen?'

'No, that's fine. I will only be a minute. You might as well stay here, Helen. Palmer cast a glance at Karen Shaw but she was already looking up at him.

'Okay, Mr. Clarke, I've nearly made all the notes I need to.'

'Very well, I won't be long.' With that, Palmer left the living room and climbed the staircase. The

265

daughter's room was tidy, and it was evident that Miss Rawlings had been doing more than just sorting out dirty washing. The room had been thoroughly dusted and vacuumed and the various ornaments and cuddly toys had been neatly arranged on the shelves. It made Palmer's task easier and in a minute he had located what he was looking for. The diary and address book had been meticulously placed on the shelf that contained the various other books and pamphlets. He flicked through it avoiding the diary section until he reached the addresses. In less than two minutes he had written down the addresses of the two girls called Michelle, and the Southfields address of the boy he could only presume was the boyfriend. This task completed he descended the staircase.

'Well, Miss Rawlings, your daughter has a very tidy room. There's not much to look round at and I'm afraid there is nothing of any use if you wanted us to pursue matters. The main thing is you know that she is at her boyfriend's for now, and he sounds the sort of person who'd tell you if she moved on. I really don't think you have very much to worry about on that front.'

'Well, Mr Clarke, I'm sorry to have troubled you.'

'Not at all, and don't worry. I have already sent my report back to the solicitors on the other enquiry and I don't think this adds anything to that report. I expect you'll hear from them in a few days, and hopefully it will be good news. Now, we mustn't take up any more of your time. I think it's time we moved on to our next appointment.'

'Well, thank you once again, Mr Clarke, for coming round.' The lone figure of Miss Rawlings smiled at the departing couple as they walked back down the path to the pavement. As soon as they were out of earshot Karen turned to Palmer and said,

'What next appointment?'

'Lunch,' he replied and laughed.

***

The Common was almost deserted as Palmer and Shaw sat on the bench by the pond eating the sandwiches they had just purchased. There was a chill in the light breeze that caused the ripples to form on the surface of the water.

'One thing we know,' Palmer spoke through a half-full mouth.

'What's that?'

'This girl, Michelle, lives not one mile from here, just above the tennis courts. I found that out from Sonia's bedroom. Seems she left in such a hurry she didn't take her address book with her.'

'But it doesn't tie in with everything else.' Karen had waited until she had swallowed the remains of the egg and cress sandwich. 'We know that Sonia is using a false name with Manning, she's involved in the group, and must have instigated the threatening letter to you. Why are you focusing on this other girl now?'

'Because whoever went into the Burnston house last night wasn't Sonia Fielding and you yourself said the writing on the sheet about the Rite of Death was left-handed and I know that Fielding is right handed – I saw her at Manning's office don't forget. So we must be looking for someone else.'

'But why would Sonia have the documents in her room if she wasn't part of it?'

'Okay, I'll have a guess. What if this Michelle was round there sometime in the recent past and she left them there by accident. Perhaps the girls were having a laugh at it – I don't know, but there are a hundred different possibilities. The main thing we have to focus on this afternoon is the fact that it's the full moon tonight and this Rite of the First Hour is about to take place and I have a strong feeling everything is about to come to a head because of it.'

'So, what do we do?'

'We find a florist and get a bunch of roses. Then we deliver them to this address, and see who's there.' Palmer showed his girlfriend the address he'd taken from Sonia Fielding's address book barely an hour earlier.

'Sounds easy, but what if she's not in?'

'She will be, it's her big night remember, and if you look at the preparation for the Rite it takes about four hours, so she'll be in getting ready. Have you finished that sandwich?'

'Yes.'

'Okay, let's get this over with. If you deliver the flowers I'll try to get a picture, is that okay?'

'I guess so, but what do I say?'

'Just pretend you work for the florists and someone asked you to deliver them this afternoon.'

'Right, well there's a florists just on the corner by those other shops. We could try there.' Karen was pointing back in the direction of the war memorial and the small parade of shops behind it.

'That will do. Let's go then.'

The couple walked back to the florists and purchased a bunch of a dozen red roses. For good measure Palmer wrote a card which simply said, 'Good Luck, with Best Wishes', and then they drove the mile to where the young woman lived.

Karen Shaw plucked up the courage she needed to impersonate the florist's delivery person and rang the doorbell. The house was large, with at least five bedrooms and with a double garage to one side. The double aspect front was imposing and provided Palmer with ample opportunity for taking pictures. Karen rang the doorbell a second time.

After perhaps thirty seconds the second summons resulted in the door being unlocked. Still secured by a chain from within the door was opened a couple of inches.

'Yes?' The female voice questioned the visitor.

'Florists. I've got a delivery of roses for Michelle Carranides.'

'Hang on a second, I'll open the door.' As the young woman within closed the door to release the chain so Shaw signalled to Palmer with a momentary thumbs up sign.

The door opened and a young woman with short, dark, hair appeared. She took the bunch of roses from Shaw, and as she did so Palmer reeled off three pictures from where he sat in the car just outside the driveway.

'Do I have to sign for them?'

'No ma'am, we just need to be sure they got to the right address. They are lovely aren't they?'

'Gorgeous. I wonder who they're from.'

'There is a card attached to the top. Perhaps it's signed.'

'Perhaps, anyway, thanks for bringing them round.'

'All part of the service.' With that Karen Shaw turned round and began to walk back down the driveway. She regained the comfort of the car, sighed and said,

'Well, did you get a decent shot.'

'Yes, not that I needed it. She's the other girl I saw at the house the other night, no question about it.'

'So, what do we do next?'

'We go and do a little research on our Miss Carranides.'

'Back to your place then?'

'Back to my place, but only for a while, because there's work to be done this afternoon. Also, I want to contact Eddie and find out what he's up to.'

Chapter Nineteen

Palmer started the car and began the twenty minutes journey back to his home. He drove much of the way in silence, his mind concentrating both on the road and on the recent developments in the case. His partner, sitting beside him, knew better than to disturb him when he was in one of his reflective moods. Instead she spent the journey wondering what lay in store for them that coming evening.

The journey over, Palmer busied himself in his study. The computer was still in start-up mode when Palmer returned to the room with two cups of coffee.

'We have got to find out what we can about this Miss Carranides. We know she is involved in Corpus Eros somehow. The question I have right now is this – is she involved in anything else?'

'There is something that I was thinking about Damien. It sounds a bit silly, but she doesn't look quite like the woman I saw in my dream last night.'

'Sorry, say that again.' Palmer was busy starting a program on the computer and he had not heard what Karen had said.

'I said that Michelle doesn't look exactly like the woman in my dream last night.'

'So?' Palmer was still concentrating on the computer. 'There, got you. Michelle Carranides, age 20, registered living at blah, blah, we know where. Lives with what look like her parents. She's not registered as being born in this country, surprise,

surprise, and she doesn't show on the directors listings – again no surprise. Sorry, what did you say about your dream?'

'Palmer, you are incorrigible. Why don't you listen to me? I said Michelle is not the woman in my dreams. She's like her, but it isn't her Damien. The more I think about it, the more I'm sure.' The woman was beginning to become excited and her voice had risen both in pitch and in volume.

'Not the girl of your dreams, that's interesting. This Michelle Carranides is registered at Merton Technical College. She's also doing an evening class in pottery. Might be interesting, I wonder what else we can find?'

'Did you hear what I said, Damien?' the voice was getting louder. Palmer stopped what he was doing.

'Yes, she's not the girl in your dream. So, it doesn't prove anything.'

'Except if the dream is as accurate as the one a few days ago. If it is, then she can't be the person who is about to kill someone, or more specifically Warren Connors.'

'There is that I suppose, but before I get too excited by this can you answer me one little question?'

'And that is?'

'If Michelle Carranides isn't the woman, who is it?'

'I don't know.'

'Exactly,' Palmer paused and then punched the air, 'but there is something else that makes it unlikely that Miss Carranides is the killer, if your dream is accurate. She'll hardly be wearing a tracksuit top and jogging pants tonight. So I agree with you, if your dream is accurate then Michelle Carranides cannot be the killer. But if she isn't, then who is? We've got a few hours until the Rite of The First Hour is likely to take place and if you reckon that the killer will turn that Rite into the Rite of Death, we have a problem.'

'Which is?'

'Without Carranides fitting the bill, we have no suspect. And we're still left with the question of who went into the Burnston house yesterday evening, and why did they do that?'

'I don't know, Damien, but I'm sure Michelle Carranides is exactly like Rawlings described her – a sweet young woman. She is neither the killer of Burnston, nor the person who I saw killing Connors.'

'Okay, so we don't have a suspect, but in some ways that makes everybody we know who's involved in Corpus Eros a suspect. Let's look at those Rites again.' Palmer picked up the sheets of paper that described the Rite of The First Hour. 'The procedure notes state that the initiate will turn up at precisely ten o'clock. She is allowed half an hour to prepare after which she will be examined by the President of the Rite. If acceptable she will attend to the needs of the elders, whatever that might mean, up to the appointed hour. Half an hour before midnight she will be escorted as part of the group to the place where the Rite will be performed. Now I'm only guessing but I'd bet that means they're going out onto the Common somewhere.'

'Hmm, and I'll bet you something else. My dream saw the stabbing in countryside. That would

273

mean whoever is the killer knows where they'll be going.'

'Of course,' Palmer sat up, 'she knows where the site is because she's been there before.' Palmer was warming to the theory that was being developed though the lack of a suspect was continuing to frustrate him.

'So, does that give you any ideas who it might be?'

'Well, it could be anyone. Might even be someone not involved in the group. What if it's someone not involved with the group, but someone who has a grudge – perhaps an ex-member?'

'It's an idea, but the only ex-member we know about is Heather Burnston and she's locked up.' Karen scratched the back of her head as she spoke.

'No, there is one other. Rachel Connors, or at least so she reckons.'

'But she's blond, and she didn't really look that much like the woman in the dream.'

'Okay, let's take a step back for a minute. We mustn't get distracted. Our objective is to prove that Heather Burnston didn't kill her husband. If she didn't then someone with a key to the house did. We know Rachel Connors has a key.'

'Yeah, and the visitor last night has a key, the one with the short dark hair.'

'Yeah, Eddie clearly saw her lock the door behind her, which means she has got a key from somewhere.'

'Exactly,' Karen was thinking fast, ahead of the discussion. 'And if she has a key now, what's to say she didn't have one in January? What's to say she didn't kill Burnston?'

'Hold on, you're going too fast for me.'

'It's not difficult, Damien, the woman Eddie saw last night has a key to the house, if she had it in January then she could have used it to get into the house so she could kill Burnston.'

'Yeah, yeah, I understood what you said, but until we know who she is we can't even begin to look for a motive, let alone a motive for her planning to kill Connors, assuming your dream is accurate. It's all getting a bit complicated, don't you think?'

'Maybe it has to, but I didn't think that the writing about the Rite of Death ritual was just fantasy, there'd been too much thought gone into it. It was a cohesive strategy, albeit that you had to read between the lines, but that was true for the Rite of the First Hour sheets. Whoever wrote the Rite of Death sheet must be planning something, and if it wasn't Sonia Fielding because she's right handed, and it wasn't Michelle Carranides, then who was it, and how come it ended up in Fielding's bedroom?'

'I don't know, but I've got an idea. Look at these.' Palmer handed her the pile of pictures he'd taken from the folder sitting on top of his desk. 'Do you recognise anyone?'

'Where did you get these from, they're disgusting?' Karen sounded genuinely shocked.

'We borrowed them from Warren Connors' photographic studio. Unless I'm mistaken that is the woman who visited the Burnston house last night, that woman bent over the horse-like contraption, only she's a good few years younger than she is now. I'd say she was in her early to mid-twenties when that picture was taken.'

'Yes, it does look awfully like her. I wonder when it was taken. Look, there's that small scar under her chin. It's the same scar as in this picture Eddie took last night.'

'You're right. Well that links her to Connors and his business and I'd take a punt that picture was taken about ten years ago. It was right at the back of his filing system, something he'd kept for posterity.'

'Okay, so from what I remember from reading the notes last night, that puts it in the timeframe when Connors met his wife and Burnston met his. Could it be an old flame trying to get even with the men for some wrongdoing? It's just a thought.'

'Yes it most certainly could be. But how would someone involved then know where they meet now, know all about the Rite of The First Hour, and also have access to the Burnston house?' Palmer looked again at the photographs as he spoke.

'Well, the person could still know someone involved in Corpus Eros, someone who kept them up to date with information.'

'Not likely, they've got a rule that you say nothing to outsiders unless you have to.'

'Even if you're being blackmailed?'

'But we have no evidence of blackmail, and certainly not involving Heather Burnston. But I like the theory of an old flame getting even with them. That at least is plausible, and it's better than nothing to go on.'

'So what do we do next? The afternoon is wearing on and we don't seem to be getting anywhere.' Karen sounded as if she was beginning to become frustrated with Palmer's approach to what to her seemed like an imminent death.

'We have no choice. We'll just have to wait and see what happens this evening. We don't know who the killer is, though if your vision is right it seems possible that whoever killed John Burnston will try to kill Connors at some point, and possibly even tonight. I think we should plan to watch some folk pretty closely this evening. Now, let's find out how Eddie's getting on.'

Palmer dialled the mobile number and was rewarded by an almost instantaneous response.

'Eddie, how's things?'

'I was just about to phone you, Damien. Connors has been at The Studio all day. A few people have been in, couple of kids for a photo I should say and whatever. I went in and made some enquiries about having my kids photographed and got shown the studio and given a price list but nothing of any use really. How are you doing?'

'Well, we're not doing very well really but Karen is convinced someone is going to try to kill Connors, possibly tonight. Could you stay with him and follow him home, or wherever he goes?'

'Sure Damien. Here listen, while I was going round the studio something struck me. They've got a small cupboard of wigs in there that was open. We must've missed it the other night because it was locked or something. Anyway I asked Tracy, she's the receptionist, what they use them for. She said some of the models have dark hair but the requirement is for blond hair so they lend her a wig for the shoot. I thought if that happened, then any of those photos we printed could be people wearing wigs, so we can't go on the hair colour.'

Palmer was thinking, a thought of such simplicity that it astounded him, a thought which instantly allowed him to solve the whole case. All he needed now was for events to unfold in the way that he now expected them to.

'Eddie, you're a genius, and I'll explain it all later on. For now though it's vital you stay with Connors. Follow him when he leaves. If it's any help I expect he'll go home from there, but he might not. When you're on the move, give me a ring on my mobile.'

'Okay, so who did it then?'

'Sorry?' It was Palmer's deepest possible attempt to sound bewildered.

'Well you sound like you know who killed John Burnston, so who is it?'

'Do I? I'll tell you later, when it's all over. I must get on Eddie. Ring me when he's on the move.'

'I will do. Bye.' Palmer heard the last three words as he ended the call. When he turned to his girlfriend he had a grim smile on his face, the kind of dark secretive smile that came with the satisfaction of having solved a case, but when the final act was still to be played out.

'You do know who did it, don't you?' Shaw responded to his smile.

'Yes, I think so.'

'How? What did Eddie say?'

'Something to do with wigs, and I'm not totally sure, shall we say ninety percent.'

'Okay, so phone the police, or Manning at least.'

'No, that would ruin everything. The less Manning knows about what is going to happen this evening the better. As for the police, I have no evidence, only a hunch, and they are not going to be interested in a hunch when they already believe the killer of John Burnston is locked up. Not only that but I don't want the killer to be deterred from giving the game away.'

'So who is it?'

'Like I said to Eddie, I'll tell you when it's all over. Now, I have a job for you to do. Rachel Connors is almost certainly at home at the moment. It's just gone four and she'll be expecting hubby home in a couple of hours. Can you get over to Wimbledon Village and park somewhere like we did the other day? I need you to stay there until she makes a move. If she comes out of the house, follow her and let me know. You've got your mobile haven't you?'

'Yes, but why Rachel Connors?'

'Because if we're right about The Rite of The First Hour taking place tonight, her husband will be going out about eight or so I should think. My guess is she'll be going out shortly afterwards, doing her own thing and that is what I need to know about. I'll have something else for you to do later, but I need to know where Rachel Connors is for the first part of the evening.'

'Okay, Damien, but it had better be worth it. I'm on my way.' She stood and kissed him on the cheek. 'See you later, and I'll call you the moment anything happens.'

'It will be worth it, I promise. We'll have a proper curry back here later on, and Eddie can come back too. Now take care and keep in touch, won't you?' He kissed her in response and waited as she let herself out through the front door. As soon as the door was closed Palmer climbed the stairs and visited the attic for the second time that day. He was looking for something, something he was sure he had put up in the loft a few years back.

One hour later, Palmer was back in his office. He had tidied up the desk and neatly arranged everything in order. As the clock in the hallway sounded five times he sat at the computer double-checking the enquiries he had made a few days previously. There was now no room to be wrong. He knew that probably in less than eight hours he would be making a monumental decision, a decision that would either bring further accolades to his career, or if he was wrong his reputation could be severely damaged. And so he meticulously checked the information he had already noted. Then, with the checks complete, he sat back and placed his hands behind his neck as he tried to stretch the nervous tension from his body.

A few minutes later his mobile phone rang. Even before he answered it the display told him who the caller was.

'Karen, where are you?'

'I'm sat just down the road from the Connors' house. There's no sign of life but her car is in the drive. Leastways the Beamer isn't, so I assume it's hers.'

'Good. Now, at some point I'm expecting Eddie to turn up following the husband home. So don't show yourself or the two of you could give the game away.'

'Okay. What are you doing?'

'I'm getting ready to join you, only I have to get a few things sorted out here first. I'm not expecting much to happen until about eight. Incidentally, you will be okay to come back here afterwards, won't you?'

'Sure, it'll be quicker than going home.'

'And do you fancy a late night curry?'

'Yeah, sounds fun.'

'Right, curry it is then, and don't forget to phone me if anything happens. I'll see you later.'

'Okay darling, bye.' Karen Shaw had parked her car about fifty metres down the road from the Connors' driveway. Like Palmer had done earlier that week she had turned the car round so it pointed up the hill, facing towards the Common. Now, as she sat in the growing gloom, she realised it would be tricky to read the novel she carried in her handbag. The evening was descending rapidly though the skies were clear and the moon would shortly be filling the night air with its eerie shine.

Five minutes after Palmer concluded his conversation with Karen Shaw his mobile phone rang again.

'Eddie, what's happening?'

'Connors has just left The Studio and we're heading back to Wimbledon. Looks like you're right and he's heading home.'

'Excellent. Keep behind him if you can. Karen's already at the house, just to let you know. Don't make a deal about recognising her when you get there.'

'Okay, but why is she there?'

'She's watching Rachel Connors for me. I have a feeling she may be going out tonight but not with Connors, and if I'm right I want to know. It also keeps Karen occupied and out of harm's way.' Palmer sounded convincing though he knew she was far from being beyond the clutches of the sinister danger they all faced that evening.

'Right, we're driving down the side of the Common now.'

'Good, just stay with him, and follow him when he goes out again. Oh, by the way, we're having a curry at my place after it's over this evening. Fancy joining us?'

'That sounds great to me. What time do you reckon that will be?'

'About two I should think. We can all have a lie in tomorrow morning.'

'We'll need it if it's one of your specials.'

'It will be. Right I must let you get on. Call me if you lose him, or when he goes out again.'

'Okay, Damien, cheers,' and the line went dead.

Palmer spent the next hour in the kitchen. The phone rang once during that time. It was Karen reporting the fact that Connors had arrived home. The evening was going well, though it was only just six o'clock and there was plenty of time for it all to go horrendously wrong.

By seven o'clock the big cooking pot was simmering slowly in the oven. Palmer turned the heat right down, thus ensuring the curry could bubble away gently all night if needs be. The rice was cooked, waiting to be reheated at the appropriate time, and the homemade Naan breads were likewise cooked and waiting to be eaten.

Chapter Twenty

Palmer tidied up the kitchen and prepared for the evening. He took the carrier bag to his car and checked that he had his survival kit, as he called it, about his person. Satisfied, he set off to follow the same route taken by Shaw a few hours earlier. The streetlights were now turned on and night had arrived. The full moon was rising through the night sky, its strange half-light bringing a shimmer to the night. Palmer drove carefully, the lights of the shops giving way to the blocks of flats and then the larger houses as he left Putney. As he neared the Common the only illumination came from the profusion of sodium lights that surrounded the Tibbet's roundabout.

Palmer thought it somehow ironic that the statue of Tibbet was bathed in the yellow light. Tibbet, some kind of olden highwayman who had frequented the area, somehow seemed to Palmer to be an inappropriate person to guard this particular corner of the Common. He was, perhaps, upon consideration, a warning of what might happen to those who perpetrated evil on the land he guarded. Palmer had never believed the rumours that Tibbet's ghost still roamed across the Common on nights such as this. He glimpsed the statue of the hooded figure with the gun as he drove round the roundabout and picked up the road that led him to the Village. For a moment he toyed with the possibility of parking in the car park next to the windmill but recalled from a previous visit that the parking area was locked after dark, something that no doubt had been instigated to keep courting couples and ne'er do wells at bay during the night.

Palmer drove to the first road on the left. He knew that if he followed the road it would eventually take him to the famous All England Lawn Tennis courts. It was a private road and Palmer elected to take the next exit off it. The next road was much more suitable for his purposes and he had driven no more than a few yards down the road before he was able to park. He'd picked up the bag that had been on the back seat, checked its contents and was about to leave when the mobile phone rang.

'Damien, this is Eddie. Connors has just come out of the house and he's walking up the road to the Common. What do you want me to do?'

'Wait until he gets to the end and then drive up. See where he's going. Do you want to stay on line?'

'Might as well, it will only take him a few seconds.'

'Is he carrying anything?'

'What like?'

'I don't know, a bag maybe.'

'No, should he be?'

'Probably not. Listen Eddie, I'm on the Common now, near to the house Karen and I watched a few nights ago. If he starts to come this way I think it's a safe bet he'll be coming to the house. In that case you can go back to the car and get over to Southfields. I want to know if Sonia Fielding is at her boyfriend's house. Have you got a pen, I've got the address?'

'Yeah, fire away.' Palmer read the address out and waited as Marston repeated it.

'Good. Where is he now?'

'He's just arrived at the top of the road. I'm going to drive up there. Hang on a tic.' Palmer waited patiently though it took less than fifteen seconds for Marston to reach the top of the road. 'Okay, Damien, he's crossed the road and is on the Common heading towards Putney. Do you want me to wait and make sure?'

'No Eddie, I'll pick him up in a minute anyway, but I'm pretty sure he's going to "CUPROSSERO"'.

'Going where?'

'"CUPROSSERO", it's the name of the house we watched a few nights ago.'

'Strange name, you realise what it's an anagram of don't you?'

'Go on,' Palmer sounded intrigued.

'Corpus Eros, mate.'

'Yes, I know. Worked it out this afternoon, and that's why I'm sure he's coming here. Okay, you'd best get off to Southfields.'

'Right, what do you want me to do there?'

'Check if the girl is in. If she is then wait and see what she does. If she isn't at home then phone me. Also give me a bell if she moves.'

'Okay Damien, I'm on my way, talk to you later.' Palmer ended the call and Marston began the ten-minute journey to Southfields. The village of Wimbledon was relatively quiet and Marston soon found the road he was looking for. Church Road led Marston to St. Mary's church, that splendid building with the spire that nestles right into the top of Wimbledon Park. From there he passed between the All England Lawn Tennis Club on his left and the park on his right until he reached the crossroads that incorporate Southfields underground station. He turned left and in a moment had found the small block of flats he was looking for. At this point he had to take a risk. He knew the flat number and in a moment he was pressing the buzzer on the intercom.

'Yes?' The female voice enquired as she picked up the phone up in the flat.

'Hi, it's Gary, is Colin there?'

'Sorry, you must have the wrong flat.'

'But that is flat ten, Colin's flat?'

'No, it's flat eight. You must've pressed the wrong button.'

'Oh, I'm sorry about that, and sorry to have troubled you.'

'That's all right.' The line went dead as the woman in the flat replaced the handset.

Marston walked back to his car, assured that he had at least discovered that a woman was in the flat, though of course he could not be sure it was Sonia Fielding.

Nearly two hours went by and Marston noticed it was now nearly ten o'clock. Suddenly, behind him, a large black limousine turned the corner, coming to a halt just outside the flats. In a moment a blond-haired woman appeared and took her seat in the back of the vehicle. The car passed Marston who took a moment to pull out into the road in pursuit. As he did so, and with his mobile phone in one hand, he struggled to dial the number he needed.

'Damien, she's on the move. Heading up the road towards Putney I'd say, missing the Village altogether.'

'I expect they're going to pick up Carranides. They'll probably turn left at the top. Be careful, it's a bit of a warren up there.'

'Sure. They're turning left. Do I follow?'

'No need to, just go straight over and take the next left. Then follow that down a couple of roads and do a left and immediately right. That should bring you back behind them and hopefully they won't think they're being followed.'

'Cor, you know the area well.'

'No, but the A to Z I've got does, and I'm looking at it now. If I'm right you'll cut back to somewhere near the top of the tennis courts and Carranides lives just down the next dip. Be careful down there. The road's pretty wide and if you stop it will look suspicious.'

'Okay, turning left now. I hope you're right about this.'

'So do I, but seeing as they're ultimately heading back to the Common it's the logical route for them. By the way, was she carrying anything?'

'I couldn't see anything other than a small handbag.'

'That's interesting. Let's see what happens next. Where are you?'

'We're coming up to the top of the Tennis Courts. Shit, they're behind me.'

'Okay, don't panic. Take a left at the top of the road and then next left. Then do a right, and stop, turn the car round and double back.'

'Got it. Turned left, this road's rutty.'

'Yeah, it's private.'

'Okay, done the left and right and they're not following me so I'm turning round.' There was a pause as Marston effected the turn. 'Right, I'm on my way back. Rutty road coming up, which way?'

'Take a left, you should go down the hill and see them ahead of you. If you take the first right halfway down the hill and go to the end you'll find my car. Park up and walk to the end of the road. If you then take a left and walk along the path about a hundred yards you'll walk past "CUPROSSERO". I'm just over the other side of the road on the common.'

'Any sign of anything happening there yet?'

'No, except that Connors arrived about an hour and a half ago. Probably had a few drinks with his mates by now.'

'Is there any news from Karen?'

'Not yet. Actually I'd better give her a ring. You know what you're doing?'

'Yes. They're parked down the road, so I'm turning right. See you in a bit.'

'Okay Eddie.' Palmer hung up and dialled his girlfriend's mobile.

'Karen, Damien, how's things?'

'I'm getting cold. The upstairs light in one of the bedrooms has been on for about an hour now. I can see a shadow through the curtains but I can't tell what's going on.'

'It's probably somebody getting ready to go out. It looks as if the party's about to get going here.'

'Where are you?'

'On the Common, pretty much where we were the other night. Connors has turned up and Eddie's watching the two women being picked up. I have to say this for Connors, he knows how to do things right. Eddie's been following a black limo for the last ten minutes or so. The girls are doing this in style.'

'Lucky them. How can I stop being so cold Damien?'

'Run the engine for a bit and turn on the heater,' he replied, 'and don't worry, it won't give the game away,' he added as if to remove any qualms she might have.

'Oh, I thought it would.'

'I doubt it. Anyway I don't expect it will be long now. Ten o'clock was the point when they were supposed to be at the house according to the preparation notes we saw. That's come and gone but it's hardly the women's fault if they're being picked up. Hang on a moment, the limo has just pulled up. Yeah, that's Fielding and Carranides without a doubt. They're off behind the iron gates. Right, I'll talk to you in a bit. Phone me if Rachel Connors leaves.'

'You think she will?'

'Oh yes, I'm sure she will. I just want to know where she goes.'

'Okay Damien, and thanks for the tip on the heater. It's warming up a bit now.'

'Okay, darling, I'll see you soon.' Palmer had just finished the conversation when he spotted the lone figure of Eddie Marston walking nonchalantly down the path. As he did so the limousine drove away. Marston passed the gateway to

"CUPROSSERO" and continued a further fifty yards before stopping. Palmer watched Marston through his binoculars as he picked his mobile phone from his coat pocket.

'Eddie, did you spot anything?'

'No. They've gone inside. I'm going to cross over the road and come and find you.'

'Good idea, actually you can take over from me here for a bit. If you cross over and walk twenty or so yards back up there's a little track leading into the Common. Go up there and I'll call you when you get close.' Marston was already walking, taking advantage of a break in the traffic to cross the road. Two minutes later he was standing with Palmer behind the row of trees that afforded them protection from being observed.

'So, what's been happening here then?' Marston had his hands in his pockets.

'Not a lot really. Connors turned up at about eight fifteen or so and went straight inside. Then two others turned up about half an hour later and then a few minutes after that another three turned up pretty much all together. Finally the limo turned up with the girls. And that is about all there is to tell I'm afraid.'

'So what happens next?'

'That depends if I'm right or wrong about this.'

'If you're right, what happens?'

'I should think they'll come out in about an hour and walk somewhere, probably onto the Common and then the fun will start.'

'And what happens if you're wrong?''

'Then we'll have wasted the evening, but I don't think I'm wrong, not now. Karen's watching

Rachel Connors and from what she says it looks to me like she's getting ready to go out as well.'

'Do you think she's coming here?'

'I just want to know where she is going.'

'Why?'

'Let's just say that forewarned is forearmed in this case.'

'So Damien, who do think is the killer?'

'Of John Burnston, I am not sure yet, and if we believe Karen's vision then Connors is in danger it could be anybody in that house, or it could be someone else.'

'Do you believe her vision?'

'I have an open mind, but I can't help remembering when she's been right before, and she certainly seemed at least as convinced on this one as she has been on others in the past. So yes, I have to give it credence.'

'You're hooked on her, aren't you mate?'

'Yeah, we're pretty close, but that doesn't change anything. You didn't see her at three this morning, and I did.'

'Okay, there's something going on.' Palmer turned to look in the direction that Marston was pointing. 'Oh great, they've ordered Pizza. I'm starving. How long do you reckon this is going to go on for?'

'Not too much longer I shouldn't think. They'll eat that and then there will be some action.' Palmer was still speaking as the muted tone of his mobile phone sounded in his pocket.

'Damien, Karen, Rachel's on the move. She's just set off in a small white car and I'm following her.'

'Excellent. Did you get the registration number?'

'Yes,' and she recited it to Palmer as he noted it down.

'Well done, now where is she going?'

'She's turned left at the top of the road, heading for the boys' school. I'm a little bit back from her but I can soon catch her up if you want me to.'

'No, you're doing fine. Are you safe to drive while talking?'

'Yeah, I'm on hands-free. She's at the boys' school and turning right onto the Common. Going past Cann... something or other house, and on towards the golf course. I'm about fifty yards back.'

'Stay there.'

'Okay. Damien, she's pulled over onto the grass at the side. What do I do?'

'Drive past and find somewhere to turn into.'

'Okay. I've slowed right down. She's turning the car round I think. I'm turning off onto this sort of track.'

'Good. Turn round and see what she's doing.'

'Okay babe.' There was a pause as Karen Shaw executed a three-point turn. Then, with the car pointing back from the track onto the road she leaned forward to assess what was happening a short distance down the road. 'She's out of the car and walking onto the common. She's got a carrier bag with her. Do you want me to follow her?'

'No. When she's out of sight take a look at her car will you?' Palmer sounded confused as if this part of the evening was not going to plan. 'And when you've done that give me a ring back.'

'Okay, Damien, bye for now.' The phone went quiet and Palmer replaced it in his pocket.

'Damn,' he said quietly, 'it looks like I was right. The Connors woman is on the Common and my bet is she's out to find out what Corpus Eros are up to tonight.'

'Is that a problem?'

'Only if she's carrying a large sharp knife and is intent on using it.'

'And you think she might be?'

'I don't know, but it's a possibility.'

The two men continued to talk for a few minutes. As they did so Karen Shaw watched as Rachel Connors walked out onto the common. Shaw watched the other woman closely but the moon's light was not sufficiently powerful to show much detail, except that the woman clearly had a scarf wrapped round her head. As soon as she reckoned Connors was a safe distance away, Karen got out of her own car and walked over to the white car. Using her flashlight she peered cautiously through the windows. There was not much of interest in the front and the back seat was also clear. However, the boot cover was missing and Shaw immediately spotted the three items of luggage piled one on top of the other. It was evident that the boot cover was missing for the very reason that the boot would not otherwise have been able to hold the three pieces of luggage.

Chapter Twenty-One

Karen Shaw extracted the mobile phone from her pocket and selected the phone number from the menu.

'Damien, it's me. She's gone off over the golf course, and I'm standing at the car. There are two suitcases and an overnight bag in the boot. Not much else to see and I've checked that the doors are locked.'

'Good work, Karen. Hello, there are a couple of folk coming out of "CUPROSSERO" as we speak. It looks as if things are about to start.'

'But it's not even midnight yet,' she protested over the airwaves.

'I know, but it's gone eleven so they could be starting a bit before twelve.'

'Okay. What do you want me to do?'

'Go back to your car. We don't know for sure what Rachel Connors is up to, but if she's carrying suitcases around the chances are she's planning on coming back to the car soon. When she does, follow her. I'll talk to you later.' Palmer returned the phone to his pocket as the woman on the other side of the Common returned to her own car.

'Right, Eddie, it's time to move. I'm going to follow that couple and see where they go. When you spot the two girls coming out I want you follow them.'

'Sure. One thing though, that couple don't look like they're wearing cloaks and hoods and all that crap. Are you sure they're worth following?'

'Yes. My guess is they're wearing it all under their coats. It avoids suspicion if they get seen.'

'Fair comment, so how do I contact you?'

'You don't from here on in, not until I contact you. The sound of these phones carries quite a way and we definitely don't want anyone to spot us. I'll see you later.' With that, Palmer set off and in a moment had disappeared from sight. The couple ahead of him had crossed the road onto the common land and were walking briskly down the towpath. They reached a track and turned off, cutting across Palmer's own track. Fortunately they were some distance ahead of him and in their animated state of conversation they did not spot him as he walked in their direction. He followed them carefully at a distance as they walked into the heart of the Common. The track became narrower and more twisted and after a few minutes Palmer lost them in the distance.

While Palmer was following the couple, Marston watched as another couple came out of the house. For a moment he reached for his phone to warn Palmer but then remembered about the need for silence. The couple set off in the same direction as the first couple had done maybe ten minutes earlier. They crossed the road and set off down the same track Palmer had taken beforehand. They reached the point where Palmer had nearly walked right into the first couple. As they continued walking, their conversation was audible to anyone within a few yards of them. They reached the point where Palmer had lost track of the first couple though by now Palmer had taken cover some distance away. He heard the couple approaching and was ready. They passed him by and turned right at the fork in the track. Palmer was immediately glad that he'd waited. He followed them cautiously until they arrived at a small clearing in the bracken and trees. The clearing was perhaps twelve feet square.

'I hope the others aren't too long, I want to get started,' the voice was clearly male.

'Yeah, it's a bit chilly out here waiting.' The response was equally clearly female.

'Don't worry about the night air. We'll son get you warmed up when we get started. Con's in a real mood tonight, so I pity those poor kids and anyone that upsets him.'

'Why's that then?'

'Apparently he had a row at home this evening. I told him to leave her when she left the group, but he didn't want to. He could have made a new relationship by now, but you know him, he wants his cake and eat it too.'

'Shush, the others are coming.' The sound of rustling invaded the still night air as the remaining four people turned up. The last arrivals included Connors, another male, and the two initiates.

'Right, it's half eleven. I see no reason why we should keep these two babes waiting any longer.' The voice was clearly Connors and Palmer could hear it from the distance he had left between himself and the group. From his position of cover he could only see with difficulty what was happening. He still had with him the carrier bag that he'd taken out of the car earlier that evening and now, as the group in the clearing busied themselves with their preparations, so too Palmer made ready for what might happen. It was five minutes before the group looked ready to start. The six group members had discarded their coats, revealing the brown cloaks with hoods which they pulled over their heads. The two initiates were not dressed in brown cloaks but a simple white smock that reached down to just above their knees. In the moonlight it looked a strange scene as the Rite began. Connors stood in the middle of the group with the initiates kneeling one on each side of him, looking up at him. The five remaining adults formed a sort of pentagonal shape around the central group. Then the chanting began, a low sound, almost a murmur, which grew in strength as the chant became more rapid. Suddenly there was silence, total silence, a silence that lasted fully ten seconds. It was at this point Palmer heard the rustle of leaves to his right. Some yards away from him a figure was moving. It was gathering momentum as it charged towards the group dressed in the cloaks. Surprised, Palmer took some seconds to react, during which time the figure had covered maybe half of the distance to the group.

Then, in an instant, Palmer saw it, the silver object in the figure's hand. Caught in the pale light of the moon the shiny metal glistened, its deadly message ever closing in on the intended target.

Leaping from his position of cover he ran after the figure. As he did so he realised the figure was wearing a dark tracksuit top, jogging pants and trainers. The runner was now less than ten yards from the group and Palmer was too far behind to catch up.

Suddenly the person ahead of him let out a loud cry, a cry intended to shock the group who were just beginning to realise what was happening.

'Connors, duck.' It was all Palmer had time to shout. Connors turned, annoyed and startled by the intrusion. It seemed he must be too late when he finally saw the lunging figure and the sharp knife. As the knife plunged towards his chest he attempted to step back. As he did so he fell over the unresisting Sonia Fielding. As if this were some bizarre part of the ritual both the initiates remained fixed to their positions. Connors fell backwards and landed in a heap on the floor.

The figure continued towards him determined that the knife would be buried deep in his body. As the tracksuit covered figure lunged a second time Palmer reached the edge of the group. The nearest person wearing the cloak and hood was still not reacting to the situation and Palmer pushed past the motionless body. As the knife sliced through the air a second time Palmer dived at the person holding the deadly weapon.

His aim was good and he secured his arms around the assailant's legs, bringing the person to the ground. The shock of the tackle made the person lose the grip on the knife and it landed harmlessly on the ground.

Palmer paused for a moment to catch his breath. It was a pause that lasted a fraction of a second too long for the person he had tackled started to struggle and broke free from his grip. The person made good their escape from his arms and headed for the direction of where the knife had landed.

'You total bastard. You lying, cheating, bastard.' Palmer recognised the voice and at the same time considered the comments had not been directed towards him. 'You two-faced bastard, you told me this was all over. Now you'll die like he did.'

The person turned, the foot of cold steel still glistening in the moonlight. Connors was still lying on the ground nursing a sprained ankle. The other group members had begun to realise what was happening and were equally minded that the person in the tracksuit had a knife. Palmer looked at the woman as he struggled to get to his feet. She had short, dark hair.

'Mrs Connors, it's over,' he began. 'Put the knife down before someone gets hurt.'

'Over, I haven't begun. Look at those two stupid pathetic creatures he's conned this time. Well, Warren, get them to move out of the way, I don't want to hurt them. Oh you can't, can you, because they're drugged? Oh well, they won't know what's going on. Now let's see who we have here.' She held the knife and pointed it at the first hooded person. 'Get your hoods off, all of you, and sit down.'

The five adults looked at Palmer, still not fully comprehending what was happening.

'Do as she says.'

The hoods were removed.

'Like lambs to the slaughter, aren't you? Now most of you know me, don't you, Major.' She walked up behind one of the men and teased the knife round his throat.

'Yes, Mrs Connors, we do.' The voice sounded peculiarly weak for a person who had held such a rank. It was also a voice Palmer recognised from his answer-phone.

'In fact, in one way or another, all of you were involved in disciplining me when I left the group. Now I want you to hear this. That discipline was so severe you ruined my chances of carrying children. You ruined my life, so now I'm going to ruin yours.'

Palmer moved forward a step.

'Get back or I start killing these idiots.' He did as he was told. He had no choice.

'Oh yes, I know you didn't all actually thrash me, but you were all there and you all saw the video afterwards. Well, I'm going to stop you from messing up these kids' lives, once and for all.' She momentarily pointed the knife at the two hapless girls dressed in white, still kneeling on the ground.

'You saw what I did to John. That's right Mr Palmer, I killed John Burnston.'

'But why did you do that? He wasn't part of the group when you left?'

'Oh yes he was, he was in it right up to the day I killed him, only that fool of a wife of his didn't know it.'

'But how did you do it?' Palmer was playing for time, time that just might save a few lives.

'Easy, I had a key.'

'But your sister Heather said you didn't.' Palmer still sounded calm.

'She was wrong. John got me one cut, so that I could let myself into the house. It was useful you see because we'd been fucking for a few years, and

301

sometimes he liked me to surprise him. He knew I wasn't getting it from Mr Floppy over there and he was happy to oblige, if only because my poor sister was such a frigid bitch, or at least that's what he said. Heather had a habit of going shopping on Saturday mornings and that's when we got together. I'd go over there, let myself in and visit the bedroom. So that Saturday, after we fucked each other senseless, and we always used a condom, it was easy to kill him. The kitchen knife was the first thing that came to hand. I got covered in blood of course, but I was naked at the time, so all I had to do was go upstairs and shower off, making sure I washed all the blood away.' She paused for a moment to walk behind the group of huddled adults, the blade of the knife passing just a few inches above their heads. Palmer was watching her every move. After a few moments she continued.

'Then I let myself out of the front door. Just to make it a bit more fun I joined Heather for coffee in the Centre Court Shopping precinct. I doped her coffee with the same hypnotic he's used on these kids, and told her what she had to do. She went home and went into the kitchen, pulled the knife out of him and by that time I'd called the cops. I was going to do each of you the same way, but I thought this might be a better opportunity.'

As she spoke she had walked round the group again and held the knife momentarily at each of their throats. She was clearly agitated that events had not gone to plan. Now she was standing just two feet from Palmer. He was sitting on the ground watching her, and he watched as she turned once more to her husband.

302

'And where better than to start with the prick that has been unfaithful to me since the day we met, and who didn't give a damn about the injuries he caused to me.' She suddenly lunged forward and the blade of the knife disappeared into the folds of the cloak that Warren Connors was wearing. The knife evidently entered his body in the abdomen for the dark stain of blood seeped onto the cloak at that point. She withdrew the knife and watched as he clutched his stomach.

'And that, you bastard, is just the start of what I am going to do. You're going to get back all the pain you've inflicted on me over the years, just like that other bastard did. Don't think he died quickly, because he didn't. It took me nearly half an hour before I finished him off.'

Connors watched his wife with a stunned look on his face. His hands were still on his stomach clutching the first wound.

'Now then, you little worms,' she began as she turned to the group of five people who were huddled together at the side of the clearing. 'Cloaks off, or you get the same treatment. And you Mr Palmer please, take off your coat and trousers. I don't want any of you thinking about running away.'

The group looked at Palmer. He in turn shrugged his shoulders and began slowly to unbutton his coat. As he did so he asked her,

'What about Kelly Southbury?'

'Oh she was easy – a simple little hit and run accident.'

'Why?'

'She was part of the group that caned me. She was the experiment, the guinea-pig, just to get a taste for getting even. She was nobody to me and so I chose her to be first.'

The group followed Palmer's lead in undressing and in less than a minute the five cloaks were lying on the ground. As the cloaks were removed it became obvious that the three men and two women were only attired with underclothes. Rachel Connors gathered the cloaks together, still watching the group and still with the knife held firmly in her hand. Palmer was undressing slowly. At the point when she was dragging the fourth cloak into the middle of the clearing he was unbuckling his belt. She was less than five feet from him and her attention was distracted when he made his move. He pulled the belt from the loops on his trousers and with a single swing he brought it down on the woman's shoulder, the shoulder connected to the hand that held the knife. She yelped in pain and immediately dropped the knife as she turned round. Palmer was moving towards her with his hand raised for the second blow, though his progress was being slowed by the pair of trousers that were beginning to fall down his legs.

For a fraction of a second she looked on the ground for the knife but it had become tangled in the cloak she had been dragging. Despite his near naked state the Major suddenly realised the opportunity. In the corner of her eye Rachel Connors saw him straighten and take a step towards her. Palmer was still advancing and in a second the belt hit her a second time. She yelped again as it connected across the same shoulder that had been hurt with the first lash.

Turning, she decided that her luck had run out. There was still one thing left to do. As she began to run off she kicked her husband once for good measure. Her trainer connected with the same area in which he had been stabbed. Palmer was lining up the third strike as she turned and ran off. In less than five seconds she had disappeared from sight. The Major reacted quickly and started to follow her.

'Let her go, she isn't going anywhere. I've had this all taped right from the start. It should be enough to get her banged up what with all your testimonies. Major, can you attend to Connors and see if there's anything you can do. You,' he pointed to one of the men, 'get your clothes back on and make your way to the main road. I'm going to call an ambulance and you'll have to show them where to come.' The man shrugged his shoulders. 'Well, get on with it, unless of course you want to end up as an accessory to murder.' The cool delivery had an unnerving effect on the man and he began to get dressed.

'Right, it's time to make some calls.'

Palmer dialled the emergency services and in moments had summoned the assistance of an ambulance and paramedics. Then he turned his attention to the fleeing Rachel Connors. The mobile phone rang twice before it was answered.

'Karen, Damien, it's all gone wrong up here. Rachel Connors tried to kill her husband, but she ran off before we could pin her down. I guess she's on her way back to you now.'

'So what do I do?' Karen sounded surprised and more than a little nervous.

'On no account approach her, she's armed and dangerous. Let her drive away, and if you can follow her then great. Put a call through to the cops and tell them what you know. Get Eddie over there to help you, or at least to give you back up. I've got an ambulance due here any minute now and there's a bunch of chinless wonders here who've got a lot of explaining to do, so I may be tied up for a bit.'

'Okay, Damien, leave it to me. I take it the curry is off then?'

'No fear, I'll talk to you as soon as I can.' Palmer replaced the mobile phone in his pocket and turned his attentions back to the Major.

'How is he, Major?'

'It doesn't look too bad, all things considered. She didn't go that deep fortunately, and the blood looks worse than it is, though I can't be a hundred percent sure that he hasn't had anything nicked inside.'

'Right, do you know what these kids were given?' He looked at the two girls who still knelt motionless in the midst of the clearing.

'Some sort of hypnotic. They take it and Connors talks to them, and then they do what he tells them. We've all had it before. They'll stay like that for a few hours at least and they'll have no memory about what has happened.'

'Right, well someone can put some coats around them. It's getting cold out here.' There was a general murmuring amongst the four people who all still seemed stunned by what had happened.

Less than five minutes later there was a rustling sound and a few seconds later three police officers appeared in the clearing. Palmer stepped forward and as he did so the plain clothes Detective Inspector recognised him.

'Mr Palmer, what are you doing here?'

'It's a long story Inspector Hartman. Thank God you were on duty. Look, that chap's wife is on the run. She just tried to kill him with the knife that's in that coat over there.'

'Did she, well she isn't going to get far. Your friend, what's her name,' he began.

'Karen Shaw,' Palmer helped him.

'Yes, her, she called us and asked for me personally. Good job I was on nights. Anyway we have a car in pursuit. The woman's heading for the A3 but she won't get far.'

'She's probably headed for Heathrow. Apparently her bags were packed.'

'Oh, she won't get that far. Our lads will stop her long before she gets that far.'

'Good.'

While Palmer had been talking to the Detective Inspector, who happened to be someone Palmer counted as a friend, the uniformed officers had taken control of the situation while the two paramedics attended to Warren Connors. They patched his wound and placed him on a stretcher. In less than five minutes they had gone. The police noted names and addresses and Palmer spent several minutes talking to the Inspector. He would, of course, have to make a full statement the following morning, but for now it was more important that Rachel Connors was stopped. In less than half an hour the group of people were walking away from the Common. As they approached the road, Palmer noted the two vans that had arrived. The small group of scantily clad people were led to the vans and driven away. Palmer turned to the Detective Inspector and shook his hand.

'It seems like we might have a long night ahead of us. See you tomorrow Damien.'

'Yes. Is there any news on the car chase?'

'Yes, it just came through while we were loading up. Seems like a car matching the description we were given was stopped just after the Hook underpass. She's on her way back here now under arrest.'

'Good. Well, John, I won't keep you, and sorry about all the paperwork.'

'Yes, still it's a bit different from most of the stuff we have to do.'

'Really?' Palmer smiled as he shook the officer's hand. 'You must tell me about it some time. Come and have dinner one evening.'

'I will.'

The two men, who had been friends for several years, parted company. Palmer walked back to his own car counting his good fortune that Hartman had been on duty that evening. Almost anyone else would have meant much more trouble for him and a late night. As it was, he could be grateful that at the end of it all the truth had come out.

Chapter Twenty-Two

It took Palmer less than fifteen minutes to drive home through the deserted streets. He opened the door and was greeted by the rich aroma of the curry.

'Sorry, Damien, we couldn't wait.' The woman appeared in the hallway as he opened the door.

'That's all right, is there any left?' he smiled as they hugged.

'Are you okay?'

'I'm fine, but what about you?'

'Yeah, I'm fine and so is Eddie. Go on in, I'll get you a plate.'

Palmer did as instructed. He was too tired to play the perfect host.

'Eddie, how are you?' Palmer looked at his colleague as he entered the lounge.

'I'm fine. What about you?'

'Oh, pretty good, considering what's been going on this evening. So what happened from your end?'

'Not a lot really. I lost the group I was following so I made my way back to where we'd been hiding. Not long afterwards one of the members of the group returned. I hid for a while but after a couple of minutes the ambulance turned up and a couple of police cars. About then Karen phoned me and I went off in pursuit of the Connors woman. That was easy, because she came almost right past where we'd parked. I just joined the convoy behind Karen. The cops finally stopped her round Chessington way on the A3 and we came back here to wait for you.'

'Thanks darling,' Palmer interrupted as he was handed the plate full of curry.

'So what happened to you?' Karen sat beside the sleuth as he took a forkful of the meal.

'Well,' he began as he chewed the food. Over the next ten minutes Palmer recounted the events on the common that evening. At the end of it Karen turned to him.

'So, when did you know it was her?'

'It was at the point when Eddie told me about the wigs. It made sense then. You see, right from the start of this case we've been deliberately fed false information and led down blind alleys.'

'How do you mean?'

'Take Rachel Connors, for instance. I first met her at the Burnston house and she was blond, long hair and seductive. That was my first impression and that was what has been playing on my mind ever since. We were made to look for a person with short dark hair and the only person that fitted the description was Carranides. And that was Connors' plan. The longer she could keep me off her back and focused on something else, the better her chances of pulling off what she tried to do this evening. You see, she's known for months when the Rite was going to take place.'

'But what about Sonia Fielding, she must have sent you the threats, surely?'

'No, I don't think so. Sonia was already involved in Corpus Eros before the Burnston murder. It was probably not a coincidence that Warren Connors went to Manning. After all, with

Fielding as the research assistant Connors would have first-hand knowledge if anything was likely to be discovered about his precious group. Incidentally I phoned Expert Investigations this afternoon, and they'd been warned away from the case as well. So the threats had nothing to do with whether Heather Burnston was the murderer, but more to do with a group of people trying to protect their sad little group. It also acted to distract me for a while. Again, Rachel Connors had more than a little input into the idea. She may have been planning her husband's death but she was devious enough to make him think she was still supportive of his activities.'

'Why?' This time it was Marston who raised the question.

'Well, she had the motive, her thrashing that meant she couldn't bear children. Then she had the means. As I think you said, Karen, any old sharp kitchen knife is adequate. What she needed was an opportunity where she could get away afterwards without getting caught. And that's why she never attacked him at home. It would have been too obvious and she knew she'd get captured eventually. No, she needed a location where she could escape and leave the country straight away. And that's what she was trying to do tonight. Using the element of surprise, and had I not been around, she would have dealt the fatal blow, possibly to more than just her husband, and then escaped. There aren't too many people who'd give chase without their clothes on, not across common land.' Palmer smiled.

'Okay, but what about The Rite of Death?' Karen had been listening as Palmer had been speaking.

'Another blind alley meant to confuse us. I remembered earlier on today that Rachel Connors was left-handed. She'd written her address out for me when she'd asked me to follow her husband. And that was yet another idea to try and distract us and waste more time. So anyway I reckon she wrote the Rite of Death, probably as an attempt to get Fielding and Carranides to change their minds about joining the group. She took it round to Fielding, probably when Marston followed her after my first visit to the Burnston home.'

'But why did she want to frame her sister for John Burnston's death?' It was Marston who sat forward as he spoke. 'How could anyone hate a sister that much?'

'I don't think she hated her at all, actually. More likely she needed to use poor Heather as an excuse, even an alibi, to give her time to sort out other members of the group. Don't forget that if Connors had died tonight then the police would doubtless have started to piece this all together and would have realised Heather wasn't the murderer at all. I think Rachel was just buying time so she could carry on with her acts of revenge. I don't think she ever believed her sister would stand trial. In fact, I wouldn't be a bit surprised if she didn't have plans to leave the country after this evening, and she probably planned to tell all when she was safely away.'

'So what'll happen next?' The woman snuggled into the sleuth.

'Well, they'll all get charged with some public indecency charge or something. Connors himself will be more thoroughly investigated and I wouldn't be surprised if he doesn't get hammered for what goes on at The Studio. As for Rachel Connors, she'll be charged with murder and attempted murder.'

'And what about Heather Burnston?'

'With luck she should be released tomorrow, or today I should say, just as soon as I've got Manning updated.'

'And Sonia Fielding, because she gave Manning a false name and address, didn't she?'

'No, she was Sonia Fielding by birth but I did a bit of probing. At eighteen she got married and became Sonia Rickman. The marriage lasted about six months and I think legally she's still married. She just used her married name and her matrimonial address. I checked with the Royal Mail and she's having her post forwarded to her mother's house. So, actually, apart from her involvement in Corpus Eros, Manning hasn't got a lot of grounds for getting rid of her, and after tonight I doubt whether Corpus Eros will continue anyway.'

'Well,' said the woman looking evenly at Marston, 'I reckon it's bed time. What's left of the night will soon fade away.'

'Yeah, I'd best be going,' Marston took the hint as the woman snuggled even more closely into the tired investigator. In turn he put his arm round her shoulder and pulled her towards him.

THE END

www.ingramcontent.com/pod-product-compliance
Lightning Source LLC
Chambersburg PA
CBHW031100260626
47172CB00001B/153